"Last night you looked, walked, talked, reacted like Amelia!"

"You were not yourself at all. You cannot remember what you said and did. You took things that were not yours, acted as I'm sure you would never dream of acting. Is there nothing to show that, when you are asleep, or weak from the effect of the injury you sustained, Amelia possesses herself of your body for some purpose of her own?"

It was unbelievable, so beyond thinking that her mind would not function. "How did I act? What can I have done to make you say such a thing?" she whispered.

Without haste he moved to take her into his arms. "Only this," he murmured gently as his lips touched hers.

Also by Jennifer Blake
Published by Fawcett Books:

DARK MASQUERADE
THE NOTORIOUS ANGEL
THE STORM AND THE SPLENDOR
GOLDEN FANCY
EMBRACE AND CONQUER
ROYAL SEDUCTION
SURRENDER IN MOONLIGHT
MIDNIGHT WALTZ
FIERCE EDEN
ROYAL PASSION
PRISONER OF DESIRE
SOUTHERN RAPTURE
LOUISIANA DAWN
PERFUME OF PARADISE
LOVE AND SMOKE

Night of the Candles

Jennifer Blake

Who is also
Patricia Maxwell

FAWCETT GOLD MEDAL • NEW YORK

A Fawcett Gold Medal Book
Published by Ballantine Books
Copyright © 1978 by Patricia Maxwell

ISBN 0-449-14093-8

Manufactured in the United States of America

First Fawcett Gold Medal Edition: January 1979
First Ballantine Books Edition: August 1989

Night
of the
Candles

Chapter
One

THE house stood stark and tired on its hill, a plain white antebellum house with four square columns across the front and two chimneys at each end thrusting toward a darkening sky. Its sloping roof was made of gray and aged cypress shingles. Utilitarian black shutters were fastened back from tall narrow windows under the shadowy overhang of the upper and lower galleries. The only concession to ornament was the black wrought-iron grilles that covered the lower half of the bottom windows, grilles that matched the iron fence with its spiked top enclosing the house with a tiny lawn of parched grass and a spreading chinaberry tree.

Beyond the fence the long dry grass was dotted with the flagrant yellow of bitterweed. A long winding drive lined with dust-coated trees curved before the house. A wagon track led away to the left to barns and outbuildings seen vaguely through the trees.

Amanda Trent pulled her hired gig to a stop before the wrought-iron gate, then sat for a moment with the reins in her hand, a frown puckering the white skin between her brows. The place looked deserted. Nothing moved behind the windows of the house. There was no sign of activity about the yard. The only sounds were the jingle of the harness as the livery horse stomped to dislodge a persistent horsefly and the sighing of the wind through the yellowing leaves of the chinaberry.

Still, there was nothing she could do but get down. She had come all this way. Her conscience would not let her retreat now.

Wrapping the reins around the whip handle standing in its socket, she looked about her for her petit point reticule. Looping it over her wrist, she bunched her skirts in one hand, placed her foot on the metal step, and jumped lightly down.

As she touched the iron gate, it swung open with a warning squawk of rusty hinges. She paused a moment, her nerves quivering, a momentary fright beating up into her throat at the loud sound in the stillness. A bleak depression gripped her, a sense of abandoned hope. Was it something within herself, in her weariness after a long day in the gig rattling over rough roads? Was it something in the atmosphere, a combination of the autumn droop of the leaves on the trees and the twilight hour? It must be. It was nonsense to suppose that it was the effect of the house before her, though in all truth it appeared barren enough to give pause to a more sensitive person than herself. With a faint curve of good humor on her mouth for her moment of foolishness, she passed through the gate and started along the brick walk, covered with the searching tentacles of Bermuda grass, toward the steps.

Suddenly there was a deep growling sound. A gray dog standing as tall as her waist appeared from around the side of the house. He had the huge head of a mastiff and the rangy body of a hound. His eyes were strange, nearly opaque, with the glazed look of cracked marbles. His yellow teeth were bared in a snarl.

Amanda stopped, standing absolutely still, her wide eyes fixed on the animal. A part of her mind recognized that this was no ordinary watchdog. She knew she must not show fear.

But the dog kept coming, a continuous rumbling in his throat. A few feet from her he dropped into a crouch, ready to leap. Blindly she flung her arm up to cover her throat and drew in her breath to scream.

"Down!"

At the harsh masculine command the dog wavered.

"Down, Cerberus!"

The dog flattened himself against the ground, his ears back. He was obedient to the voice of authority, but in his peculiar eyes there seemed to burn a lust for the taste of her blood.

Amanda breathed a trembling sigh of relief so deep it was almost a shudder. She dropped her hand, clenching it on her reticule, then raised her eyes to the dog's master.

He stood in the open doorway, one hand braced against the frame, his face hidden in the dimness. He wore an open-necked shirt with the sleeves rolled above his elbows and rough breeches tucked into riding boots. Amanda received the impression of height, of darkness, and of a closed-in countenance hastily assumed, as if something about her had shocked him.

"I apologize for your fright," he said in clipped tones that were devoid of feeling. "Cerberus does not like visitors."

Cerberus—the three-headed dog with a collar of snakes who guarded the underworld. It was not so unusual here in the South to find people and animals named for mythological characters. In the not-too-distant past many had had the leisure and, due to the classical revival the inclination, to study Homer, Virgil, and Ovid. Her own grandfather had been addicted to the Greek and Roman poets and was fond of classical allusions. Still, few, when the time came to choose a name, settled on the more repellent characters of the ancient legends.

"I . . . I'm sorry. I didn't mean to trespass."

He glanced toward the gig waiting before the gate, then returned his gaze to her. His eyes merely passed over her, but she was sure he had missed no detail of her toilette—the polonaise and skirt of smoke gaberdine trimmed with black braid, her bonnet of black straw, her side-buttoned shoes. Acutely uncomfortable, she wondered if there was dust on her face or in her auburn hair.

"You came alone?"

"Why, yes," she answered, startled by the sharp tone.

"It wasn't a very intelligent thing to do. It will be night soon, and the roads have been thick with . . . unpleasant characters . . . these days."

She took in his meaning at once. The carpetbag rule in Louisiana was entering its sixth year. There was great political unrest in the state. The dark—and robes made of sheets—was being used to cover much of the struggle for power that was taking place. But many crimes other than political could be covered with the night and a sheet.

Though she was aware of the dangers, she felt bound to defend herself. "I have always driven myself. In any case, I didn't intend to be out so late."

"Are you lost then?" he asked with the economy of words of a man with other, more important, things on his mind.

"I don't think so. I was for a time, but then I was directed to this house. I'm looking for a man, Jason Monteigne."

At the name a stillness came over the man in the doorway. Slowly he straightened and stepped forward into the evening light. When he spoke there was a soft note of dread in his voice mixed with a timbre that was somehow menacing.

"What need have you with Jason Monteigne?"

The dog growled again at the sound, his hackles rising.

"Truthfully, nothing," Amanda said, quelling the impulse to step back a pace. "I really wanted his wife, Amelia Trent Monteigne. She is my first cousin."

The change came from within. His eyes seemed to catch flame with a blazing pain before they hardened into the frozen fire of emeralds. The color drained from his face, leaving it like a bronze mask with his features chiseled upon it—the thick arched brows and high cheekbones, the high-bridged nose and firmly molded mouth.

Amanda knew, and she wanted to stop him, to keep him from voicing the words that would give such hurt. She could not.

"My wife is dead," he said, and the burning light in his eyes was suddenly gone.

"I . . . see." Amanda dropped her gaze to her gloved fingers as she began to tear at the strings of her reticule. "We didn't know. I . . . don't know what to do, but perhaps . . . that is . . . my grandfather wanted her to have this. Perhaps you would . . ."

Fumbling in the small cloth handbag attached to her wrist, she drew forth a necklace of opals and garnets set in gold and thrust it toward him. Her fingers, she saw, were trembling so violently that the sections of gold made a faint clinking sound.

"What is it?" he asked, making no move to take it from her.

Behind Jason Monteigne a woman moved from the house, a conscious expression in her brown eyes, as if she had been listening. She sauntered to his side with a lazy insouciance and placed a possessive hand on his arm. She had hair like fluffy white cotton and a mouth that wore a look of sullen stubbornness.

"Why, Jason," she drawled. "Anybody can see what it is. It's a necklace." She flicked a glance at Amanda, the glitter of self-interest barely hidden behind long, blond, almost white, lashes.

"Not just a necklace," Amanda corrected her. Without realizing it she brought the piece of jewelry closer to her own body. "It is a legacy from my grandfather. It belonged to his wife, my . . . our, Amelia's and my own . . . grandmother. She is dead now, and my grandfather died a month ago. He left this to Amelia in his will, to his only grandchild, beside myself. He called it the collar of Harmonia."

"Take it, Jason," the woman beside him said. "You are your wife's heir."

Jason did not answer her. He lifted his head, staring down at Amanda. "The collar of Harmonia was a bribe."

"You're right of course," she said, her words tumbling

over themselves, the effect of his unnerving stare. "But this one was called by the classical name because it was a wedding gift from my grandmother's father on her wedding day more than fifty years ago. You must remember that in mythology the collar was originally given to Harmonia by the god Vulcan on her marriage to Cadmus. It was only later that it was used to curry favor. I have come a long way to bring the collar to . . . to its rightful owner. However, if you don't want it . . ."

She could sense the stiffening of attitude in the man before her. So could the blond woman.

"Oh, come. Let's not be hasty," the other woman said, pressing her fingers into the muscles of Jason's arm in a silent, physical appeal. "Why don't you ask this lady to come into the house where we can talk about it in comfort? I'm sure she would like to wash the dust from her face and hands and take some refreshment."

Amanda smiled, grateful for the offer of hospitality though it was not hard to recognize the motive behind it. She was torn between what she conceived to be her duty to turn over the necklace and a reluctance to see the collar of Harmonia fall into the hands of the woman before her. She would be glad for a few moments to think. Jason hesitated, his reluctance to proffer his hospitality patent. His green eyes moved from the expectant woman beside him to Amanda's tired and pale face. His lips tightened, then he gave way with a shrug and a mocking half bow, inviting Amanda to mount the steps and go before him into the house. As she went she could feel the eyes of the dog boring into her back.

Inside, the house was well furnished but shabby. It was obvious it had not been refurbished since the years of bounty before the War Between the States. The Turkish carpet which stretched the length of the entrance hall connecting the front and back galleries was threadbare down the center and before the doors of the principal rooms. The wallpaper, in a stylized pineapple pattern indicative of hospitality, was faded almost beyond recognition. Overhead, the bronze chandelier had only a handful of candles in its brackets instead of the five dozen it was designed to hold. Its teardrop lusters were dull, sadly in need of a vinegar bath. The sideboard against one wall also showed the effect of neglect. Its foot pieces were gray with dust, and the silver tea service which occupied one end was purple with tarnish.

Through the open door, Amanda caught a glimpse of the front parlor. Cold ashes lay caked beneath an Adams mantel. The straight lines of Federal furniture were plain in a small secretary and a pair of armchairs.

In keeping with the simplicity of the earlier era in which the house had doubtless been built, a plain staircase with a square newel post mounted to the second floor. If the house ran true to form, the upper rooms would follow the same plan as the lower with six spacious rooms, three on each side, leading off the main hall.

"If you will come with me?" the woman called Sophia said, irony lacing her tone as Amanda stood staring about her.

"Yes, of course," Amanda said, flinging an embarrassed glance to where Jason Monteigne leaned in the doorway. The intensity of his gaze as he watched hastened her steps, and she mounted the stairs at the side of the white-haired woman.

"I appreciate your offer of hospitality," Amanda said as they reached the upper landing.

The woman slanted her a small smile, but did not answer.

The bedroom into which she was shown was large and comfortable. It had its own fireplace with a white Carrara mantel flanked by windows on each side. A Brussels carpet strewn with pink cabbage roses on a maroon ground covered the floor. Crimson velvet draperies hung at the windows with lace curtains beneath them, while matching draperies were drawn back from the head of the great walnut tester bed. An armoire took up almost the whole of the opposite wall but for a tall connecting door into the next room. The wallpaper was of silver stripes with a heading of red roses entertwined with silver lace ribbon. At a glance the room seemed to have seen little wear. It had not been used in some time. A layer of dust covered everything, even the white drawn-work spread and pillow shams on the bed. A brown spider had made his web in the bowl on the washstand.

"This was Amelia's room. I thought you might want to see it," Sophia said expressionlessly.

"Yes," Amanda answered slowly, aware of an odd undercurrent without being able to see the reason for it.

"I'll bring you some water and a towel."

"Thank you." She stripped off her gray leather gloves then reached up to remove her bonnet. As the door closed behind the other woman, Amanda stared after her in perplexity.

With a tiny movement of the shoulders, she thrust the jet tipped bodkin through the crown of her bonnet and, placing it on the washstand, laid her gloves on top of it.

A quiet descended on the room. The smell of disturbed dust and a musty perfume too faint to identify lingered in the air. Glancing around her as she waited for Sophia to return, Amanda slowly began to realize that here in this room was an opulence foreign to the rest of the house. There was a slipper chair, half hidden by the tester bed, in a silver brocade trimmed with purple tassellated braid. The china pitcher and bowl had been painted with a design of violets, pink roses, and cherubs, and silver tissue cloth formed a sunburst beneath the tester over the bed, held in place at the center by a gold medallion. In the corner between the front and side windows stood a dressing table covered with silver-topped boxes and jars and surmounted by a large mirror in a walnut frame.

It was curious. The other rooms on the lower floor had been furnished with good pieces but with a lack of color that bordered on austerity. Also, her first impression had been right, she saw now. The furnishings in this room were not nearly so old as those in the rest of the house. Who had fashioned this lavish retreat? It must have been Amelia, but who would have thought that her taste would have run to such heavy luxury?

Smoothing her hair that had been ruffled by the removal of her hat, Amanda moved toward the dressing table with its mirror. She felt a derisive smile curve her lips, for she expected to see a terrible color clash when her auburn hair was reflected against the background of red and pink and silver. Then the smile faded. The vibrant colors behind her seemed to bring burnished life to her smoothly styled hair and to give a glowing sheen to her complexion while the silver was repeated in the gray of her eyes. She suited that room more perfectly than she would have believed possible.

A peculiar feeling moved over her so that she shivered

without realizing it. It was like *déjà vu,* a term she had heard but never fully appreciated before. It was as if she had been there before, in front of that mirror, with the room at that precise angle behind her.

As she stared, her reflection dimmed. Turning, she saw that the light in the room had faded also. Beyond the window it appeared that night had fallen with amazing swiftness, but as she moved to stand peering out she saw that the effect was caused by a black cloud looming up from the southeast. The wind had risen; she could see the tops of the trees threshing in the woods some distance from the house. The gray-blue light had drawn the color from the grass leaving it without life, flattened by the wind.

As she watched she saw her gig, with a man at the reins, being driven along the wagon track toward the barn among the trees. Perhaps Jason had given orders for her horse to be watered. It was a thoughtful gesture. It had been a long dry drive.

Aware of her own thirst, she turned quickly when the door opened behind her. She would be glad to return to the parlor downstairs for her refreshment.

A woman stood in the doorway. She gave a gasp followed by a single word that rose to a shriek.

"No!"

Amanda swallowed, a nerve throbbing in her throat. Then she moved into the center of the room toward the large woman.

"What is it? What is the matter?"

"Grüss Gott," the woman breathed, putting her hand to a massive bosom. "You gave me a turn."

"I didn't mean to startle you. I was waiting for Sophia to bring water."

"*Ach,* that one! She says to me, 'Look in Amelia's room. There is a surprise.' The mischief maker. I'll have her eyes some day! But don't be alarmed. I have no anger for you. I know well it is the doing of that one. It is no fault of yours that you have the size, the hair, and the eyes of Madame Amelia."

Amanda summoned a smile. "Amelia and I always favored. However, you will notice that my eyes are gray. Hers were almost the color of violets."

Ponderously the woman moved closer, squinting to see in the dim room. "Yes. It is so," she agreed, nodding. "Ah, the violets. How Madame Amelia loved them, their scent, their color . . . You knew Madame Amelia? You are her kinswoman, it may be?"

"A cousin. Our fathers were brothers. We were brought up together by our grandparents."

"Of course! You will be her dear Amanda, *nicht?* She spoke of you sometimes, when her heart turned toward home. She told me of how your fathers were killed in the war and of how your mother died of the fever and her own mother remarried a man with no use for a child . . . especially another man's child."

In the guttural accents of the woman, Amanda thought she recognized a member of Louisiana's German colony. Lured to Louisiana by John Law's Mississippi bubble, they had made a section above New Orleans, known as the German Coast, their own. Their culture had added a soupçon more flavor to the already rich blend of French, Spanish, Scots-English, African, and Indian heritages in the state.

"I didn't mean to be so long . . ."

Sophia, coming through the door with a pitcher of water in one square, rather brown hand and a towel over her arm, spoke to Amanda. "I see you have met our capable Marta. Has she told you her life's story yet? Never mind. She will, given the chance. I advise you to be ruthless. Tell her at once you don't want to hear anything so boring."

"At least I am a decent, God-fearing woman," Marta retaliated, a scowl drawing her small, pale blue eyes together. "I have no need for the prayers of other people."

"Pray for me, Marta, when you fall down on your knees tonight before your stern God. Pray for my wicked soul."

"Do you dare to mock the Lord, you blasphemous creature? Sin lies upon you like dirt upon the ground. You should always go robed in scarlet. The Lord knows your sins, he knows, and he will mete out punishment, you will see, you will see."

"Don't be tiresome, Marta. Go away." Sophia gave the big woman a push toward the door.

Marta shook her off. "Don't order me. You have not the right. I go, but it is because I have no liking for seeing your sly face."

Sophia closed the door with a vindictive snap while the other woman was still speaking, then moved to place the pitcher on the washstand. "That Marta," she said with a touch of scorn. "I can't see why Jason keeps her on. She is no use anymore."

"No use?" Amanda asked, seeing that some contribution to the conversation was expected of her.

"She calls herself a nurse, in imitation of Miss Nightingale, but lady's maid would be more like it. She was Amelia's slave from the moment Jason brought her here. For me, I doubt she could help with a hangnail." A grimace twisted her lips.

Amanda walked to the washstand. She wiped the grime from the bowl with the towel and then tipped water into it. Picking up the soap she asked, "Amelia needed a nurse?"

"Didn't you know?"

"We . . . didn't hear from her often. My grandfather never approved of the marriage."

"Yes, I know. Stupid of him. Jason could have been of invaluable aid with his resources."

Her grandfather had not needed Jason's aid, but Amanda made no comment. She patted her face dry then let her gaze go to the window where a streak of lightning flashed.

"Was she ill long?"

"Several months. She was delicate from the first, complaining of headaches and lying about in her dressing gown."

Delicate? Amelia had been a normal, healthy girl. There had never been any questions of weakness or ill health of a chronic nature before her marriage.

"When exactly . . . did she die?"

"It must be over three months. Odd, it seems longer. I suppose that's because Jason has been so hard to live with."

"What caused it . . . how did it happen?"

"The doctor from town said it was a growth in her head. She couldn't stand the pain. In the end she took her own life. She drank an overdose of the laudanum she had been taking to ease her."

"Amelia? Take her own life? I can't believe it." Amanda whispered. "She would never have done such a thing."

"No? You should have been here to hear her cry

and beg for death," Sophia said with a callous authority that forbade contradiction.

As they made their way back downstairs Amanda could not rid herself of her first conviction. Amelia could not have committed suicide. She had been so gay, so carefree. She loved all the bright things in life, sunny days, parties, music, pretty clothes in brilliant colors. She had loved to laugh, to meet new people. When they had gone away to boarding school, the seminary for young ladies, Amelia had been the one who was taken up by everyone. She had been the one with the most friends, the most secrets to giggle over.

When they were children together they had been close, she and Amelia, dependent on each other for help and companionship, and they had remained good friends within the framework of the school, but Amanda could not help feeling left out.

She had been a quiet solemn child, a reserved young woman with a strong practical streak that had been fostered by her grandparents. She was apt to choose materials for her clothes for their durability and failure to show soiling rather than for beauty. Lacking the outgoing personality of Amelia, she had never really cared for the gregarious life of the boarding school, and so she had not been upset when she had been called home to look after her grandmother in her last illness.

It was in the last months of the final term, after Amanda had gone, that Amelia had met Jason Monteigne. It had been at a house party near Christmas, a party given by the parents of one of her many friends. She had been, for Amelia, strangely secretive about the meeting. She had known their grandfather, a Scotsman by birth and a staunch Presbyterian, would not approve of a man whose mother was half French and half Indian of the Caddo tribe, whose father had made his fortune as a riverboat gambler, and who was himself a follower of Popery. The week after Amelia had returned to school from attending her grandmother's funeral, she had eloped with Jason.

With a shake of her head, Amanda pushed the memories of that time, more than three years past, from her mind. She could not allow herself to dwell on those days now.

In the front parlor they found a small but cheerful fire burning beneath the Adams mantel. Its warm glow dispelled some of the gathering gloom, lending an air of spurious hospitality to the room. A pair of lamps illuminated the corners, a condition the room tolerated in stiff discomfort, like an elderly matron enduring the revealing light of the sun upon her patched and faded garments.

The flickering lamplight also disclosed a portrait hanging above the mantel. It shone on gold buttons and braid and slid gleaming along the length of a dress sword. The figure was a soldier in the tailored gray of an officer of the Confederate Army. One hand rested on the hilt of his sword, the other held a broad-brimmed campaign hat, letting it lie against his gold-striped trouser leg. There was pride and confidence in every line, from the set of the straight, broad shoulders, to the firm placing of the booted feet. In the background was the spread of green field with long, arrow-straight furrows pointing toward a white pillared mansion on a hill. The house was Monteigne and the soldier, young, carefree, faintly reckless, was Jason.

22

"A handsome devil, isn't he?" Sophia mocked as Amanda stood gazing up at the portrait.

Amanda looked away at once, moving to hold out her hands to the flames beneath the mantel. "I hadn't realized . . . that is . . . Amelia never mentioned that he had fought in the war."

"Amelia had no use for unpleasant things. She tried very hard to forget them, and she usually succeeded."

"You seem to have known my cousin well," Amanda said. She could not disagree with this appraisal of her Amelia's character. It was true enough, though she could not, as Sophia's tone suggested, consider it a fault.

"We . . . my brother and I . . . have been neighbors of Jason's all our lives. We have always been in and out of each other's houses. And, of course, I have been serving as Jason's housekeeper since we lost our plantation."

"I see."

"No, I'm sure you don't," the other woman said, smiling at Amanda's carefully neutral tone. "We could not pay the back taxes, and a slimy carpetbagger bought our home at a Sheriff's auction. Jason took us in. Since Amelia was ill, I made myself useful."

There was nothing surprising in the tale. People in the South had been put to stranger shifts in the last few years. What was odd was the satisfaction Sophia seemed to feel in the arrangement.

Before she could comment, footsteps were heard in the hallway outside and a man appeared in the doorway. Of average height, he was broad in the chest and shoulders, creating an impression of stockiness. His hair, the color of cornsilk, lay fine and thin across his skull. A mask of pale gold freckles covered his face, testifying to his outdoor occupation. With his blue eyes and pale lips he was obviously related to Sophia, though the smile which lit his features was warmer by several degrees.

"Allow me to present my brother, Theodore Abercrombie. Theo, this is Amelia's cousin, Amanda Trent." Sophia performed the introduction with bad grace.

"Delighted, Miss Trent," Theo said, inclining his head. "If I had known we had a visitor, I would have taken more trouble removing my dirt. I am afraid I've only just come from the fields. We're harvesting, you know, trying to get the last cotton boll before the fall rains begin."

"Miss Trent isn't interested in your problems," his sister said, a cutting edge to her voice. "She only came on a small errand. She will be leaving shortly."

Theo glanced beyond them to the window which framed a towering mass of dark clouds roiled by the wind. A frown creased his brow before he spoke. "Oh? I'm sorry to hear that. I take it you have come to see Jason, Miss Trent. Can I run him to earth for you, or have you already spoken to him?"

Sophia answered for her. "He was here only a moment ago. I can't imagine where he has disappeared to."

"Or that he would dare to do it without telling you?" her brother murmured in a tone meant for his sister's ears alone. Sophia moved away with an angry swish of skirts. Taking up a poker, she prodded the logs in the fireplace, making them blaze up.

There was a smell in the air of dust and old wallpaper, of smoke, burning oak logs, and the sulphurous taint of the storm. Moving out of the way of the other woman,

24

Amanda took a seat on the slippery hardness of the green-striped silk settee.

Somewhere in the house a door slammed. The draft stirred the window hangings and caused the flames in the lamps to shiver. His footfalls loud in the stillness, Theo stepped to a chair opposite the settee and lowered himself into it. The change of position placed Amanda in the full glow of the lamp on the table beside her. Theo made a small sound in his throat that turned into a difficult cough. Glancing at him with a smile of ready sympathy, Amanda found him staring at her above the clenched fist he held to his lips. He looked away at once, but the freckles stood out on his face like blotches and for an instant his eyes had been dark with what had every appearance of shock.

Sophia, her attention also drawn to her brother's face, laughed. "You didn't expect that, did you? Isn't it just what you needed, what we all needed, to have the lovely face of dear dead Amelia return to haunt us?"

"Sophia," her brother said, a warning in his voice.

It was not needed. Sophia swung away, her lips tightly folded, as Jason strolled into the room.

As a concession to his guest he had donned a brown cord jacket. His dark hair was damp and newly brushed, and his trousers had been pulled down over boots wiped free of dust and dirt from the field. His eyes scanned the company, missing nothing, neither Theo's uncomfortable silence nor Sophia's sulky chagrin. His green gaze locked with Amanda's for the length of time it took her to recognize his iron self-control, and then he looked away.

"I believe, Miss Trent, that you were promised some

refreshment. On a night like this I think something with strength in it is in order."

Jason walked to the sideboard just inside the dining room which led from the parlor. Through the wide entrance that normally closed with tall double doors, she watched as he used water, already heating over a spirit lamp, to mix two glasses of negus. When he brought a glass to Sophia and herself, she thanked him without demur though she would have preferred plain water.

Returning to the sideboard he poured drinks from one of the bottles with silver tags, drinks with a much stronger color, for Theo and himself.

There was the distant rumble of thunder. Amanda looked up in time to see a brilliant streak of lightning crackle before a deafening roll of thunder exploded just above the house. She could not repress a start nor the frown that drew her brows together.

"There, did you see that?" Theo asked leaning forward in his chair to send her a smile. "The rain will break any minute. You can't mean to try for town. You must stay."

There was a warmth about Sophia's brother that inspired liking. His bright blue eyes held genuine concern for her safety and well-being. Waiting for her answer, he seemed completely oblivious of the fact that the hospitality he was pressing upon her was not his to offer. "I couldn't impose," Amanda said, flicking a glance on her host.

Theo caught the implication of that flutter of the lashes. "No imposition. Isn't that so, Jason?"

"By all means, stay," Jason answered, looking briefly from his glass with an expression devoid of either concern or welcome.

As his eyes slid over her, Amanda felt that he was deliberately keeping his face blank, as if he was enduring her presence as best he might until the time he could be released from the memories the sight of her inevitably brought back to him. The grieving widower. Was it a pose? she wondered, and then flushed as Jason looked up to catch her watching him, the speculation plain upon her expressive face.

"I would really rather go back into town," she said dropping her gaze to the glass in her hands.

"Nonsense. Think of the danger," Theo insisted with a seriousness hidden by a gallant air.

Sophia intervened. "Perhaps if Amanda insists on going back, one of you could act as her escort."

"An excellent idea, Sophia," her brother exclaimed, "I volunteer."

"Really, there is no need," Amanda protested.

"None of us here at Monteigne would be able to forgive ourselves if anything happened to you. If you must go, I go with you." He glanced at Jason as though for support. Their host was in the process of pouring himself a fresh drink. The look he sent Theo was quite unreadable to Amanda, still it had the effect of sending the hot blood rushing to Theo's hairline.

A species of indignation stirred in Amanda's breast. Theo was, so far, the only one who had tried to be kind to her. It was the outside of enough to see him belittled for his efforts.

"If you are certain you won't mind the drive, then I confess I would be glad of the company," she said. It was true enough. An escort, a man at the reins, would be a comfort on these unknown roads after dark. She had lost her way once this afternoon, there was nothing to keep her from doing so again. Too, although she had seen no sign of unusual activity earlier, she was not blind to the possibility of being molested if her assailants discovered she was a woman alone.

"I will not mind," Theo answered so simply no one could doubt the truth of his statement.

Thunder vibrated through the room. Hard on the sound Sophia spoke. "Even with an escort, it really is foolish of you to think of leaving now, you will be soaked to the skin, or worse, blown off the road. What would it hurt to stay a little longer, until the rain stops? And as long as you are waiting, you may as well take dinner with us. Theo, I'm certain, will want to fortify himself for the long drive into town and back."

It would not be fair to expect Theo to wait until his return for his meal. Reluctantly Amanda agreed.

"Good. That's settled," Theo said, setting down his glass and rubbing his hands together before holding them out to the fire. "Getting cooler, be Hallowe'en in little more than a week."

"Will it? Yes, I suppose so," Amanda said, mentally counting up the days.

"All Hallow's Eve. We shall have to lay in a stock of candles."

"Candles?"

"For the Night of the Candles."

"I don't . . . oh, you mean for the cemetery. Do you keep that custom?"

"We, Sophia and I, have French Catholic ancestors like so many in this area. If you have never seen the cemetery glimmering with candlelight to keep away the demons on All Hallow's Eve, you should make the effort. As a custom it has a certain macabre charm."

"Don't let my brother persuade you, Miss Trent," Sophia said in her husky voice. "The occasion has a religious significance, it's true, but it is also an excuse for the most diabolical and disgusting tricks ever to be invented by a childish mind. I have no liking for cemeteries at the best of times, but I keep a wary eye out on The Night of the Candles."

"I resent the implication!" Theo said, then sobered with a quick, slanting glance at Jason. "I don't imagine any of us will be in a frolicsome mood this particular year."

He referred, of course, to the still fresh bereavement, the new grave with Amelia's name on the stone. The thought cast a pall on the company that Theo tried to break by turning brisk and matter of fact.

"Well, when do we eat?"

His sister lifted her feathery blond lashes in a languid sweep. "Dinner will be ready when Proserpine is ready and not one second sooner, you know that. This evening she was late starting dinner because her second granddaughter has a cold, and she had to carry her some peppersauce for her cough."

Amanda sipped her hot, watered wine with sugar and spices. She was not very hungry. She had taken a lunch hamper from the hotel this morning and eaten it along the way. How long ago that seemed. Then she had thought to find Amelia alive. She had expected that they would have a comfortable gossip and she might visit a day or two. Her bags were in the gig. She had missed Amelia, her sprightly ways and infectious laugh, missed having someone to talk nonsense to now and then. Amelia had been such a happy person and so young to die. But she must not go on thinking in this vein or she would be crying, here in front of these strangers. She took a deep, resolute breath.

"You must be alone in the world now, Amanda, if what you say about your grandparents is true. What are you going to do with yourself?" Sophia's voice was polite but a new curiosity gleamed in her brown eyes.

"I won't be alone for long. I am engaged to be married, probably in the spring."

"Your fiancé allowed you to come here alone?" Jason asked.

"I can see you don't approve. Women have had to become independent here in the South since the war, Mr. Monteigne. There are not enough men to escort all the women left alone."

"That doesn't answer my question."

"No, perhaps not. To be perfectly honest, I didn't tell Nathaniel I was coming. He was away on business in New Orleans. He is a lawyer, you see, and interested in politics. I had the opportunity to travel as far as Natchitoches with friends who were going on to Shreveport, and I could not allow the chance to pass. It isn't as if it were a journey around the world, you know. It's only a matter of some sixty or sixty-five miles from my grandfather's plantation."

"Oh, your grandfather had a plantation? What will become of it now?" Sophia probed, ignoring her brother's frown of disapproval.

"It will have to be sold. It is too far from town to be practical for Nathaniel and me to live there, as much as I hate the idea of leaving the old house. It was nothing very grand, since it was built before the cotton boom, but I love it." Amanda had the feeling that she was being drawn, but it could not matter, and it was necessary to pass the time somehow.

"You have moved then?"

"I'm just on the verge of doing so. Most of my things are packed away. But I wanted to clear away all my obligations first. Nathaniel and I are going to build a new house on the edge of town."

"An edifice suitable for a rising young lawyer-politician, of course," Sophia commented. "I'm sure your grandfather's money will come in handy."

Amanda was silent a moment, long enough to quell the impulse to answer such cynicism as it deserved, before she replied. "That is not the case at all."

"No? Tell me, Amanda. With whom are you going to live until the wedding?"

"Why, with Nathaniel's parents. They have quite a nice home themselves. Nathaniel is hardly a pauper."

"That may be, but politics is notoriously expensive, and it appears to me that your young man is being very sure of you. So sure that you felt you had to escape him the moment his back was turned."

"That isn't true!" Amanda exclaimed, staring at Sophia with real horror.

"Pay no attention to my sister," Theo said with a dismissing wave of his hand. "She enjoys the pose of the worldly wise cynic. Don't let her infect you with the disease."

"I'm sure there's no danger of that," Jason drawled. "Amanda hasn't the look of the easily disenchanted."

"Are . . . are you suggesting that I am gullible?" Anger boiled up suddenly. Why should they bother when she would go out of their lives in an hour or so, never to see them again? Why should they attack her with their verbal barbs? Although uninvited she was still a guest, and this was the height of discourtesy.

Thunder rumbled again and then, in the midst of the sound, came the ringing of a handbell.

"At last!" Theo got to his feet and gave his hand to Amanda as she rose, then tucked her hand into his elbow, and led her toward the dining room, leaving his sister to follow with Jason. They were met at the foot of the stairs by the nurse, Marta. The woman, her face almost purple from the exertion of hurrying, fell in behind them.

Jason took his place at the head of the table. The cook, Proserpine, standing behind his chair, ran her eyes over the company, and then, a carefully blank look hiding her displeasure, went away to bring another place setting for Amanda. Amanda glanced at Sophia, but if the woman had been made to feel she had been derelict in her duties, she gave no sign. Sophia took her place, automatically on Jason's right and watched with an amused expression as her brother held the chair on the left for Amanda, then sat down beside her.

It was a simple meal. Vegetable soup was followed by crisp golden chicken stuffed with herbs, fluffy biscuits the size of a silver dollar, gravy, rice, smoked ham with sweet potatoes, and some of the eggplants of the season mealed and fried. Dessert was a pie made with fresh pecans and cane syrup, still warm from the oven.

The courses were accompanied by wine, and Amanda noticed that Jason refilled his glass often from the decanter at his elbow.

Halfway through the meal the rain began, falling thick and heavy on the roof, while the lightning flickered continuously beyond the muslin curtains over the windows.

There was not much conversation. The storm seemed to have a depressing effect on the group around the board, excepta for Marta who ate with a stolid unconcern for the other diners, pushing the food into her mouth by the forkful. Theo and Sophia spoke now and then, employing the short swift comments of those long used to each other's thoughts and opinions. Jason sat morose, staring at his wine glass, now and then raising his eyes to let his gaze slide over Amanda as if he would like to stare but would not allow himself to do so. A scowl drew his brows together, and she wondered if his anger was directed at himself or at her.

As Prosperpine, a big woman with a round face on which ill nature had stamped strong lines, brought the last dessert plate, she stopped beside Jason.

"Yes, what is it?" he asked without looking up.

"That tramp, the crazy Carl. He's done come in out of the rain. He's eatin' in my kitchen right now."

"And?"

"And this time he's got a lizard with him, feedin' it off his plate!"

"A lizard?"

"One of them . . . change-lizards."

"Chameleon."

"That's right. I ain't puttin' up with no such carryin'-on in my good clean kitchen. You tell him to take himself off. I ain't havin' no lizard runnin' around on the table where I eat!"

Jason sighed. "What can it hurt? You have to make allowances for Carl."

"I'm through making 'lowances. A kitty-cat I can stand, but I ain't standin' no scaly lizard with beady eyes and a wicked, forked tongue! What if that little beast gets loose in the stranger's bedroom tonight? It's me that'll . . ."

"All right, all right. I'll speak to him."

Mollified, Proserpine nodded and moved with head held high and a slow step from the room, her skirts rustling from the paper she had sewn to her petticoats to imitate the sound of taffeta.

Chapter
Two

"IF you will take my advice, you will throw that madman out of the house for good," Sophia said dispassionately.

"I can't help but agree with Sophia," her brother supported her. "I never have understood your soft spot for that crazy man. Nobody else would let a lunatic have the run of the house to the point of keeping a bed ready for him. What's he to you?"

"He is a victim of divine wrath. You remember. *Those whom the gods would destroy they first make mad*. Let us say I have a certain fellow feeling."

"Oh come, Jason. Don't let's begin in that vein again," Sophia said in a scathing tone.

"Why not? It is a perfect night for it. My dear wife has returned to me in the image of her cousin. We have gloom enough for a dozen morbid soliloquies. Let us speak then of love and madness and despair, and, finally, of death. It was not so long ago after all, the night Amelia died. Amanda, lovely Amanda, who is so like our own Amelia, burns with curiosity—a curiosity she is too much the lady to display. Let us remember then the night Amelia died. Drag forward the shuddering memories of flowers and funereal draperies. Put them on display. The coffin on its bier, her marble face, her crossed hands, the golden gleam of her wedding ring in the glow of the candles, her hair, so alive. God, so alive!"

Theo stirred uncomfortably. "Jason . . ."

"Let us remember. Why forget? Why should we try to suppress the memory of the pain and the screams in the night or the terrible pleading in her eyes? There were demons in her head, she said, tiny monsters slowly cutting her mind into slivers with sharp knives. Don't stare so, Amanda . . . the end was near, no one could help, no doctor would try. And so the nights and the hot cloud-less days of July ran on, and then one midnight that is nothing more than a miasma of cringing horror and fatigue and helplessness—she died. She died at last, and we were glad."

It was with an effort that Amanda looked away from the twisted smile on his bronze face and the glitter of his eyes. With a trembling hand she crumpled the napkin in her lap, dropped it beside her plate, and got to her feet. She felt raw, lacerated, by the intensity of the grief Jason had shown her. Vaguely she was aware of a noisy sobbing, coming from the nurse, Marta, and of tears standing in her own eyes. She felt torn between a desire to offer some form of comfort to Jason and a longing to get away from him.

But as she stood she was brought up short. The hem of

her dress was caught beneath the leg of Theo's chair. Hastily he rose and touched her elbow. "Perhaps you would like to come into the parlor?" he asked. "Proserpine will bring coffee there."

"I . . . no. No coffee. I would just like to go. Please."

"You can't, not in this storm. Try a little coffee."

"No, really, all I want is to go."

"I insist," he said, drawing her away from the table.

For the first time in her life Amanda found herself hating all the polite mouthings that people use to cover their real feelings. What did Theo care whether she went or stayed? It could make no possible difference to him. "I only want my bonnet, my reticule, and my gloves so that I can remove myself from this house!"

"I'll get your things," Sophia said.

"No," Theo said, but his sister paid no attention, moving past him toward the door.

"My . . . horse . . . and gig?" Amanda clasped her hands together, trying to appear imperious, determined —wishing her voice would not tremble so when she was upset.

Without a word Jason rose and left the room. In a moment they heard the slam of the outside door.

Theo shook his head. "It's folly, but if nothing can turn you away from it, at least come in and sit down in the parlor while you wait. I hope Jason has the good sense to put my mare on a leading rein and my saddle in the gig. I still mean to come with you, and I will not take no for an answer."

Amanda obediently moved beside him, leaving Marta alone, hiccuping at the table and consoling herself with a second piece of pie. In the parlor Amanda seated herself on the green striped settee. There was a crewel-embroidered cushion beside her, and she began to play nervously with the long green fringe that edged it.

Somewhere in the house, in the hall, she thought, there was a grandfather clock for she could hear it ticking. The sound of the rain had dwindled. She was glad since it made her leaving easier.

Theo stood beneath the brass chandelier in the center of the oriental carpet of once rich colors on gold. "You mustn't blame Jason for what he said just now. He took Amelia's death hard. I have the idea sometimes that he blames himself, though it's hard to see what else he could have done for her. You . . . the way you look . . . brought it all back."

"I can see that. However, Jason seems to have forgotten that I can feel grief too."

"Possibly. Grief is a selfish emotion bound up with the sense of personal loss. Still, he meant nothing against you, and I don't want you to . . . to take too much to heart all the hurtful things he said."

"I appreciate your concern . . ."

"Theo . . . call me Theo," he broke in.

". . . Theo. Really there's no need to worry about me. I'm not, truly, a very emotional person. I don't believe a few words spoken in anger can hurt me."

That was certainly true. Now that she was calmer she could feel her usual self-control returning, wrapping around her like a protective comforter. How often in the past had she regretted her inability to expose her emotions. Amelia had not been like that. Amelia had been quick to anger, her rage flaring up, then quickly dying away. Her joy had known no bounds, her affection had been swiftly given, conveyed without restraint or embarrassment. When she cried she had wept aloud, not suffered the aching constriction of silent tears that Amanda knew. How had it come about? *Look at Amanda,* her grandmother had said often in those early days. *She knows the conduct becoming in a lady.* And the young Amanda, only a year older than Amelia, had tried to be a model of poise and reserve to keep her grandmother's approval. Well, it didn't matter now. Still, how wonderful it must have been for a time to be loved with such desperation. Desperation—a strange word to use in conjunction with love. What she had meant was that degree of intensity.

Theo was still standing before her.

"Are you sure you wouldn't like something else while you wait? Another glass of wine?"

"Thank you, Theo, but no. I'm all right. It . . . it is nice for you to be concerned about me . . . and about Jason."

He looked almost embarrassed. "As to that, Jason has been a good friend. We grew up together, neighbors, until after the war. My family lost everything. The shock was too much for my parents. They're still living, if you can call it that, with an older sister in town. Jason's people died during the war—his father on the battlefield, his mother and younger brother of typhoid—along with quite a few of the hands here. We were alone. Jason took me in as a sort of overseer. And then, of course, Sophia came to help keep house when Amelia got so bad. Yes, we owe Jason a great deal."

Amanda murmured something agreeable, looking up as Sophia came into the room carrying her things and also a long cloak, thrown over her arm.

Sophia handed the bonnet with the gloves inside it and

the reticule to Amanda, then draped the cloak over the arm of the settee. "I thought you might need this to protect you from the rain. It is coated with rubber. Theo will have one like it, and this will keep him from having to play the gallant and give it to you."

"Sophia . . ." Theo began.

"Well I'm sure Amanda has no wish to shelter with you under yours, and the gig does have open sides."

"Thank you," Amanda said, quietly holding the other girl's chilled gaze. Sophia did not look away.

"There is an oiled silk umbrella beside the door you can use. You can give it, and the cloak also, to Theo when you get into town."

"Yes, I'll do that." When had the other woman become so antagonistic? Had it been when she had learned that Amanda was independent with property of her own? Or was it later, when Jason had shown himself so disturbed by her presence, when he had called her lovely?

Sophia started to speak again, then stopped as the sound of footsteps crossing the gallery came to them. Amanda rose as Jason, his hair and his clothes dripping with rain, came in the door.

He stood a moment staring at Amanda, then abruptly he moved to one side. "The gig is ready," he said tonelessly.

Theo reached for the cloak and, shaking out its folds, placed it on Amanda's shoulders. With fingers gone suddenly numb, she placed her bonnet on her hair and thrust the bodkin through the crown to secure it. Then pulling on her gloves, she walked past Jason out onto the dark gallery. Theo and Jason followed her. Sophia came last, carrying a lamp to light their way down the steps.

Then at the top of the steps Sophia suddenly exclaimed, "Wait!"

Theo swung around. "What is it?"

"The necklace, Jason."

"Oh, yes." Amanda began to take her purse from her wrist.

"Never mind," Jason said. "It is yours. Keep it."

"What necklace?" Theo asked, his eyes moving from one to the other. "I don't understand."

"The collar of something. A valuable piece of jewelry Amanda was bringing to her cousin, a part of some legacy. It belongs to Jason now." Sophia spoke impatiently, her eyes on Amanda, her face hard in the lamplight. Beyond the circle of light a soft rain fell. The horse snorted, shaking his head so the bit and harness jangled. Out in the dark behind one of the tall columns a shadow moved, or was it only a wind-blown gust of rain?

Then Amanda had her bag open. "Here," she said, distaste for this house and the people in it making her voice cold as she pushed the collar of gold and gems at Jason. "Take it. I don't want it."

His brows drew together in a scowl. "You think I do? What use would I have for that, or for all the jewels of Arabia? Let it adorn your own milk-white skin. Let it be a token of remembrance for you. For me, I need none."

For a moment longer Amanda stood there, then she let her hand drop. Turning she started down the steps.

At that moment the shadow beside the column started forward.

"My Madame!" The cry was loud, joyous. A shambling form came running toward her. A bearded and wild-eyed man took the first of the steps, then dropped suddenly to his knees and caught up the hem of her dress, lifting it to his lips.

Amanda, already beginning her descent, was thrown off balance. She lurched, reaching blindly for support, then she was falling, falling away from the shouts and clutching, jostling, confusion into a bright well of pain with darkness at the bottom.

Her head was on fire, her brain burning with a flame that flared high as she was lifted, but left her body cold. There was a roaring of an angry voice in her ears, and she felt as if she was tied by steel bonds to a moving rock. Andromeda, she thought dazedly, sacrificed to the sea serpent. Then she knew no more.

Amanda opened her eyes. Above her was a silver cloud pierced by a gold sun . . . the underside of the canopy of Amelia's tester bed. Within her skull a drum beat a monotonous rhythm to the pulsation of her heart. Beneath her were sheets of smooth starched linen, and over her was a comforter of padded silk. The nightgown she wore was her own plain dimity, laundered many times into a soothing softness.

She turned her head a little, frowning in concentration that sent throbbing waves between her temples. What was she doing here? Then as she remembered the night and the storm and her fall, there was a rustle nearby, and a wide white figure moved into her line of vision.

"How do you feel now?"

With difficulty Amanda focused on the woman. She was familiar, and yet the name hovered out of reach. She wanted to answer the question that had been put to her, but there seemed to be a great distance between her mind and her lips.

"I'm Marta. Don't you remember?"

Slowly she nodded. Marta, a sickroom nurse. For Amelia. She moistened her lips. "My . . . head."

"You hit it when you fell. You have a concussion, I think. I have seen it before, during the war. It should not be so bad."

No, it couldn't be. The steps were not high, little more than five or six feet. The throbbing went on and on. She lay very still, hoping it would diminish if she did not move.

Two lamps were burning in the room, one on the marble-topped washstand, one on the table near the bed. Darkness still lingered beyond the windows, and she thought she could hear the whisper of falling rain on the wooden shingles above.

"It was kind of you to put me to bed."

"It was nothing. I can't say to you how shocked I was when *Herr* Jason came carrying you up the stairs with you pale, so pale, and that great bruise there just under your hair. Such a commotion. One would have thought you were dead with that Carl weeping and wringing of his hands, and Sophia cold, so cold, toward her brother while *Herr* Jason just walked away from them all, his face, as he carried you, *ach*, so . . . so like death."

The German woman's eyes were wide with wonder, but there was a sympathetic understanding also in her face.

"My head aches," Amanda said, her voice sounding faint to her own ears.

"Yes, I have just the thing. Eau de cologne in water cold from the cistern. Let me put this cloth on your forehead . . ."

The smell of violets, sweet and fresh, scented the air as the excess water was squeezed from the pad made of a small linen towel. It was cool and refreshing, but it did not stop the pain. In a few moments the smell of the violets, warmed by her skin, began to intensify until she felt as though she were drowning in the scent.

"Take it away. Please, take it away." Lifting a hand she pushed at the cloth.

"But it will help the ache inside your head," Marta protested, setting it back in place.

"No, no. It makes me feel ill. Take it away."

"All right, all right, if you say so," the nurse agreed as Amanda's voice began to rise. "I'll just go and pour this out and bring some cold water, without the cologne. It is all I can do. There is not another thing in the house."

The door closed behind her, and Amanda lay very still, fighting the lingering feeling of nausea. When the door opened a moment later she did not open her eyes, thinking it was Marta returning. It was only when the shuffling whisper of soft, hesitant footsteps on the rug came to her that she slowly turned her head.

"My Madame . . ."

Amanda caught her breath remembering the hoarse voice, the bearded face with wild eyes that had come at her from out of the rainswept darkness just before she fell. Then she saw the apprehension that drew the face of the creature before her into a caricature of woe, and she managed to smile.

"Oh, Madame. You have come back."

He was a small man, or seemed to be because of the permanent stoop that bent his shoulders. His sandy hair was a tangle of thick curls tied back with a piece of grime-blackened leather. If the damp clothes he wore had ever had shape or color, they had lost it. There were no shoes on his feet with their thick, calloused soles. In his hand he carried a battered gray hat with a tarnished insignia of some kind, and over his shoulder was slung a cloth bag which bulged at the sides. The gray-streaked beard that covered his lower face made him seem ancient, but from his cheeks and forehead and the squint lines around his pale brown eyes, Amanda thought he could not be much older than Jason and Theo. He had brought with him into the room the freshness of the outdoors combined with the taint of woodsmoke, nothing else. Still there was something of the animal about him. What was the name the cook had used? Crazy Carl? It had to be him.

"What do you want?"

"To . . . to see you," he said in a voice that was nearly a whisper. "Just to see you." He inched nearer the bed, his eyes fixed on Amanda's face. As she stared at him she realized that tears were tracking slowly down his cheeks.

He thinks that I'm Amelia. The realization came with a sudden clarity. He thinks that I'm Amelia, returned from the dead.

Slowly he advanced toward the bed. When his foot touched the set of carpet-padded steps beside the tall four-poster he glanced down, then went down on his knees, his mouth open and the light of reverence in his tear-filled eyes. Gropingly he reached for her hand that lay curled on top of the coverlet.

Amanda shivered as she felt the damp warmth of his fingers. She wanted to draw away, but she knew that the slightest movement would make her head pound.

"I . . . I'm so happy that you are back," he said in a

husky stammer. "Don't ever go away again. Don't let them make you go. I cannot live if . . . if they make you go away again."

"What is this! What in the world are you doing in here!" The high, strident voice belonged to Sophia. She stood in the doorway in her dressing gown of white satin trimmed with blond lace, her hair spilling over her shoulders.

At the sight of Sophia, a vacant look came over the man's face. He got slowly to his feet and stood staring at Sophia, his hat in his hands and his shoulders sagging.

"Get out! Get out, I say. I've told you time and time again. Why can't you understand, you stupid idiot? I won't have you up here. I can't stand the sight of you, your drooling face and sly ways. If I catch you up here again I'll . . . I'll have Jason throw you off the plantation!"

"Sophia, please," Amanda whispered, closing her eyes against the waves of distress that broke inside her mind, mingling with the throbbing ache.

But the protest seemed to add to Sophia's ire. Glancing about she saw a small hearth broom beside the fireplace. A quick movement and she held it in her hands, brandishing it at Carl.

"I told you to get out," she cried, taking a step toward him.

A slow smile grew on Carl's face and with a cunning look in his eyes he shuffled forward, not toward the door but toward Sophia.

A look of alarm appeared on her smooth ivory face. She stopped and uncertainly lowered the broom. Carl moved a bit more.

"Here now! Here . . ." It was Marta, standing in

the hall doorway, a pan held in both hands, her wide face pale as she took in the scene with amazed eyes.

"What is this?"

At the harsh voice they all froze and then turned guiltily toward the door that led into the room next door. Jason stood there just tying the belt of his dressing gown with an angry jerk.

"What is all this noise? Marta is the only one who should be here."

"I found this creature in here bothering Amanda," Sophia began. "He is obviously out of his head. He thinks she . . ."

"I just went to bring some fresh water without the cologne in it, which upset Miss Amanda. Her head . . ."

"All right!" Jason cut off both explanations. "Out. Everybody but Marta. Carl, come. I'll see you downstairs." He waited politely for Sophia and Carl to precede him, then left the room, closing the door softly behind him.

Marta crossed to the washstand to set down her pan, then came toward the bed to lay the cool cloth once more upon Amanda's forehead.

"There. Is that better?"

Amanda nodded slowly, clenching her teeth with the effort. She found herself longing to be alone, to lie very still in the darkness, perhaps to sleep.

Marta fussed about, twitching the covers straight on the bed, picking up the hearth broom where Sophia had let it fall, and putting it back in place, wiping dust from the furniture. She gave the appearance of great efficiency, and it was with the attitude of someone interrupted in an important task that she turned to face Jason as he came quietly back into the room a few minutes later.

"How is she?"

At the ragged sound of his voice Amanda opened her eyes. It must be difficult for him, she thought, to see a woman who resembled his wife with her hair spread out upon the pillows where his wife had lain in her illness.

"She is in agony, *Herr* Jason." Marta answered his question in a low voice. "She needs something for it, but there is not a thing. You threw it all . . . every bottle . . . out, remember?"

Jason raised his head a fraction, staring at Marta, then he turned away without speaking and moved toward the bed.

"You are in pain?"

Amanda tried to nod but she could not. "Yes," she whispered.

"Fever?" he asked, looking at Marta.

"I think not," she answered. " 'Twas the blow to the head when she fell."

Jason's face tightened, but he reached out to lay his fingers against Amanda's cheek. "No, no fever . . ." he murmured, then stopped as his fingertips touched the track of helpless tears running from the corner of Amanda's eyes into her hair. His face tightened, and he seemed to grow pale beneath his tan.

"Concussion?"

"I am almost sure of it, *Herr* Jason."

He did not move for a long moment, then he sighed. "Wait," he said and swung away, moving to the door of his room. He reappeared in a moment carrying a small green bottle with a black stopper.

"You kept it!" Marta exclaimed, then shut her mouth, swallowing the rest of what she had been going to say.

Jason ignored her. A carafe of water had been placed on the table beside the bed, and he took up one of the small glasses turned upside down on its tray. With the stopper from the green bottle, he measured five careful drops into the glass, then slipped the bottle into his pocket. He added a little water and swirled the liquid to mix it. At last he moved nearer the bed and placed the glass in Amanda's hand, then stepped back with a brusque gesture to Marta indicating that she assist Amanda.

With Marta's strong arm beneath her shoulders, Amanda drank the elixir of opium. Then she lay back, her eyes barely open as she waited to be released from her pain.

She heard Marta set the glass down and move to sit down on the slipper chair as if she intended to keep an all-night vigil. Jason swung away, moving back toward his room.

She opened her eyes. "Thank you," she murmured. But if Jason heard her he gave no sign.

The blackness in her mind grew lighter, brightening until it had the glow of a spring day. She stood in a field of pink and white poppies, their fragile heads blowing in the wind. Coming toward her, running lightly without a sound, her hands outstretched, a smile of welcome on her face, was Amelia. She wore a dress of summer muslin sprigged with violets and green leaves, its flounces trimmed with purple ribbon. Her hair was loose, blowing in the gentle wind. There were gems, emeralds to match Jason's eyes, in her ears, and the collar of Harmonia around her neck. Running at her side was the great dog, Cerberus, his tongue lolling out with joy.

"Amanda!" the bewitching vision cried. Catching Amanda's hands, she swung her around dizzyingly, like the child's game of flying statues, relief mixed with the happiness sparkling in her pansy purple eyes. "I am so glad to see you. You are just the one I need. We always helped each other, didn't we? You will help me now, won't you?"

In her dream Amanda felt gladness, but it was overlaid by the impulse to draw back, to retreat from a suffocating fear.

She awoke, her heart beating high in her throat. She felt strange, disoriented, the effect, she supposed, of the opium. It was dark in the room. The lamps had gone out, leaving a smell of smoking wick and warm oil. Marta was a white blur in her chair from which issued a wheezing, even breathing. Then she heard the sound of music, a faint melody drawn from a Spanish guitar, sad, steeped in regret. She lay listening enthralled, strangely soothed. As the last notes died away she closed her eyes and slept, the pain in her head banished.

Chapter
Three

"YOU are awake, *fräulein*? *Guten Morgen*. How do you feel?" Marta, coming into the room with a breakfast tray containing coffee and hot rolls, brought Amanda's eyes open.

"Much better," she said, smiling up at the round concerned face of the nurse.

"That is good. The head, it still aches?"

"A little, but not as badly as it did last night. Marta . . ."

"Yes, *fräulein*?"

"Last night . . . it's nothing but confusion in my head. Was Mr. Monteigne here in this room?"

"Indeed yes," Marta answered as she placed the tray on the table and helped Amanda to sit up against a pile of pillows. "But 'twas nothing to disturb yourself about. He was concerned only with your welfare. He gave you medicine to stop the pain. It was most extraordinary, *fräulein,* you cannot know what it meant."

"Oh?" Amanda accepted the tray across her lap.

"*Ach,* your cousin, his wife, lay there in that bed crying with the terrible pain in her head. It was like the return of a bad dream to see you so."

"I can imagine. I'm sorry, terribly sorry."

"There is another thing. The medicine in the green bottle. It was this, the laudanum, the elixir of opium, that my *liebchen,* your cousin, used to take her life."

Shaking her head, Marta sat down in the chair and folded her hands.

Amanda was silent. It was no wonder Jason had looked so grim. Still, what could she have done? She could not help the accident that had placed her in this invidious position.

"Now, *fräulein,* you must not blame yourself. It may be that you would not have needed the laudanum, your condition might not have been called to the master's attention at all, if it had not been for that woman and the madman from the stranger's bedroom."

"Oh, yes . . . Sophia . . . and the one they call Crazy Carl. I remember now." She did remember, but it seemed fantastic, the shabbily dressed man kneeling beside her bed pressing his lips to her hand.

"Why was he here . . . that is, I know he thought I was Amelia, but why would he care so for her? What did she have to do with him?"

"That poor lady. She could never resist a stray. Carl now, no one knows his last name. He just came walking along the road one day. Near as anyone can tell he had been wandering, living hand to mouth, since the war. It seems sometimes, from what he says, that he was in a large battle with much . . . much artillery . . . is that the word? He was struck perhaps, or maybe it was only the noise, who can say? Madame Amelia took him in. She fed him, gave him clothes. He had been sleeping in the ditches, but she let him have the stranger's bedroom."

"Stranger's bedroom?"

"You don't know the custom? We are not so far from the river here at Monteigne. There is much traffic, of people going to the West, looking for something new, different, they know not what. A small bedroom is kept ready for the travelers caught nearby when night falls. Families, those who are kin or friends of kin, the traveling preacher, the circuit riders . . . all are welcome. It was so before the war when hospitality was a part of the life. It is so now."

"I had forgotten how soft-hearted Amelia was. But yes, she could never stand to see anything hurt or killed. She was fearless when it came to righting what she felt was an injustice."

"*Ach, ja,* that is my *liebchen.* No animal could be mistreated in her presence. Let me tell you. It was only last spring, just after I came to be with her. We were driving in town when she saw three or four boys with a half-grown puppy. They were tormenting the poor thing, dipping it into the water of the river, letting it near drown, laughing at its feeble struggles. She marched up to them and took it away. Perhaps you saw it in the yard? She named it Cerberus because it so nearly crossed the river . . . what was the name, I cannot think . . ."

"Styx."

"That is it! The dog stayed with her always until he grew too big to be in the house. He had no love for anyone but her. She had his whole heart. When she died he transferred his trust to that mad man, Carl. He obeys *Herr* Jason and tolerates the rest of us who live here at Monteigne; everyone else is an enemy. I shudder to think of how he howled the night she died. There was nothing that would make him stop."

"It is strange that you should mention the dog. I saw them together last night, in a dream."

"It is not so strange to me that you dreamed of her . . . not here, lying in her bed."

"No, but the dog . . ." But perhaps that was easily explained by the fact that he had frightened her earlier. The dream had been so real. There was something about it she felt she should remember, but it had faded away as dreams do in the light of morning. All she could recall was the great dog . . . and Amelia, wearing the collar of Harmonia.

"Marta?"

"*Ja, fräulein?*"

"What became of the collar of Harmonia . . . the necklace?"

"Necklace?"

"I had it in my hand when I fell. Did someone pick it up?"

"I have seen nothing of a necklace, *fräulein*. No one has said anything to me of it."

"Would you look in my reticule?"

"*Ja,* that I will," she answered and getting heavily to her feet, moved to the armoire and took down the small petit point purse. But though she turned the contents out onto the foot of the bed, there was no sign of the necklace.

"It could be that the master picked it up," Marta suggested.

Amanda nodded but in her thoughts she added . . .

or Sophia. The woman had wanted the necklace badly. What was to keep her from pocketing it on the spot, hoping that once it was in her possession Jason would relent and allow her to keep it? She had no right, no right at all. Or did she? Perhaps if she and Jason were planning to wed? But could that be so? Jason seemed so torn with grief. Amelia had been dead only a few months. It seemed unlikely that he could propose marriage again so soon. And yet Sophia had insinuated by her actions that there was some relationship between them. Men were human, and Amelia had been ill a long time. Sophia was an attractive woman, and she had been living under this roof nearly a year, according to Theo. She was not a girl anymore. If she was going to marry, it must be soon. There was no denying that Jason was a catch, a man still in possession of his home and with the necessary men and equipment to work the land, an attractive man, no more than thirty-five. Women, for the sake of security, had given themselves in marriage many times before to men with much less to recommend them. Would Sophia stay on here at Monteigne if she was not sure there was something to gain?

"Have you eaten, Marta?" Amanda was not used to constant care. Privacy had always been important to her, and it made her nervous that Marta sat watching her so that she could anticipate her every need.

"*Ja, fräulein.*"

"Is there nothing you need to do? I could entertain myself, reading perhaps, if you do."

"There are many books in *Herr* Jason's study. Shall I bring one or two?"

"Yes, please. Marta . . ."

"*Ja?*" She turned at the door.

"How long will it be before I can get up? I won't stay here, imposing on Mr. Monteigne's hospitality, a moment longer than is absolutely necessary."

"I cannot say, *fräulein*. It would be better if you did not leave your bed for two or three days, perhaps more if your headache does not leave you." She closed the door gently behind her.

Two or three days. Amanda let her shoulders sag against the pillow. She couldn't stay that long. Two or three days of strain, of feeling like an intruder, of stirring up the memories of the dead girl who had occupied these rooms, and who even now seemed to be keeping them alive. She couldn't bear it.

Marta returned with the books, but the effort of remembering, of speaking, and of trying to concentrate on the answers had made her head begin to ache again. She lay back with her eyes closed.

A short while later a knock came on the hall door. Marta moved to open it, and Amanda heard the murmur of a masculine voice.

"Marta?"

"It is *Herr* Theodore. He was asking after your health."

"Oh, would you ask him, please, about the necklace?"

"Certainly, *fräulein*."

Amanda could hear snatches of the conversation, enough to know that Theo was denying all knowledge of the missing piece of jewelry. She sighed, a frown flitting across her brow. It could not have disappeared.

When the door was closed, Marta came toward her. "*Herr* Theodore wishes me to convey to you his sorrow that you were injured, his joy that you are going to stay on for a time at Monteigne, and his most fervent hope that you will be able to come downstairs soon."

Amanda smiled a little as Marta heaved a sigh of relief at having delivered her message.

The nurse began to grumble, smoothing the coverlet and patting the pillow. "Don't fret yourself, *fräulein*, about the bauble. It will turn up; you will see."

The morning passed. Marta braided Amanda's hair, plied her with pungent tisanes of mint and spices and currant syrup, and insisted on laying a cool cloth over Amanda's forehead. Amanda submitted to her ministrations in the hope that she would be that much closer to returning to town—and from there back to her own life on her grandfather's plantation, her packing—and her plans for the wedding.

It was just before luncheon that Sophia came to see her.

"How are you?" she asked without preamble as she swung through the door, her brown eyes without warmth.

Marta looked up and a queer expression crossed her normally stolid face. She got to her feet.

"I'm much better," Amanda said, but Sophia was hardly listening.

"Is there anything you wanted to do, Marta?" she asked coolly. "I'm sure Amanda doesn't need a nurse at her side constantly, but I will be happy to stay for a few minutes if you have something that needs your attention."

"Yes," Marta licked her lips. "I was wishing for a bit of busy work to occupy my hands, not that I'm that much of a seamstress, but the time does lag." There was a nervous flutter in her voice but the look in her eyes as she let her gaze slide over Sophia was malignant. She moved through the door that Sophia had left open, closing it behind her with a slam.

Sophia laughed then turned toward the bed. "What have you been doing with yourself?"

"Reading—a little. Talking with Marta."

"I'll wager you have. What has our invaluable Marta been telling you?"

"Nothing really, we spoke of Carl and of the big dog, Cerberus."

"Oh, Cerberus, Amelia's pet. He's a vicious brute, but I don't suppose he can help it since it was Amelia who made him that way."

"Amelia?" Amanda couldn't keep the surprise out of her voice.

"Yes, dear Amelia. She couldn't stand to have him care for anyone else, even Jason. She was like that. Of course, Jason can control the beast by sheer strength of will, but Cerberus has no feeling for him or for anyone else now that Amelia is gone. If it were left to me, I'd have him destroyed."

"Amelia, my cousin Amelia, made him brutal? I can't believe it."

"No? I find that odd. You must not have known her as well as you thought . . . or . . . how long is it since you saw her last? Two . . . three years? People change."

"Amelia could never hurt anything."

"I never said she deliberately set out to hurt anyone," Sophia protested. "But there was something about her that inspired a fanatical loyalty. Well, look around you. There is Jason, hating you because you are not her. There is Marta, pathetically grateful to be allowed to serve you because you were connected with her. And Carl, worshiping at your feet because he thinks you are she. No one escaped her spell."

"Except you."

"Not even I. Look at me, twenty-six years old and a housekeeper, unnoticed, unappreciated by the only man I ever loved. She took him from me, took him, bound him to her so tightly that even in death she holds him. No, she had no hold on me. I hated her too much."

"Are you sure it isn't hate that has made you see her as you do?" Amanda asked quietly.

"Am I . . . oh, I see. You are another one of her dupes. After three long years you still remember her as gay and beautiful and happy. Well then, forget it. Forget I said anything. She is dead now. She can't hurt anyone anymore."

Sophia, her face hard, walked to the window.

After a while, to ease the strain, Amanda asked, "Where is everyone this morning?"

"Jason planted sugar cane this year, not too much, just enough for syrup for the family and plantation workers. There is a coolness in the air after the rain, the first hint of fall, perfect syrup weather. They are down below in the barns now, crushing the sugar cane and boiling the juice. Would you like some of the fresh juice? We have some in the outdoor kitchen."

"I don't believe so, thank you. Marta has been bringing me hot liquids all morning."

"This would be cool and pleasantly sweet. No? Then let me apologize for inflicting my views of your cousin on you . . ."

"Wait. I . . . the collar of Harmonia . . . the necklace," Amanda explained as Sophia stopped, a blank look on her face.

"Yes, what of it?"

"It's gone."

Sophia frowned. "Are you sure?"

"Marta looked. I had it in my hand when I fell, but now we can't find it. I thought that you might have picked it up for me."

"No . . . no, I haven't seen it. I remember that you had it . . . but I have no idea what happened to it. We were so concerned about you."

There was nothing in her face to make Amanda think she was telling anything but the truth. Still, the necklace had not simply vanished. If neither Sophia nor Theo had taken it, there was only Jason and, perhaps Carl, left. "I . . . I hate to be a bother, but would you mind asking Jason about it when he comes in?"

"Yes, of course, I will. Don't trouble yourself over it. A beautiful thing like that couldn't be lost. I expect Jason is holding it for you."

"Thank you. I . . . do appreciate your asking him for me."

"Not at all."

When the woman had gone Amanda lay staring up at the tester above her, thinking of Sophia. She seemed bitter, a cold type of woman, and yet she had poured out her feelings for Jason and her opinion of Amelia and the others in the house with a surprising fervor. It might be because Amanda was a stranger, and she did not expect to see her again after this interlude was over. She had hinted, too, that it was because she expected Amanda to share her feelings, but how could she? Amelia was not like the picture Sophia had painted. Was she?

Thinking back Amanda could remember little things, petty bickering, a few childish tricks while they were growing up. It was only natural for the two girls, left alone in the world, to compete for the affection of the only two people who cared about them, their grandparents. Amelia had always said that Amanda had an unfair advantage since she had lived with them longer, but that wasn't so. If her grandparents had preferred her, which she was not prepared to admit, it was because she was quieter, less troublesome, less volatile in her emotions. The elderly set great store by peace.

No, she could not accept Sophia's view. What of the things Marta had said? What of Amelia's pity for frail things, her rescue of a near-drowned puppy, and of Carl, a derelict? Marta had no reason to make a saint of Amelia. On the other hand Sophia's view of Amelia, by her own admission, was colored by jealousy. Why, then, had she let herself be disturbed? It must be that she did not care for the idea of anyone spreading a false impression of someone who had been so close to her.

After luncheon she drifted off to sleep for a time, but every movement that Marta made dragged her back to consciousness. She wished the woman would go away and leave her in peace. However, no suggestion seemed to penetrate her absorption in what she took to be her duty. Amanda decided at last that she was holding on in a determination to make the most of a post that gave her importance and tended to prolong her stay at Monteigne.

Amanda had at last, in the middle of the afternoon, given up trying to sleep and taken up a copy of *The Lady of the Lake* when the sound of a carriage was heard in the drive.

"Who can it be?" Marta said and moved with a surprising quickness to the window looking out over the gallery. From behind the muslin curtains she stared down at the drive. Amanda, as she watched her, wondered if her own arrival only the day before had caused such naked interest.

"It is a man," Marta informed her. "He is in his own gig. He is a gentleman. He wears a dark brown suit with a cream waistcoat and green breeches . . . and also a little hat like a bowl with a brim."

"The . . . gig . . . is it black with red wheels . . . and is the horse black with a blaze and stocking feet?"

"*Ja, ja.* Do you know this man?" Marta turned toward her.

"I . . . think it must be Nathaniel Sterling, my fiancé."

"Your . . . but what would he be doing here?"

"Looking for me, I would imagine. He will be furious that I came here without telling him."

"Do not distress yourself. I will not allow him to upset you. If he wants to take his temper out on someone . . ."

"Oh, Nathaniel never loses his temper. He has too much self-control."

"I see," Marta said in a grim tone.

"No, I don't think you do. Nathaniel isn't at all unreasonable. I will explain, and it will be all right."

"That is not the way he appears to me. Hah!"

The last exclamation was for the barking that erupted below as Cerberus challenged the new guest. There was shouting and a yelp.

"What is happening?" Amanda cried as Marta hurried back to the window.

"I think Cerberus has torn the arm of your fiancé's suit, and it looks as if he has struck the dog with his cane. Now he is back outside the gate, but Jason approaches from the barns. He will bring him safely in."

Amanda threw back the covers. "I must get up."

"Why, *fräulein*?" Marta exclaimed, hurrying to put a restraining hand on her arm.

"I can't let Nathaniel find me like this. It will be odious enough to have to tell him of it, much less having to lie flat on my back while I do it."

"Now, *Fräulein* Amanda. Only lie back down. You will find you are not as strong as you think."

That was certainly true enough, for at the too quick movement her head had begun to whirl and the dull far-off ache at the back of her skull had moved forward. She allowed Marta to ease her back against the pillows.

"Tell Marta that you don't wish to see this man, and I will stand guard at the door, *nicht?*"

Amanda raised one hand and then let it drop in a small gesture of futility. It would do no good to keep Nathaniel out. The facts must be faced some time. She had come on a fool's errand, trusting too much to luck and her own competence. No doubt Nathaniel would not go so far as to tell her so, but she would see the truth, and the disappointment, in his eyes.

It was a short while later that Sophia tapped on the door and then stepped into the room.

"You have a visitor," she told Amanda, an arch amusement lacing her voice.

"I know, Marta saw him from the window," Amanda admitted.

"Then do you want to receive him or not?"

"I . . . perhaps it would not be the thing?" she suggested doubtfully.

"Your fiancé? Unexceptional, I would think. It would not do if he were only a suitor, but in this case I don't see how it can hurt, especially if you are in company . . ."

"I take your point. You will stay then?"

"Gladly," Sophia answered promptly, not bothering to hide her curiosity.

Accordingly, while Sophia went to show Nathaniel upstairs, Marta fetched her dressing gown to put around her shoulders and cover her nightgown. Amanda smoothed a hand over her hair and down the long auburn braid that hung over her shoulder, pinched her cheeks to bring color to her face, and composed herself for the meeting with her hands folded in her lap.

Sophia opened the door and stepped aside. Nathaniel walked to stand, ill at ease, his color high, in the center of the room.

He was not a handsome man, but a high forehead and a certain severity of expression in his hazel eyes gave him a distinguished appearance. His dark brown hair was brushed back to fall in a loose wave at his temple, and he wore deep sideburns to the point of his jaw. Annoyance at his errand, concern for Amanda's predicament, and a degree of embarrassment made his manner stiff.

"Well, Amanda?" he said.

"Nathaniel."

"Miss Abercrombie has been telling me about your fall and the situation here. How are you?"

"Well enough. A bit of a headache still. But . . . why are you here?"

"Why am I . . ." he caught himself with a flicking glance to the two other women, Sophia and Marta, in the room. "I returned from the state capital to find you gone on this long journey without a word . . ."

"I left you a letter explaining . . ."

"Yes. I had it. Really, Amanda. There was no need for

such haste. I would have come with you; I told you as much."

"Yes, after we were married. I tried to make you understand that I wished to clear this from my mind before. I know there will be little enough time for jaunts of this sort later on. You are always so busy."

"Don't let us go into that again. I have come to take you home."

"It was kind of you to bother, Nathaniel. However, I don't believe . . ."

"*Fräulein* Amanda," Marta broke in in a decided voice, "cannot possibly be moved. Not now, not tomorrow, not for several days."

"See here, who is this woman?"

"I am a nurse-companion, *mein herr*."

"Surely there was no need to go to that extent," Nathaniel protested.

"Not in this case," Sophia explained. "Marta was called in for the late wife of Mr. Monteigne."

"I see. Your effort in coming here was for nothing then, Amanda."

"It seems so," Amanda was forced to agree.

"What of the legacy?" Nathaniel, ever practical, went straight to the sore point.

"You mean . . . the necklace?"

"Yes, of course."

"I . . . I tried to persuade Jason, Amelia's husband, you know, to take it. He is her legal heir. But he refused."

"Very right of him. Then you are to keep it?"

"I suppose, if I can find it."

"If you can find it?"

"I had it when I fell, but now it is gone."

With his customary self-control Nathaniel said nothing,

though his lips tightened and his eyes narrowed thoughtfully.

"It was a pretty bauble," Sophia drawled. "I'm sure Amanda thinks that I took it while she was unconscious."

"Not at all," Amanda said, aware of a warmth stealing into her cheeks. Under the circumstances, she found Sophia's bluntness disconcerting, almost as much as Nathaniel's critical attitude.

"I'm sure you must be mistaken," Nathaniel said with a touch of gallantry. "I can't imagine anyone suspecting you of a crime."

"How nice of you to say so," Sophia returned at once. "Still, I must admit I did covet the necklace." She gave a wry smile as if to deprecate her feminine weakness, but Nathaniel turned away.

"Are you comfortable, Amanda? Do you have everything you want?"

"Oh, yes. I'm fine," she answered in a slightly warmer tone in response to his show of concern.

"What about a doctor? I suppose a decent man has been consulted?"

"I'm afraid not. You see . . ."

"There was not the least need. I am fully competent to deal with this situation." Marta drew herself to her full height, a formidable figure with her stoutness, every bit as tall and probably heavier than Nathaniel.

He frowned. "You won't object, however, if I seek another opinion?" Without waiting for a reply he turned back to Amanda. "I'll have to go back to town now, but I'll be back early in the morning with the physician."

"All right, Nathaniel."

"I don't particularly like leaving you. You know I wouldn't if it wasn't necessary."

"Yes," she said smiling a little. "Don't worry. I'll be fine."

He stood still a moment longer, his eyes on her face. Finally he gave a short nod, then turned on his heel and left the room.

"My!" Sophia said lightly, "the masterful type. I wonder, Amanda dear, how you ever dared cross him?" She smiled and then went from the room after Nathaniel to show him out of the house and to the front gate.

Marta made a sound between a snort and a grunt. She moved with a heavy step to the front window, and though Amanda refused to allow herself to question the nurse about what she saw below, it was some time before she heard the sound of the carriage leaving.

Amanda had an early dinner with Marta in her room. Actually it was not dinner at all but a high tea with pekoe, chicken sandwiches, a heavy, spiced fig cake, and honey on toast dripping with butter. It was satisfying and faintly stimulating. It put Amanda in the mood for a bath before the fire in the fireplace. Marta dragged an old copper sitz bath into place, along with its bath screen to enclose the bather in the warmth from the fire and keep out chilling drafts, then she trudged up and down the stairs with the water cans.

The bath itself was a long, slow process. It took some time merely to get from the bed to the tub with Amanda leaning heavily on Marta's arm to conquer her dizziness after each step. But at last it was accomplished, and feeling deliciously clean and drowsy, Amanda sat in a chair before the fire while Marta loosened her heavy braid and brushed her hair until it shone with the gleam of the fire in its waves.

"You are very good-natured, Marta," Amanda said. "You make a wonderful nurse."

"I only live to serve my patients," she answered in a muffled voice.

"You must have done this often for my cousin. I'm sorry if I have brought back hurtful memories. I think you were fond of her."

"Yes, *fräulein*, I was fond of her, but you must not trouble yourself about looking like her. It is not so marked a resemblance, once a person gets to know you, and even if it were, it is not something you can help. Me, I remember how she suffered. So. It is not to grieve that she no longer feels the sorrow in her heart."

"The sorrow, Marta?"

The brush stilled then began to move again. "Why, *fräulein*, the knowledge that she would never be well, the knowledge that she must leave her dear husband forever."

"Yes, I . . . see."

"You needn't sit with me tonight," she said a little later as she lay against the pillows settled for the night.

"I do not mind," Marta protested.

"No, but I do," Amanda said firmly. "I forbid it. Truly, it bothers me to know that someone is losing sleep because of me. I don't want to take laudanum tonight, and I'm sure I couldn't sleep with you awake in the chair beside me."

"Well, if the *fräulein* is certain . . . but I'm not at all sure that *Herr* Jason will agree."

"If he doesn't, just send him to me."

"Yes, *fräulein*. If it is all right I will stay here beside you until you grow sleepy. That you will not mind?"

Seeing that it was the best she could do, Amanda agreed. Whether it was the presence of the nurse, the bed rest she had been forced to take during the day, or the persistent tiny ache behind her eyes, her drowsiness evaporated once the lamp was blown out. She lay staring at the walls in the last flickering orange light of the dying fire, unable to sleep. The silver stripes of the wallpaper reflected a reddish fire glow, as did the turnings of the polished wood of the armoire. The brass of the fender around the fireplace gleamed.

Marta sat still, so still that several times Amanda looked toward the slipper chair, wondering if she had dozed off, but each time the German nurse's eyes were fixed unwavering on the bed of coals beneath the mantel.

At last she heard footsteps outside in the hall as the others went up to bed. She had opened her mouth when a scratching came on the hall door, a soft sound that would not have awakened a sleeper. Moving quietly, Marta rose.

Amanda closed her eyes, hoping to encourage her to leave her post. She heard Marta round the end of the bed, then reaching the door, ease it open. There was a whispered consultation, then Marta stepped through the door and began to close it behind her. As Amanda opened her eyes she could not see who Marta had spoken to, though before the door closed she saw the shadow of a man stretching, elongated, across the floor toward her, projected into the darkened room by a light behind him in the hall. The man's shape was wide and long, tapering as though he wore a long cape or a set of waterproof oil skins, something which enshrouded him from shoulders to ankles. As she watched, he raised an odd stocking cap to his head, slipping it down over his face to his neck. His resulting appearance struck a chord of memory. She groped in her mind for the dark image, without being quite able to capture it. A blue flame dancing on the red coals in the fireplace leaped higher then died.

The change in light attracted the attention of the couple at the door. There was a flutter of white, and then the door closed. Amanda was alone in the dark.

She was awake and yet she was not. She felt suddenly free, and at the same time, compressed, pushed back, into the depths of her mind. It was a strange feeling but not entirely new. It had been growing, even as her breath moved regularly in and out in the rhythm of sleep. It had been a gentle sensation, gentle but unrelenting, one that paid no heed to the gossamer beat of a fluttering spirit of resistance. Weak, she was so weak, and half inclined, in her inner confusion, to succumb willingly. She had always given in to this smiling invader, this companion of her loneliness, sharer of sorrows. She allowed herself to be thrust aside and sighed, moving deeper into blackness. Aware that now she was twain, and yet unaware. She felt detached, as unconcerned as a dreamer dreaming of a stranger.

When she opened her eyes and looked about the room, her own room, it was no dream; she was no dream. She stared up at the canopy above her, at the tissue cloth of silver, and she smiled. Glancing down she ran her hand over the silk coverlet, enjoying the tactile sensation. She stretched, raising her arms above her head, then as the movement brought the ache in her head back she put a hand to her temple, an expression of surprise on her face.

She gazed about the room anxiously, as if searching for a change. Finding none, a look of satisfaction gleamed for a moment in her eyes. Then she threw back the covers and levered herself into a sitting position.

When her head had stopped spinning she stood up, holding to the tall post at the head of the bed. The wash-stand with its lamp was close. She reached out and took up a sulphur match, striking it on the rough underside of the marble top on the washstand. With trembling fingers she lifted the globe and touched the match to the black-ened wick. It caught slowly, then as she turned up the wick, flared into a steady light. She replaced the fragile glass globe and turned away.

Standing there in the light she stared down at the nightgown she was wearing. It was simple, unadorned white dimity. Typically Amanda. Not at all right. She would prefer something soft and fine with lace and em-broidery perhaps, in a pretty color, yellow or lilac. And this heavy braid. She had never been able to bear to have her hair confined at night.

Stronger now for being on her feet, she moved, staying near the bed until she was certain she would not need its support, toward the armoire. Bracing her forearm against the side she turned the handle and pulled the door open.

The dresses hung on their padded silk hangers, dresses covered with braid and tassels, with lace and embroidery, dresses in bright hues with all the extravagances of fashion dreamed of in Paris and New Orleans and Philadelphia. Shoes in neat canvas cases were in the bottom of the armoire while parasols of lace and satin, silk and tassels, stood closed in the corners. Fans lay on the shelves along with neatly piled lingerie, with corsets and camisoles and a scattering of garters. There was also a pile of folded handkerchiefs, each delicately embroidered. With a thoughtful frown she took one from the top of the pile and turning, tied it quickly to one of the tall posts at the foot of the bed. It hung, a white signal, and an odd smile tugged at the corner of her mouth before she turned back to the armoire.

She chose a nightgown of white silk with a panel of green embroidered leaves set into the bodice and a green ribbon threaded through the *décolletage* to gather it up for modesty.

She stepped out of the dimity gown and threw it on the bed and then let the white silk one flow down over her with a delicious coolness. She pulled the green ribbon, drawing it closed over her breasts and tied it in a graceful bow.

That little exertion left her faintly nauseated with a swimming feeling behind her eyes. As she made her way to the dressing table she held to the furniture, then half collapsed onto the stool before the mirror.

This would not do, she told herself dropping her head into her hands. She must be stronger.

At last, looking down, she noticed the end of the braid that fell over her shoulder. With trembling fingers she slipped the ribbon tie off and began to separate the plait into strands. Finally she picked up the brush. As she began to pull it through the lustrous tresses she automatically raised her eyes to the mirror then she stopped, staring. Gray eyes. Lashes and brows slightly darker than they should be, a firmer chin and wider mouth. For a moment tears threatened, then she took a deep breath, compressing her lips. What had she expected?

She shivered a little, becoming aware of the chill of the room. On her right was the fireplace from which a little warmth still emanated, she could feel it against the skin of her arm. Strange, she thought as she took up a hair-brush, how you noticed little things like that at times.

Carefully she brushed her hair, spreading it out over her shoulders, curling the ends around her fingers and pulling tendrils free of the mass to curl about her temples and before her ears. Taking up a scent bottle she sniffed the glass stopper, violets. It was a lovely fragrance, light but lasting, memorable. She touched the liquid to her wrists and the hollow of her throat, then passed it over the shining strands of her hair.

With deft hands she opened jars, applied softening cream to her face, her hands, and arms. She used rice powder papers to remove the shine from her face and then, humming a snatch of a lilting song beneath her breath, she touched a bit of oil of carmine to her lips.

There. That was much better. She could do with another length of ribbon to go around her hair but she now looked much better, more . . .

The thought and her soft singing broke off as a faint sound came from behind her. Her heart fluttering in her throat, she turned on the stool.

A man stood in the doorway in his dressing gown.

"I heard someone moving about in here, and I thought perhaps you were ill," he said, a frown between his eyes, his eyes bleak and withdrawn despite his words of concern.

"Jason!" she said, jumping to her feet and going toward him, her hands outstretched and a teasing light in her eyes. "Jason, my love, don't you know . . ."

But she had not taken more than three steps before the fragile darkness caught up with her, and she sank, like a boneless doll with a white china face, to the floor.

Chapter
Four

"WHY, *fräulein*, were you perhaps uncomfortable in the other gown? You should have called me." The nurse smiled, surprise in her eyes as she moved into the room, then her face changed and she stared fixedly at Amanda as she came closer to the bed.

"You . . . you didn't . . . you weren't in this room last night?" Amanda asked, her eyes wide.

"No, *fräulein*, not after I left you when you dozed off."

"You didn't attend me, not at all?"

Marta shook her head slowly.

"Who did?" There was an undertone of anger combined with a touch of something like fear in her voice.

"I don't know, *fräulein*, I heard nothing after I retired to my own small room at the back of the house."

"Marta, please. I . . . I woke up this morning wearing this gown I have never seen before, my hair was down, and I can't remember how it came about! I can't remember!"

"The gown, *fräulein*, it belonged to Madame Amelia. It was one of her favorites. *Herr* Jason chose it for her on his last trip to New Orleans."

Looking down, Amanda plucked at the green satin ribbon, "Marta . . . if you didn't help me . . . Why can't I remember? Is there something you aren't telling me? Have I been in a delirium and you are afraid to let me know of it?"

"Oh, no, *fräulein,* nothing like that."

"Perhaps Sophia . . . but no, I would still remember it even if it was necessary for Sophia to help me to change."

"I am sure you could not have awakened her without waking me," Marta said.

"Then . . . I must have done it myself . . . and yet, I wouldn't dream of going through Amelia's things. I would certainly never think of wearing them."

"Look, what is this?"

The nurse moved to the foot of the bed where she removed a handkerchief that had been tied about the post. "Why, it is one of Madame Amelia's handkerchiefs. See, it has her initials embroidered in the corner, surrounded by a laurel wreath."

As Marta turned it first one way, then the other, in her large hands Amanda stared at it. It reminded her of something. Oh, yes. It was only a ridiculous childhood memory.

It had been a game she and Amelia had played the rainy summer during the first year of the war. They had pretended they were spies for the confederacy. The top floor of their grandparents' house had been enemy territory. Amelia most often took the active part, spying out the lay of the land while Amanda lay on watch across the river, the lower hall. They had nearly driven their grandparents mad with their skulking and peering around doors. When Amelia had discovered something she had thought worth reporting, she would creep out and tie her handkerchief to the banister as a signal. *Have information. Am returning.* Then she would sneak down the back servants' stairs while Amanda tried to meet her outside on the gallery. If at any time either of them were seen, they were "caught" and were assumed to have paid the extreme penalty for spying, death.

It had been a harmless game. Amanda smiled a little, remembering their excitement and pleasurable sense of mock fear. It was ridiculous to connect such a childish message to the handkerchief tied about the post of her bed. What was she thinking of? She must have been more affected by the blow on the head than she realized.

Amanda was a practical young woman with very little superstition in her make-up, and yet, as she watched Marta put the handkerchief away in the armoire, she shivered.

"Perhaps . . . perhaps I put the handkerchief there at the same time that I took her gown. I . . . I must have. There is no other explanation."

"Fräulein . . ."

"Yes . . . what is it?"

"Have you ever sleepwalked?"

"Never."

"Well, try not to worry, *fräulein*. Injuries to the head are strange sometimes. It is not uncommon to find forgetfulness associated with them."

Amanda did not reply, but the distress died out of her face, leaving her calmer.

It returned, for a moment, when later that morning as she ate her breakfast she touched her lips with her napkin and it came away with a trace of lip color, something she never used. She stared at it for a time, but she did not mention it to Marta.

She did speak of it to the doctor when he arrived.

A middle-aged man with gold rimmed spectacles, a paunch, mutton-chop whiskers, and wearing gaiters with his charcoal gray suit, he pursed his lips, staring at the floor as he spoke.

At last he said, "I wouldn't worry too much about it. As the nurse pointed out, amnesia, the loss of memory, is not too unusual a complication with concussion."

"But, Doctor, why did I do things I wouldn't ordinarily think of doing? It is this that disturbs me more than the fact of the forgetfulness."

"I can't give you an answer to that. We don't know too much about it actually. In any case, it is not so great a thing. I would advise you to forget it. It may not happen again."

"But it could?"

"Well, yes, I suppose it could. We have no way of controlling these periods of amnesia. You must not frighten yourself by giving rein to an overactive imagination. There is probably some perfectly rational, normal explanation for your behavior, you have only forgotten what it is. I'm going to give you some drops for the headache. They are to be taken only when you need them, and I will leave them with the nurse here. She will see to it."

He glanced up at Marta standing back out of the way

near the fireplace. "You are . . . ah . . . familiar with this?"

She gave a curt nod without speaking, her eyes going to Amanda who grimaced. That the good doctor should treat her like a child or someone wanting in sense was an irritation. She was not ordinarily a nervous person, and she didn't believe she was being overly concerned. It was only the vague feeling that there was something more to the incident the night before than had yet come to light.

Now the doctor was staring at Marta. "Are we acquainted?" he asked suddenly.

Marta's face took on a stolid, almost bovine look. "I'm not sure, *Herr Doktor*. You did not, I believe, attend Madame Montcigne in her last illness."

"No. My practice is in the next parish. My colleague is out of town for several weeks. During his absence I've been holding a surgery twice a week for his patients in town, in addition to my own. I make no secret of the fact that I will be heartily glad to see his return. I'm still persuaded this is not our first meeting. I have a good memory for faces. Comes from recognizing patients, you know. If we have met before, I'm sure it will come to me."

"Yes, *Herr Doktor*," Marta replied politely.

The man picked up his bag. "Well, young lady, I want you to take care of yourself, don't be too anxious to be up and about. Time is a great healer, you know, a great healer." With a few more similar bromides he got himself out the door.

When he had gone down the stairs where Sophia waited to give him some light refreshments before she showed him out of the house, Amanda lay staring at the ceiling. What did the man think, that she was a hysterical female, glorying in her illness and determined to dramatize it? It was a weird enough tale, but she had not imagined it. The gown, the cosmetics were there as proof, or had been before she had removed them.

Marta was very quiet. Amanda glanced at her, seeing her frown of preoccupation. What was she thinking? It was hard to tell what might be going on behind that broad white face. The woman had been most attentive, she was grateful to her. But she could not help remembering what Sophia had said, that Marta was extending herself for the sake of her job and her position at Monteigne, not for any liking she might feel toward Amanda herself.

Marta had not seemed to care too much for the doctor. Perhaps she was apprehensive over losing her position at Monteigne, and she was afraid that he would say Amanda had no use for her. Or it might be a kind of professional jealousy; she was miffed that, with her experience available, Nathaniel had felt it necessary to call in a doctor. Whatever the reason, Marta had certainly been less than cordial. Moreover, when at last they heard the clatter of his buggy as it went down the drive, Marta seemed to relax, allowing the tension to drain from her face and her lips to form the semblance of a smile.

She went to the window, drawing back the curtain to peer around the edge, a frown creasing her brow. She jumped, swinging about, as Sophia swept into the room.

"So," the blond woman said with the flash of a smile, "you have the official verdict. An interesting one, I must say."

"The doctor told you . . ."

"Certainly. I had only to ask him. Few men of his style are immune to a smile. About these spells, have you ever had them before?"

"Spells? You make it sound like I have some sort of

seizures, Sophia," she answered, trying to laugh. "It is only that something happened to me last night I can't remember. I'm sure it was nothing, but I felt I should ask the doctor about it."

"Yes?"

She obviously wanted to be told about it, but perversely, because her curiosity was so obvious, Amanda did not want her to know. It was embarrassing to think that Sophia had discussed her so openly with the doctor. She could just as easily discuss anything Amanda might tell her with Nathaniel or Theo, or even Jason. No, she would not gratify her to that extent.

She gave a small shrug. "It was nothing really."

Sophia sent her a sharp look before she turned to Marta.

"I spoke to the doctor about you, too," she informed the nurse with an unpleasant edge to her voice.

Marta did not speak but she raised startled eyes to Sophia's face.

"He remembered where he had met you before."

"Did he, *fräulein*?" the nurse asked in a toneless voice but her face, if it was possible, grew paler.

"It was some years ago and in a town farther south, for, as he pointed out, you are a memorable person."

Marta opened her mouth as if to question Sophia, then her eyelids dropped. "I have worked with many doctors in my life, but I can't remember this man. He is mistaken."

"I think not." Sophia said, a malicious look in her eye as she stared at the German woman. "But we will talk about it later, tonight after dinner?"

"There is nothing to talk about," Marta asserted, but

her voice lacked conviction, and Sophia turned away satisfied.

At the door she looked back. "Oh, Amanda, I nearly forgot. Your fiancé arrived from town while you were with the doctor. Jason has invited him to stay with us until you are able to travel. It will save him having to make the long trip out every day to see you. I was just going to make the room at the end of the hall ready. Marta could help me, that is, if you have no need of her."

"No, I'm perfectly comfortable, though I can't answer for Marta, of course. It was good of Jason to think of Nathaniel. I'm sure he appreciates it."

"Oh, yes, he said all that was proper. But then he is a very proper man, your fiancé, isn't he?"

"He . . . observes the conventions, if that is what you mean," Amanda said stiffly, forced by a note of amusement in Sophia's voice into defending Nathaniel.

"Jason may not be so proper, but hospitality comes naturally to him. You needn't think it is a mark of favor that he has thrown his home open to you. He would have done the same for anyone."

"I'm certain you are right," Amanda replied. "I'm in no danger of . . . misunderstanding, I assure you."

"When I left the parlor just now, I believe your fiancé and Theo had formed the intention of riding over the property. However, I'm sure I heard Nathaniel mention that he would visit with you here after luncheon."

Amanda did not answer. Sophia gave a brief nod of good-bye and, rather graciously, held the door for Marta to go before her from the room.

As she lay listening to their receding footsteps, Amanda smiled wryly at herself. Surely she wasn't jealous of the other woman? Regardless, something about Sophia set her teeth on edge. When had she been invited to make herself free of Nathaniel's given name? And while it was, on the surface, nice to be kept informed of the movements of the others in the household, why did she have the feeling that Sophia had had a hand in Nathaniel's decision to put off making his appearance at her bedside until a later time?

It was not that she wanted Nathaniel to rush to her side with flowers and protestations of concern and devotion, but it made him appear callous to go off riding before even inquiring after her. Surely he could have seen that? Perhaps he had inquired. What was a man to do if he was told, possibly, that Amanda was resting . . . ?

Lying there thinking, however, she could find no reason for Sophia to have done what she suspected. No, she was being fanciful and overly sensitive. Nathaniel was not a demonstrative man, that was all. There was no need, none at all, for him to be concerned. All it would take to get her back on her feet was a few days of rest and quiet. It was enough that Nathaniel had brought the doctor to examine her. She was satisfied.

Amanda let her mind wander. When gentlemen rode over a plantation they were usually looking at the fields, the harvesting, and at this time of year, the livestock, cribs, and barns filled with the fruits of their toil. She had seen the plantation outbuildings among the trees, but where were the fields? They must be at some distance from the house, and behind the rise on which it stood, possibly, or else farther away, beyond the encroaching woods. She could visualize the three men galloping through the forest trails, skirting the edge of the fields, their horses hooves throwing up clods of dirt. Sophia had not mentioned Jason, but it was usual for the host to act as escort on a tour of inspection.

Her speculations were so certain that she jumped, startled, when a firm knock sounded on the door. It was a moment before she could gather her wits to make a reply.

The knob turned and Jason stood in the doorway.

"Miss Trent," he said formally with the faintest hint of a bow, "I hope you are well?"

"Yes, thank you." Unconsciously her hand went to the high neckline of her cambric gown.

He took a few steps into the room, his green gaze intent upon her face. He studied the plait that hung in a thick shining rope over her shoulder and the plain texture of the nightgown that covered her from throat to wrists as she lay propped on her pillows beneath the covers. A slow blush mounted to her cheeks, and her eyes widened in puzzlement. For a long moment tension held them motionless, then his eyelids flickered down.

"I understand you are still troubled by your head. There is no need for you to suffer without aid. If you will send Marta to me when you are in need of something for the pain . . ."

"There is no need. The doctor left a vial of laudanum for me."

"That's good then. If there is anything I can do, any way I can be of help, you will let me know?"

Once again she thanked him, then went on. "It was kind of you to offer hospitality to Nathaniel. I do appreciate it as much, I'm sure, as he. And I wish I could tell you how sorry I am that you have had me an invalid inflicted upon you! I know you cannot like it, and I don't blame you. Believe me, I would not stay if it wasn't necessary."

"You are most welcome at Monteigne, Miss Trent. I only regret that you were injured on my property. As for your fiancé, I'm sure this is where I would rather be, were I in his place. But enough. Let us not talk of gratitude. There is no need."

"But surely . . ."

"As a relative of my wife you have a right to hospitality."

She was silenced, as much by the hardness of his face as by his words. Then as he turned she put out her hand.

"Mr. Monteigne . . ."

"Yes?"

"About the necklace . . . did Sophia speak to you about it?"

It was a moment before he answered, and Amanda received the impression that he was reluctant to answer.

"I have searched near the steps but found nothing. No one has mentioned finding it. I . . . am at a loss, to be honest, to understand what has become of it. I apologize."

"You apologize? Why should you?"

"Come, let's not be polite. Someone has taken the necklace. It is perfectly plain to me—it must be to anyone of sense. I regret that it has happened on my property. I will do everything in my power to return it to you, but in the meantime . . . I am sorry for it."

"I . . . I appreciate that. But I wish I could persuade you to take it."

"I have no need of it."

"Surely . . ."

"In addition it has much more sentimental value than actual worth. I will not consider taking it out of your family."

"You are very . . . kind."

"Is that a surprise? You did not, perhaps, expect kindness from the man Amelia married?"

"I didn't know what to expect," Amanda replied, meeting his gaze squarely.

"You . . . none of you . . . ever troubled yourselves to come and find out. I might have been anything, any kind of man, but you abandoned Amelia to me."

"You ran away with Amelia without consulting her family. Wasn't that what you wanted, for her to have no contact with her relatives?"

"I would have been just as happy, if you want the truth. The point is that Amelia was not. She felt that she was forsaken. Family ties mean much to a woman. Amelia died with no one other than myself to care."

"Whose fault is that? We were never told that she was ill."

"You never bothered to ask."

It was an impasse. Neither of them was able to concede the other's point of view. Yet, as Amanda stared at his set face and saw the sternness that marked his features, like a mask to hide pain, Amanda began to see the trend of his thoughts.

"You think that . . . that if someone, someone other than yourself, had been here with Amelia to offer her love and sympathy, she would not have . . . taken her own life?"

Even as she spoke his face relaxed and a tiredness came into his eyes.

"Don't. Don't think of it, don't take on a useless burden of remorse. There is no need, and I did not intend it, I promise you. That burden is mine."

That burden is mine. When he had gone Amanda lay thinking of that strange statement. Why should Jason carry a burden of remorse? He had been here, hadn't he, when Amelia died? He had given her his love and support, hadn't he? What did he have to reproach himself with then, unless it was the fact that he hadn't been able to prevent her from taking her life? Yes, perhaps that. That would weigh on a man like Jason. A man like Jason. What did she know of the kind of man he was? The answer was nothing, nothing at all.

Marta returned, bringing her luncheon tray. Not a talkative person ordinarily, she seemed even quieter than usual as she moved about the room with lowered eyes.

What had Sophia said to her? Something disturbing, it appeared. Why should she do such a thing? Did she like stirring up trouble? Was she one of those people who cannot bear the quiet dullness of peace? What was it to her where the doctor had seen Marta? Was it the lure of mystery, however mundane it might prove in reality? Or was it only the idea of knowing, with the realization that knowledge is power?

Now she was being entirely too fanciful. It was the effect of having too much idle time with nothing to do but think and watch the people around her for hidden motives. With a tiny grimace of self-derision Amanda picked up her fork and began to eat.

It had been an eventful morning. She had not been able to rest, and it was not surprising that she found her headache returning after luncheon. In an effort to sleep it off, she had Marta pull the drapes against the bright encroaching sun. When the heavy woman had left with her quiet tread, Amanda lay with her eyes closed. It was dim in the room, and the silence of the afternoon somnolence lay heavy around her. Though it was cool in the morning and late evening, it grew warm during the day and after a time she threw back the comforter, leaving only the sheet to cover her arms.

Comfortable, finally, she had just began to feel drowsy when a knock sounded.

She must have been nearer to sleep than she had realized, because it was a moment before she could rouse herself sufficiently to struggle up on one elbow and speak the necessary words.

At her invitation Nathaniel stepped briskly into the room, leaving the door open behind him for the sake of convention.

"Resting, Amanda? Good, good. It's just what you need to put you back in good frame. I didn't wake you, did I?"

"No, no," she said, forcing herself to smile and appear alert. "Marta tells me you are staying here. I hope you are comfortable."

"Ah, yes. It was decent of Monteigne to offer me his hospitality, don't you think? But he seems a decent fellow—a trifle moody but accommodating above average, under the circumstances."

"Yes, I feel it, too. After all, Nathaniel, we are complete strangers to him."

"Hardly that. You are a relative, by marriage."

"But with no real tie, especially after the way Grandfather felt about him. I never realized how it must have seemed to him, Nathaniel, our ignoring Amelia like that. Grandfather was so ill, we were so worried, and I couldn't have gone against him myself without upsetting him terribly. Still, I could have written to Amelia."

"To what point? I doubt it would have made the slightest difference in the end, and you could not, of course, risk an estrangement from your grandfather at that crucial time."

"It would have disturbed him. I wonder, though, if he would not have become reconciled to the marriage, given time. He was not an unreasonable man."

"Not unreasonable, but mighty proud. But I meant, rather, that there was little point in endangering the succession, not but what he would have left you something extra, still he might, you know, have relented to the point of making Amelia an equal heir so far as the money went."

"Nathaniel! As if I would have minded it if he had!"

"Perhaps not, perhaps not, but we must look on it from a practical viewpoint."

She frowned without answering. She could not fault Nathaniel for having a practical outlook on life, but it was annoying at times. She looked at his face with its strong jaw outlined by his sideburns and the firm mouth. He had a straight nose and wide-spaced eyes. His brown hair was meticulously combed, his entire appearance neat. He was a well-set-up man, of average height, and if he lacked a romantic temperament and background, he made up for it by being steady and dependable with the drive necessary for success.

As if grown nervous under her oddly intent gaze, he looked about.

"Isn't it stuffy in here to you? Shall I raise a window? The smell of that perfume is stifling."

"Perfume?" Amanda took a deep breath.

"Can't you smell it? I wonder you aren't swooning from the strength of it."

"It seems I can . . . but it isn't strong."

"You've just gotten used to it. It's stifling. I've got to raise a window," he said, moving to pull the drape aside and raise the curtains to push the casement up. That done, he glanced back over his shoulder as he repositioned the drapes. "I've never noticed your wearing a fragrance such as this one before. What is it?"

"It isn't mine," she answered as she turned to look at him, then let her gaze go to the dressing table on the wall beside her.

"It hardly seems suitable for a nurse."

"It isn't Marta's either. It belonged to Amelia."

"Amelia? Then who . . ."

"No one has been wearing it. Marta used some night before last . . ."

"Oh, you mean the nurse has spilled the stuff? Why couldn't you say as much? I can't say I'm sorry that it isn't yours, Amanda. I've always liked the light fragrance you use."

"Soap and water, Nathaniel," she pointed out with a wry smile, letting the matter of the perfume go. Scents had a way of lingering. That must be it.

"Very nice," he said dismissingly as he moved to sit on the bed beside her and pick up her hand. "Tell me, how do you feel?"

"A trifle headachy but really quite well. I hate being an invalid."

"I know you do. Your Puritan nature won't let you enjoy it, will it?"

"I'm afraid not. I like to be up and doing."

"I understand. I'm the same way, really. You know, it's no great wonder that we are to be married. We are very well suited."

Amanda looked down at his firm hand covering hers

before she glanced up to meet his smiling hazel eyes. Despite his sometimes irritating practicality, there was something stable about Nathaniel, something as firm and sure as his handclasp that found recognition in her own nature. "Yes," she told him, "you are right."

"Good," he said, covering her hand so that it was held between both of his. "I knew you were all right."

"All right?"

"It crossed my mind that you might be enjoying all this attention, this room that looks as if it were furnished for a sybarite. There has sometimes, in the past, been a touch of envy in your manner when you spoke of Amelia, my dear, though I'm sure you didn't realize it."

"Why, Nathaniel, you must be mistaken."

"I assure you I'm not. I've marked it several times."

"But it's ridiculous. Why should I envy Amelia?" She was genuinely puzzled, and not a little distressed that Nathaniel, not a man of imagination, should make such a statement.

"Now, now, I didn't mean to upset you. I realize there is nothing to it. It was only a thought, and you must see that I would never have mentioned it if I considered it had any real basis."

"Yes, I do see," she was forced to agree, but the damage had been done. The warmth that his presence had brought was gone. They exchanged a few more commonplaces, and then during the first lull in the conversation she told him she believed she could sleep if he didn't mind.

He got to his feet. After a moment's hesitation he leaned to brush a kiss across her brow. It was an indication of his concern since he would not normally have risked being seen from the open doorway.

"Sleep well," he murmured and left the room pulling the door to behind him.

She did not sleep. For some reason that she couldn't explain, the suggestion that she was enjoying taking Amelia's place disturbed her. She knew it was not so, but she could not dismiss a feeling of uneasiness. The more she thought of it the more unlikely it seemed that such an idea had originated with Nathaniel. He had not known Amelia well. His relationship with Amanda had developed in the years since Amelia went away. Before that the two young women had been away at the seminary, and he had been busy setting up his law practice. He might have seen Amelia during the holidays but seldom, if ever, had he seen the two of them together.

No, he had no basis to suppose she had ever been jealous of Amelia. How could he have come by such an idea? Who could have planted the seeds of doubt in his mind?

It was possible that it had been her grandfather. He had always considered Amelia as someone special, which was one reason his disappointment and anger over her conduct had been so intense. It had been his custom to speak of Amelia as of one dead, always eulogizing her good points, never speaking ill of her, placing the entire blame for the fiasco of her marriage on Jason's shoulders. He had said up until the day of his death that she would come to her senses and, after a suitable show of repentance, he would allow her to return. It had made Amanda angry to hear him speak in such a manner, angry for Amelia and for her grandfather, too. Angry for Amelia because he treated her love . . . and her lover . . . so lightly, and anger for her grandfather because

Amelia did not understand his stiff-necked pride and love, would not make the necessary effort to bring about their reconciliation. It was possible, she supposed, that there had been some jealousy mixed with that anger, but she did not think so.

She could remember once, however, when she had felt hurt. Amelia and she had been friends as well as cousins but, shortly after they had started going to the seminary, Amanda became aware that Amelia no longer needed or depended on her as she once had. It was not until then that she had realized how much she had relied on her for gaiety and brightness in her life. Deep inside she had been hurt that Amelia could desert her so easily for new friends and pleasures. She had tried once to explain how she felt to her grandmother. What was it that the wise old woman had said? It had not made much impression at the time, but now the conversation came back as if it were only yesterday.

"I know, my child, that it isn't that you do not want Amelia to have other friends."

"Oh, no, that's not what I meant at all . . ."

"Good, good. Are you sad then because you think you have lost first place in her heart? You would have lost that eventually anyway, to the man she marries."

"Yes, I know, Grandmother. No, I think it is that I feel . . . I feel as if she had betrayed my confidence. I can't explain it exactly . . ."

"I think I see. My child, there are those who are born to quick and easy laughter, to charm and happiness. They are like the yellow butterflies fluttering in the garden, never still, never . . . constant. It was much the same with Amelia's mother, otherwise she would never have left her child here while she began a new life with another man. To say they are shallow is to be unnecessarily cruel. Such terms hardly seem to apply. They draw people to them so easily but they do not understand the nature of the emotions they cause others to feel. They do as they will with no thought of the effect of it. Amelia has no idea that she has hurt you. It is, I think, a form of self-love, but it is unintentional, and so it is useless to be distressed. The butterfly is beautiful, but it gathers nectar for itself alone. It is the bee, not quite so lovely, but steady and loyal to its own, that gives the sweetness of its honey to the world."

Chapter
Five

I T was late in the afternoon, for the light outside the windows had begun to fade, when Amanda heard a commotion in the hall. There was the sound of a man's voice raised in anger and then a loud, despairing wail, followed by cries of alarm and the clatter and thud of running feet.

Amanda lay still, listening, until a strained quiet fell. She thought of calling out, but she did not wish to be a nuisance during a time of possible crisis.

At last, when she thought she could bear the suspense no longer, there came a tap on the door, and Theo stepped into the room.

"Forgive me for the intrusion, but I thought you might have been disturbed by the noise just now."

"Yes. Tell me what is happening."

"There, I knew you would be upset. I promise you, it's nothing to worry about. It was only that tramp, Carl, trying to sneak upstairs again. He is becoming obstinate. Really, I think Jason is going to have to do something about him. He had the audacity to tell me I had no right to order him to take himself off. Said he answered to no one but Jason and his Madame. You should have heard the bloodcurdling scream when I laid hands on him. Pure histrionics . . . but no doubt you did hear?"

She nodded. "He wasn't hurt?"

"Carl? Never. He's as tough as a hickory nut, physically, at least. Mentally is another question. We have looked on him as harmless, and he has been most biddable in the past. Now—well—I have my doubts. He has something on his mind. I'd be careful around him, if I were you. Sophia says that he believes that you are Amelia. He was very fond of her, used to follow her about like a lap dog. Amusing up to a point, still . . ." He shook his head.

"You think he might have wanted to talk to me—as Amelia, I mean?"

"Talk to you? I hardly think so. Half the time the gibberish he speaks doesn't make sense. More likely he just wanted to be near, like a pet near his master . . . or mistress, in this case."

"Surely that could not hurt."

"Maybe not, but the idea is unacceptable to me, totally unacceptable. I can't imagine why Jason ever allowed it to get started. The idea of letting a blubbering imbecile like that fawn on your wife . . . why, the whole idea is disgusting. Especially with a woman like Amelia."

A woman like Amelia. Here was someone else then who looked on Amelia as special. A bleakness that she could not understand settled over her. She tried to thrust it aside, chiding herself for being petty, but it did not help her depression.

"Did I hear you mention Amelia, brother mine?" It was Sophia moving into the room with her sinuous glide. "You mustn't pay too much attention to his opinion on the subject. He is a most practical man—except where women are concerned. And there, like most men, he is searching for a goddess of beauty and purity."

"Really, Sophia. You make me sound like a half-wit. I hope I'm not so gullible as all that. I consider myself a fair judge of character . . ."

"And you considered Amelia all that was truth and beauty and light. In short you were as besotted as Carl!"

"Nonsense. She was an excellent woman, but she was also my best friend's wife."

"When has that ever made a difference?"

"It makes a difference to me."

"Now it does."

"Now that she is dead, you mean? I find that as outrageous as anything you have said so far."

"Do you? Well let me tell you . . ."

Their voices washed over Amanda. She found herself trying to shut out the angry sounds that were making her head throb. Carl, crazy Carl. How sad it was that the poor deluded creature should want to be near her. It made her feel odd, as if she wanted to cry, and at the same time, to rail against Theo for preventing the poor man's simple wish. He was so pathetic with his pitiful whisper of *My Madame*. How could Theo be so cruel? How could he speak of him in such despicable terms?

Perhaps it was not Theo's fault. Men did not have the same feeling for helpless creatures that women had. Their first thought was not to help them but to put them out of their misery. The traditional answer of the strong for the weak, the perfect for the imperfect. Theo, hardy and handsome in a rugged way with his heavy blond brows, ruddy complexion, and broad cheekbones. He stood with his feet firmly planted, slightly apart, the only sign of the unease he felt at being in a young, unmarried woman's bedroom, the awkwardness of his large, square hands hidden in his pockets. He had the appearance of a man of action with little regard for sentiment except as it applied to a pretty woman. Such a man had to be forgiven for his intolerance of other weak creatures.

Now he was saying, rage in his voice, "The trouble with you, Sophia, is that you are a jealous jade. You were jealous of Amelia from the moment Jason brought her home with him, jealous because she was in the place you wanted, and because she filled it much better than you could hope to do."

"That's not true!" Sophia cried, breathless with indignation.

"Don't try to cozen me. I'm your brother, remember? I was there when you first heard the news. I was the one who picked up the pieces of the Sèvres vase you threw at me for being the bearer of the ill tidings."

"Is it a crime to be angry because one of your childhood friends was fool enough to run away with a chit just out of school, a stupid, immature girl too frightened and self-centered to even try to give him an heir?"

"Don't be indelicate . . ."

"Why not? You know it's true. You know half her illness was in her mind. She was terrified of the thought of having a child and being ill was a good excuse . . . the eternal headache."

Theo stared at his sister's scornful face. "She died of that headache."

"Did she? She died of fear. She took her own life because she knew Jason was aware of her fraud."

They stared at each other, their breathing harsh in the quiet room. Amanda looked from one to the other. Then, before she was even aware of the impulse, she blurted out: "But weren't they happy together?"

There was a surprised silence. It was as if Theo and Sophia had forgotten her presence. They glanced at each other warily, reluctant to speak. Then at last Theo cleared his throat.

"It was hard to tell. At times Amelia would be wildly happy, singing, dancing about, hanging onto Jason's arm, drinking in his every word. Other times she was . . . quiet, depressed."

"Ah, you admit then that our precious Amelia wasn't perfect. She was, in fact, a moody witch, mooning about of an evening with that big dog at her side, her hair flying loose in the wind like a gypsy, and Carl following her like a faithful henchman."

"Sophia! You make her sound crazed! I will not have you talk about her like that!" Theo glared at her, his hands clenched, his face red with anger.

"Temper, Theo. You'll give yourself apoplexy. But you see, Amanda? She was a witch. She evoked either love or hatred, nothing in between."

"And which, my dear sister, did she arouse in you?"

"She was spoiled, selfish, a woman who could not rest until she had attached every man she saw. She used her charm like a weapon to get what she wanted, and she did not care who got hurt in the process."

"Remember, Sophia, that she was a relative of Amanda's."

"That is true, but I'll warrant it makes little difference. If she knew Amelia she has probably been hurt by her. No, I wouldn't go so far as to say that I hated Amelia, but I certainly had no love for her."

Suddenly Theo smiled, looking beyond Sophia to the door. Sophia turned, then swung back to cast a look of loathing at her brother.

In the doorway stood Jason, his face still, one eyebrow lifted in sardonic inquiry. No one spoke. They waited, frozen in a guilty horror for what they had said about the wife of the man in the doorway and his relationship with her.

"This is not the place for this discussion," Jason said at last, his soft tones carrying a flick of the lash.

"Jason . . ." Sophia began, but he cut her off with an upraised hand.

"Now don't get on your high horse," Theo said. "It was my fault for baiting Sophia. I can never resist pushing her to the limit, you know. Come on, Sophia. Jason's right. We picked a bad time for our quarrel."

Jason looked for a moment as if he intended to make an issue of it, but then he stepped to one side.

Theo took Sophia's arm in a firm hold. "Forgive us, Amanda. I never intended to upset you. Thoughtlessness and temper, pure and simple. My apologies."

"Of course," Amanda murmured, acutely embarrassed, feeling as chastened as if she had been at fault, wanting only for them all to leave her.

Abruptly there came a rasping sound as someone cleared his throat. It was Nathaniel, standing in the hall, one fist to his mouth as he made that polite sound. Amanda felt a hysterical desire to laugh at the puzzlement of his expression as he sensed the tension in the room.

"I . . . I was beginning to wonder where everyone had disappeared to. The woman in the kitchen could give me no satisfaction. I felt I should do something about my appearance before dinner, but I have no idea in which room my valise was deposited."

"How very remiss of me," Sophia said, obviously happy to have a legitimate reason for detaching herself from her brother's hand and leaving them. "You'll be thinking I am not much of a housekeeper. Come with me, and I will show you to your room at once."

Their voices receded down the hall. Theo looked at Amanda as if gauging her reaction to Sophia's ushering Nathaniel away, then he slanted a glance at Jason. "I could do with a drink," he said tentatively.

It was a moment before Jason gave any sign that he had heard, then with a curt nod to Amanda he turned and walked out, leaving Theo to follow if he chose.

It became plain as soon as Marta returned that she had heard the argument. "You must rest, *liebchen*. Close your eyes while I go down for your supper tray. I know how exhausting having a quarrel raging around your ears can be. Many is the time when I've heard . . . but no matter. I keep out of the way. For someone like me there is nothing else to be done. Stay and be quiet and you are accused of being nosy and sly. Stay and give your opinion and the wrath of all descends. Either way, you are out of a position. It is best to go away until the storm is over, then employ oneself in soothing the wounds. Would you like a cup of tea?"

Amanda smiled as she declined the palliative. "I haven't any wounds," she said.

"No, no, I didn't mean it to sound so," Marta exclaimed, clasping her long thick white fingers together. "I only thought after such a . . . a trying experience you would like the calming effect of a nice, hot cup."

Amanda could see that Marta wanted to pamper her, perhaps in part because she felt that she should not have stayed away from her patient during the fracas. With good grace, she gave in and admitted that she would enjoy the tea if Marta would be so kind.

Marta had been gone only a few minutes when she heard footsteps outside in the hall. They were so loud that she glanced at the door realizing that Marta had not pulled it quite shut behind her. Listening, she thought the footsteps sounded like Nathaniel and half expected him to stop in and see her, but after only a momentary hesitation he passed on by.

A wry smile touched her mouth. She was being ridiculous to feel slighted. It was not as if she wanted him dancing attendance on her.

Her thoughts were broken off by the slamming of a door followed by raised voices.

Sophia and Theo again, she was almost sure. Why did people have to flail at each other with words? What was so important that they must tear at each other, hunting verbally for the most vital spot? Was there something lacking in herself that there seemed to be little worth the agony of that mental rending?

Though the voices were muffled, unintelligible through the thick walls, Amanda wanted to cover her ears to shut out the vicious spate of words that went on and on.

Marta brought her tea on a tray with her own small

pot covered by a knitted cozy. As she placed it on the washstand and gently poured the tea into the cup, their eyes met, then they looked away. They were not eaves-dropping, but it was impossible to ignore the noisy altercation.

Marta was just handing her the cup when there came the sharp crack of flesh on flesh. Amanda jumped, spill-ing the tea into its saucer. Then before they could move or speak, they heard another slap and a woman's cry of mingled rage and surprise.

For a second Marta's lips compressed into lines of disapproval, then her expression turned carefully blank.

"Marta! It was Theo . . . and Sophia . . . wasn't it?" Amanda could not have said what made her ask the question, but it seemed important.

"I couldn't say," was her answer.

"The voices . . . they came from across the hall, didn't they?"

"It seemed so."

Irritation with the short, noncommittal answer made her tone sharp. "Then whose room is it?"

"It belongs to *Herr* Theo, *fräulein*."

"Then it must have been he and his sister."

Marta did not answer. She made a great show of re-placing the tea cozy and examining the rug to be certain that no tea stained it.

Amanda was left with a sense of dissatisfaction. Sip-ping the brew Marta had gone to so much trouble to bring, she found herself breathing quietly so she could listen. As she realized what she was doing, she grimaced, forcing her thoughts away. After all, it did not concern her. She didn't know why she was troubling herself about it. Soon she would be gone from here, and it was unlikely that she would see these people again. The thought, she discovered, was not a happy one. It was strange how you could meet people and learn something of their lives, then part never to meet again. It was as if there was no purpose, no plan to life, only a vast accidental meshing of people and events.

Pensively, she decided that she would be sorry to see the last of the people here at Monteigne. It would be like saying a final good-bye to Amelia and the part she had played, for so many years, in her life. It was as though once she had left everyone who had ever known Amelia behind, the memory of that lovely child-woman would disappear and it would be as if she had never existed.

Supper came and was disposed of with a minimum of fuss. The food was good but nothing out of the ordinary. There had been a sweet potato pie that Amanda enjoyed since it was in season. The sweet potatoes, just dug a few weeks before, were at their freshest and sweetest now.

When the meal was over and the tray removed, there came a period of letdown. It made her restless to think of the others below, deep in conversation around the fireplace. She wondered if her name was mentioned.

Marta had returned to stay with her, but the German nurse was quiet, too, almost morose in her gloom. She had brought her tatting with her, and she sat like a large gray spider, weaving a fine web. Her small, silver shuttle flew back and forth in her capable hands, and the pattern of lace emerged, intricate and fine.

Once or twice Amanda tried to make conversation, but she soon desisted. Each time she spoke Marta at once stopped her tatting, and Amanda was afraid she was distracting the other woman from her pattern.

Seeing Marta with busy work made her wish for her

own needle. She felt the need to be doing something, even if it was only petit point. Tomorrow she really must get up. She could not stand to play the invalid much longer. It gave her too much time to think, nocturnal thoughts with an undertone of melancholy.

Oh, come, she scolded herself silently, looking toward the window. It was dark now but that was no excuse for blaming her depression on the night. Unconsciously she sighed.

Marta looked up then followed her gaze to the window. "Did you want the curtains pulled?" she asked setting down her work. "I should have done it when I lit the lamp, but it was not quite dark outside."

Since she had already gone to the trouble of getting up out of her chair, Amanda did not object.

The woman reached to twitch the panel of heavy velvet along its rod then stopped, staring out into the night.

"What is it?" Amanda asked.

"I'm not sure, *fräulein,* but I think . . . *ja,* I'm sure it is that Carl."

"What is he doing?"

"Sitting."

"Just . . . sitting?"

"*Ja.* Just sitting, with a candle."

"Candle?" Amanda threw back the cover and swung her legs off the bed.

"No, no, *fräulein.* You mustn't."

But Amanda had already got to her feet. She stood a moment holding to the side of the bed, then she reached for her dressing gown and pulled it about her shoulders. An excuse, any excuse, for action was what she had been waiting for. It was not that she was so terribly interested in poor Carl, she just wanted to do something besides lie flat on her back.

She saw first the glow of the candlelight and the shadow of a figure, like an ancient deity, sitting cross-legged behind it. As she and Marta stared, Carl leaned forward, his face glimmering pale, and lit a second candle from the first.

"What can he be doing?"

"I could not say, *fräulein*."

"It is cold out there, and the dew is on the ground. Perhaps he is only trying to get warm."

"*Ja, fräulein*," Marta answered tonelessly.

"You don't think so?"

"It has the look, I think, of a vigil."

"Oh," she said, casting Marta a half humorous look. "He must be practicing . . . for the Night of the Candles Theo mentioned the other night."

"Three candles . . ." Marta murmured as if she hadn't heard. "He is lighting a third candle."

A look confirmed the words of the nurse though Amanda could not see what significance there might be in it.

"Poor thing," she said at last. "Do you suppose he is sitting out there because Theo wouldn't let him in?"

"It is possible."

"I don't like it. I can't bear to have an animal in the cold at night, much less a human being. Perhaps if I spoke to him . . ."

"You needn't trouble yourself. See, now. *Herr* Theo goes toward him."

"It's about time!"

They turned back into the room as the voice rang

out behind them. It was Sophia, a spot of color in each cheek, who had walked into the room. She moved to the window to stand between them, staring out at the scene taking place in the dark velvet of the high grass on the lawn.

"What an idiot! He gets stranger every day. I never feel safe, not with him roaming at will. We will be lucky if he doesn't set fire to the grass and burn the house down!"

"It will hardly do that, not after the rain."

"There has been a drying wind blowing all the day. You can still see it. Look at the trees."

The tops of the trees in the far woods, their branches still holding scattered rags of leaves, were swaying back and forth in the pale moonlight. Higher up, the wind sent a low bank of clouds scurrying, its grayness catching a silver sheen as it flew.

Striding up to Carl, Theo took a commanding stance. Carl got slowly to his feet. As they spoke the wind whirled the sound away, leaving those in the house to watch a pantomime.

After a moment Carl began to slowly shake his head. Theo gestured, and again Carl shook his head.

Then Carl appeared to look beyond Theo to the house. What he saw there gave him courage for suddenly he began to caper about, his hands moving in time to some weird music that could only be in his mind. His patched and misshapen clothes fluttered and flapped in the wind, like the garments of a scarecrow. In the light of the moon, he looked like a demented thing, a pitiful caricature of a human being.

Amanda found herself wanting to cry out for him to stop, for him not to play the fool and increase the chances of being declared mad. She was so involved in the drama below that she scarcely noticed when Marta had stepped back, relinquishing her place to Sophia with a subservient murmur.

Now Carl pranced away, as if in obedience to Theo's dictates, then he came creeping slyly back, his mouth curved in an open, gleeful grin.

Theo, pushed beyond endurance, took a threatening step forward. Stopping, Carl swept up one of the candles and thrust it at Theo.

Amanda expected to see the candle flicker and die in the wind. It did not. It fluttered briefly before flaring brighter still. Carl brandished it like a weapon, forcing Theo to dodge and stumble back a pace before the dancing flame.

Again Carl looked toward the house, as though for approval. Theo turned his head, looking also, then he called out, a faint swell of sound as the wind began to fall.

"Why in God's name doesn't he do something?" Sophia muttered in fierce contempt.

And then Jason moved from the shadows near the front gallery. His head was thrown back, and he was laughing, caught in the grip of a dark mirth. He raised his arm, motioning to Theo, and made some humorous comment.

Theo turned away reluctantly, moving to join him. Together they went back into the house, leaving Carl to his candles and the wind and the cold, damp night.

"Oh, for . . ." Sophia made a sound of disgust in her throat. "Jason is a fool, almost as great a fool as that imbecile out there!"

"I don't understand, Sophia. Why do you hate the man so much?"

Sophia stared at her, her pale lashes almost invisible

in the weak light so that her eyes seemed to have only naked rims. There was a look of hauteur and concentration on her face, as if she wondered what gave Amanda the right to question her and what she hoped to gain by it. As the silence stretched, Amanda thought she was not going to answer.

Then she spoke slowly. "I don't know. I cannot bear cripples, but that isn't it entirely. It's like . . . like living in the shadow of an overhanging rock; he gives me a feeling of constant dread. He . . . he makes me nervous."

And living with dread made her irritable and vindictive, Amanda thought, though she was given no chance to show her understanding. In aggravation with herself for saying too much, Sophia had gone, in a swift swirl of skirts, from the room.

"She is not a very happy person," Amanda said, feeling as she spoke the inadequacy of the comment.

"No, *fräulein*," Marta agreed, moving heavily from the shadows. *"Fräulein . . ."*

"Yes, Marta."

"Would you object if I brought a pallet and slept here in this room with you?"

"Why, no, I wouldn't object . . . precisely."

"It is that man out there," she went on, a little too quickly. "I do not trust him. Like all his kind, may God watch over them, he has only one idea."

"You mean, that I am his Madame Amelia, returned from . . . from the grave."

"Exactly so. I have no idea that he would harm you. In fact, I would say it would be the last thing he would do. Still, he is not . . . not accountable."

Amanda nodded in slow agreement, and Marta went

away to return shortly bearing the mattress from a single bed, a pillow, and several blankets and sheets in her arms. Her pallet she placed before the fireplace to take advantage of the warmth of the floor there and the heat that lingered in the bricks.

For a time after they had finally lain down, Amanda felt ridiculous. It seemed so medieval to have someone sleeping at the foot of her bed for her protection.

She had become a little chilled from standing before the window, and now she pulled the covers up to her neck. She was not very sleepy, and the presence of another person in the room did not help. She lay staring up into the inside of the tester letting her mind drift.

What was it Sophia had said of Amelia, that she had no wish for children? She had said that her illness was feigned, an excuse to keep from having to produce an heir. She could hardly credit that, not with Marta, a special nurse, in attendance on her. Surely that would not have been necessary for an imaginary illness? And yet, she could remember that once, when she was thirteen and Amelia ten years old, Amelia had pretended to have a sprained wrist. She had kept it tightly wrapped and cried out at the least touch for more than a month during the summer because she hated putting up the plums, blackberries, and peaches, making them into jelly, preserves, and sometimes wine. These were housewifely skills their grandmother had insisted that every girl should know. Amanda had watched the younger girl bind up her wrist every morning and take off the bandage at night without ever mentioning a word to their grandmother.

Yet, if it was true that Amelia had somehow faked her illness, then why had she taken her own life? Why would she do such a thing when she had everything to live for, youth, beauty, a loving husband, a lovely home, a life of comfort and leisure? No, she had no reason to kill herself. What did that leave? An accidental death? An attempted suicide that was never meant to be fatal, simply frightening for those around her? Or . . . murder?

No. She mustn't allow her imagination to run away from her. There was no use indulging in wild speculation, all on the evidence of a jealous woman who was only too eager to step into Amelia's shoes. No, she must stop it. She must think of something—anything—else. Nathaniel. Her wedding. The house they would build, white, with an octagonal tower housing a study and library for Nathaniel. And for herself a sunroom where she could grow ferns and have a settee of rattan with green and white printed cushions. She would buy a baby carriage of rattan, and on warm spring days she would roll the baby out into the back garden, and he could sun while she did needlepoint for her dining room chairs . . .

Candles, bright pinpricks of light shone in the dark night, hundreds, thousands of them. They grew, blossoming, moving closer. She turned as they came nearer. She began to run along a dirt track. She could feel the warmth of the tapers growing behind her and then, in the way of dreams, the candles were before her, sweeping in upon her in a smothering wave, burning, setting her on fire!

She came awake with a jerk, staring wide-eyed into the dark, her breathing quick and uneven. Then she sighed in relief as the tension faded. Turning her head, she could just make out Marta on her pallet, her chest rising and falling with her stentorian breathing. She smiled a little in the dark. Stentorian from Stentor, the Greek herald with the loud voice.

Looking beyond to the window she saw the starshine

gleaming through a crack between the drapes. It reminded her of Carl and his tireless vigil.

Obeying an impulse, she slid out of bed and padded to the window. There was a faint swimming in her head but, other than that small weakness, she felt well.

The moon had set, leaving the ground below in much greater darkness than earlier. There was no sign of candlelight, no capering figure. Then as she strained her eyes she saw him.

Carl, crazy Carl, still sat below her window, cross-legged before the burned out stumps of his candles, his hands dangling over his knees, his head slumped upon his chest.

Pity such as she had never known before swelled her chest. It caught her so unaware that she gasped with the force of its pain, her vision blurring with a rush of tears. Poor human creature, wayward, contrary, but infinitely vulnerable. Why should he be forced to wander, lost and alone, bereft of the source of kindness?

Amanda grew suddenly chilled. Numbness crept over her, paralyzing her limbs. Eyes, wide and blank, she clung to the drapes of ruby velvet as to a lifeline, her fingers crushing their soft folds.

Then below her Carl stirred. He lifted his head in a listening pose, his body going rigid. An instant later he surged to his feet, and with swift, incongruous grace, melted into the shadows toward the rear of the house.

Almost at once, Amanda saw what had alerted him. It was a horseman, cantering along the road toward the barns. In the blackness of the night it was impossible to identify either horse or rider. They were no more than moving shapes in the night heralded by the faint clop of hooves. So Amanda thought until she realized there was one other circumstance that helped make them apparent to her gaze. The rider was dressed in robes of white, full robes billowing in the night wind, flowing back over the rump of his horse. He wore no hood to define the shape of his head however, giving him, for one brief instant, the look of a headless phantom.

A slow frown creased Amanda's forehead as memory stirred. Once before, not so long ago, she had seen something similar. Where? When? She could not quite bring the moment into focus. The harder she tried, the more it receded into dark mists of pain and an odd mental malaise.

Did it matter? What was important was that someone at Monteigne rode encased in the white, sheetlike robes of the nightriders. Riding in secret, hiding under the cover of night, they joined with others to perpetrate deeds of darkness.

Shivering violently, Amanda turned from the window. She tumbled into bed and drew the cover to her chin. Though she closed her eyes and sought desperately for the oblivion of sleep, its simple, mindless comfort would not come. Chilled and awake, she was left to face her fears, both known and unknown.

Chapter
Six

TOWARD daylight, when the dawn at last pushed the shadows out of her room, Amanda finally slept. It was a heavy, unnatural slumber like the effect of a sleeping potion. She was awakened in midmorning by Marta, bringing a breakfast tray.

Roused, she recovered her vigor to the point of getting out of bed and declaring her intention of going downstairs. Her small hidebound trunk had been delivered to her room, and from its depth she took a morning costume of brown fustian which featured a high-necked polonaise with slashed sleeves to show a white blouse, and fullness which was drawn to the back exposing a white underskirt of the same material. It was as near to mourning wear as she had brought with her, and, with the addition of a black ribbon at the neck, should be unexceptional.

Marta helped her with her laces and buttons and putting up her hair, though she did so in the heavy silence of disapproval. Amanda did not let that deter her. She was tired of the bed, tired of the coming and going in her bedroom, and of the feeling that the commotion and disruption in the household was her fault. She was not so simple as to think that she was well enough to travel with only a lone male to support her, but she refused to be bedridden a moment longer. She could see no difference between staying in bed and lounging at ease on one of the sofas in the parlor. It would be more convenient; Marta would not have to run up and down the stairs with trays; and she would not have to feel that she was putting everyone to needless trouble.

More than these, she would not have to lie helpless, at the mercy of her own imagination and the foreboding that crowded her mind.

She left her room and went down the hall with its narrow strip of carpeting. Marta trailed behind her, smelling salts grimly at the ready.

The stairs presented no problem going down, though she was silently doubtful of getting back up so easily.

Nothing moved in the quiet house. The front and rear doors had been left open, allowing the fresh coolness of the wind to sweep through the hallway. Amanda took a deep breath, feeling better already, as she stepped into the parlor.

No one was there. A wry smile curved her lips as she recognized the pangs of disappointment. She had no real need for congratulations on her show of fortitude, still it would have been nice to have someone share her elation.

She had accomplished the feat. She was downstairs. Taking up a book on farming methods that had been left lying on one of the tables, she lay down upon the settee. Marta piled cushions at her back, then settled herself into a chair and took her tatting from a voluminous apron pocket.

They sat for some time, Amanda trying to find something of interest in contour plowing and green manures, Marta keeping a wary eye on her patient. It was almost as if she expected her to keel over at any moment, Amanda thought with the beginning of exasperation.

She was saved from this severe test of her nerves by Jason. He strode into the room with his hat in his hand and a preoccupied frown on his face. He checked as he saw her, then came on more slowly. Tossing his hat into a chair, he took a seat, a species of concern replacing his frown.

"I didn't expect to see you today," he said, leaning forward with his elbow on one knee. "Are you sure you are strong enough?"

"Quite sure. I feel much better for the effort. I do believe if I had stayed in bed a moment longer I would have had a nervous attack."

A slow smile lit his face, changing him beyond recognition. "You surprise me. I would have said you were not the type."

"It is difficult to say what type a person may be until he or she is tried."

"True," he conceded. "And what, if I may ask, has tried you? Tell me, and I will see what can be done to change it."

How could she answer that? He could not be expected to change his household to suit her whims. She dismissed the impulse to demand that he refrain from riding with the nightriders during her visit to say instead: "The fault is in myself. I haven't the temperament to be an invalid."

He gave a slow nod. "I can believe that. Amelia used to say how conscientious you always were, how full of energy."

"Did she?"

"She admired that in you. We often admire the qualities in others we lack ourselves."

Once more Amanda was at a loss. She was grateful to Marta who chose that moment to get to her feet.

"Your pardon, *fräulein, mein herr*. I find I come downstairs without my spare reel of thread. While you, *Herr* Jason, are here, I will fetch it."

A casual wave of long brown fingers signaled his acquiescence. As Marta's heavy tread sounded on the stairs he leaned back, so at ease anyone might have been forgiven for thinking he was content to be where he was.

"I . . . haven't thanked you for having me here," Amanda began as the silence stretched.

"Not at all. It was the least I could do when you were injured on my front doorsteps, wasn't it?"

Amanda shook her head at his dismissing tone. "Nonetheless, I am grateful for the care you have given me."

"As to that, Marta is your benefactress, and I'm sure she is happy to have a patient to practice her skill upon again."

"She has been extremely kind."

"Marta is a person of strong likes and dislikes. I don't believe anything or anyone could prevail upon her to care for a person she took in aversion. She may have her faults, but I have never known her to stint herself when the welfare of her patient is at stake."

There was an undercurrent in his voice, almost as if

he was defending the German nurse. Amanda did not pursue the subject however. It could only lead to the illness of Amelia with its painful end.

From the corner of her eye Amanda glanced at him, aware of a peculiar magnetism about his still form. He was staring at her, his elbow propped on the arm of his chair and his chin resting on his fist. His gaze moved slowly from her brow to her cheeks, blooming with color, to the curves of her mouth, pausing a moment there before dropping to her hands clasped tightly in her lap. He frowned.

"You say you are engaged to Sterling, but you don't wear his ring," he said abruptly.

Instinctively Amanda covered her naked finger. "No. Such things aren't that important since the war. We decided a wedding band would be enough."

"Very practical," he murmured.

"Yes," Amanda answered, her tone abrupt. Glancing about in search of some inspiration for a change of subject, her gaze alighted on the portrait above the fireplace. "I never realized you fought in the recent conflict."

"Didn't every man in the South who was able to stand?"

"Not every man," Amanda said unhappily. Claiming he was needed by his parents, both of whom were plagued by ill health, Nathaniel had never gone to battle. Oh, he had drilled with the home guard and worn a tailored uniform, but that had been the extent of his effort. It was nothing short of amazing the way his mother's health had improved after Appomattox, though his father still claimed a heart condition. "I believe from your insignia that you were with the cavalry?"

"Gray's Brigade," he admitted.

"I think I have heard of them. You were at Bull Run and Chattanooga . . . "

"At Bull Run, yes. During the Chattanooga offensive our main target was the M & C railroad."

"Vicksburg?"

"Grant's supply depot. We only slowed the inevitable. If Lee had relieved the seige . . . Never mind. We lost. It's over."

"Is it?" she asked slowly. "Is it over as long as the South is garrisoned by Federal troops and no man who fought in the war can hold office, when the people of the South are forced to remain in the Union but are treated as disenfranchised citizens, required to swear fealty to the victors? How can it be over when men ride at night to right old wrongs and make new ones in the process?"

"In ancient times warriors were put to the sword and women and children enslaved. You must admit the methods today are more humane."

"More humane, perhaps, but the intention is the same—to cripple and humiliate the enemy."

"Do you approve of the nightriders then?" he asked smiling a little at her vehemence.

She slanted a conscious glance at him, the image of the man on horseback cantering toward the barn the night before vivid in her mind. A shade of coolness crept into her voice as she said, "No. They only invite retaliation and give those with old scores to settle or covetous instincts a cover for their wicked deeds. I will, if you like, admit to ambivalent feelings on this score. It goes against the grain to accept the treatment being meted out and do nothing about it."

He shifted in his chair to cross one ankle over his knee. "What do you suggest?"

"I don't know. I suppose we shall all have to swallow our pride and take the oath of allegiance. Until we do this there will never be enough men of like mind with the right to vote the scalawags and carpetbaggers out of office. The trouble is that some, like my grandfather, would rather die than so compromise their honor."

"Your grandfather?"

She nodded, her eyes clouded with remembrance. "Oh, they blamed it on the privations of the war years and the death of my grandmother. It wasn't that—not entirely. It was watching everything he had worked for all his long life lose value, seeing the fortune he made disappear along with the gallant traditions he believed in and the honor he held most sacred. He no longer cared to live, and so he died."

"Leaving you alone to face all he had left."

"Someone must," she said simply.

"For all your much vaunted self-control, I think you felt it more than most."

His tone was quiet, gentle, and disconcerting in its understanding. She met his open green gaze for a long moment, a breathless eon of time in which she felt a fleeting, perilous comfort . . . and something more she could not quite define. Admiration? Affinity?

Softly, almost to himself, he added, "It is the ones who allow themselves to feel the most who are easiest for others to use . . . and to hurt."

This was too close for bearing. She made a swift, negative gesture, sitting forward. One of the cushions behind her slid to the floor, but she scarcely noticed. "I don't believe that," she said.

In a single smooth movement, he rose from the chair, picked up the cushion and loomed over her to place it behind her back. "Don't you?" he asked, his face so close to her own she could see her own pale face reflected in the pupils of his eyes, see the ridged muscles of his jaw and the blue shadow of his beard under the skin. Even if she could have found an answer, she could not have voiced it.

A sound in the doorway behind them cut across the moment. "Well," Sophia said, her voice overloud. "This is where you are. I could not believe it when I found your room empty just now."

"Just the person we want to see," Jason said straightening, stepping to the fireplace without hurry or visible change of demeanor. "The occasion calls for refreshment, don't you think? What shall it be, Amanda? A glass of wine, or a cup of tea?"

"Tea, please," Amanda replied.

"Certainly," Sophia said. "I will be happy to tell Proserpine. For three, I presume?"

"Yes, I suppose so," Jason replied, "since Marta seems to have deserted us."

Her silvery blond head held high, the other woman went away. Despite her words she did not look happy to relay the orders of the master of the house, even though she was to be included in partaking of the refreshments.

"It's getting warmer, don't you think?" Jason said. Moving to the window, he brushed the curtains aside and raised the sash, letting in a breeze laden with the musty midday warmth of Indian summer. Sophia returned before he was done and took the chair he had occupied.

"Marta hasn't deserted Amanda," the other woman said as if taking up a conversation where she had left off. "I saw her upstairs a while ago. Since she was free I asked her to turn out her room. It has been some time since it was cleaned last, and I wanted to gather the linens for the laundress. She comes tomorrow, you know, Jason."

He gave her an indifferent nod.

"For myself, I don't see why Proserpine couldn't do it. When I went into the kitchen just now she was perfectly idle," Sophia went on. "Luncheon has been ready this hour and more, except for a caramel custard baking in the oven."

"You know Proserpine has never been anything but a cook. She takes pride in that."

"We cannot afford to pay her for pride."

"Perhaps you would like to let her go and take on the cooking as well as the house?" Jason asked in a mild tone that held in its softness a hint of mockery.

"You must be mad," Sophia said with a shudder.

"Only practical," he answered.

"You know I can't cook."

"I was forgetting. I would wager Amanda can," he said, a peculiar smile tugging at the corner of his mouth.

As he quirked an eyebrow in her direction, Amanda admitted it.

"You see?" he said.

"What an odd humor you are in today," Sophia said with a shrug.

"Yes," he agreed and smiled at Proserpine as she brought the tea tray.

"The house is very quiet," Amanda commented as she accepted her cup from Sophia who sat behind the silver teapot.

The other woman looked up, a bright light in her brown eyes. "How remiss of one," she exclaimed. "No doubt you are wondering why your fiancé isn't in evidence. I was supposed to have told you that he and Theo were going riding this morning."

Amanda had meant nothing of the kind, but she let

the matter stand, turning to Jason. "It is very generous of you to provide a mount for Nathaniel."

"Not at all," he answered, his gaze pensive as he stared into his teacup.

Her tone falsely bright, Sophia said, "Don't worry, in no time at all you will be well enough to ride again. Then I suppose you will be leaving us."

"Yes," Amanda said, and there was nothing she could do to keep her answer from sounding ungracious. She sipped her tea, helplessly aware of the growing constraint in the room. An instant later she gave a slight, impatient movement of her shoulders. She was a guest in this house, and as such, it was her duty to be polite and pleasant, but no more than that. It was up to her host to keep the conversation going and provide an atmosphere of friendliness and conviviality. If he could not do that, then she need feel no guilt.

"Is something wrong?" Jason asked, a disquieting indication of how closely he was watching her.

"No," she answered, summoning a smile. "I'm fine."

"Your tea is all right?"

"Perfect."

"Don't fuss so, Jason," Sophia said. "It was only a bump on the head."

He made no reply, but it was not long afterward that he said something about seeing to the estate accounts, bowed to both Sophia and Amanda, and went away. Sophia did not linger. Murmuring something about the laundry, she swished from the room, leaving the tea things on the table.

Amanda sat staring into space with a frown between her eyes, more disturbed than she liked to admit. For the first time she began to see what had attracted Amelia to Jason Monteigne, that quality within him that had prompted her to elope with him, giving up family and friends. There was no doubt that he could be charming. What troubled her—one of many things that troubled her—was a feeling that there had been a purpose behind his charm. What could it be? The necklace? When found, it was his for the asking. Had he, perhaps, been sounding her out on the nightriders, checking to see if she could be trusted to remain quiet about his activities if she should discover them? Or was he, for some reason as yet unperceived, seeking to influence her opinion of himself? When she had first arrived he cared nothing for what she thought; why should her opinion trouble him now?

She was being ridiculous. He had been surprised, even shocked, to see her on the night she first came to Monteigne. Saddled with an unwelcome guest, he had been under no obligation to exercise charm.

She picked up the farming book, then set it down again. She stared around the room, noting each sign of age and neglect, wishing for a good polish and a cloth to bring the shine back to the fine old furniture. The portrait over the mantel seemed to draw her gaze, and she returned to it again and again. It had not been such a long time since it was painted, ten, perhaps eleven years. And yet in that time the dashing young centurion has become a bitter and grieving philosopher, a rider of the night.

Grown too restless to bear with her own company a moment longer, Amanda got to her feet. Soon it would be time for luncheon. She should make herself ready for it. Moving slowly, a precaution against the faint swimming in her head, she made her way to the stairs. By gripping the railing tightly, she made it up the steps though she was dismayed at her weakness. She was standing at the landing waiting for her knees to stop trembling when she heard voices. They were coming from the middle bedroom on the right across from the head of the stairs.

"You heard me," Sophia was saying.

"No, *fräulein*. It wasn't so."

"Explain it to Jason. I doubt he will believe you."

"Why? Why do you do these things?"

"Never mind. I want you to think about what I've said."

"I will think."

"Think hard. Two deaths? It seems to need some explaining to me—perhaps to the sheriff."

"*Fräulein* Sophia! You cannot!"

"Be quiet! Unless you want the whole house to know?"

Their voices became muted and Amanda moved on, her weakness forgotten as she revolved in her mind what she had just heard. Two deaths. What could it mean? Why should Marta be afraid of Jason? And why was Sophia involving herself?

Luncheon was a long meal. They were all gathered around the board to partake of the bounty, most of which had been grown on Monteigne. Amanda felt a reserve in her manner toward Jason, but she seemed unable to do anything about it. She felt the tension between Marta and Sophia also. Nathaniel and Theo, telling of their ride, were the only ones who seemed unaware of the crosscurrents.

Toward the end of the meal a strained silence fell. Jason looked up as if suddenly becoming aware of his duties as a host. He turned in his seat, to speak to Nathaniel. "I believe that you plan to go into politics?"

"Yes," Nathaniel answered. "I have my eye on a Senate seat in the State Legislature."

"Interesting," Theo observed. "My father was a State Senator."

"Before the war, I suppose?"

"Oh, yes, of course. It's been quite a while since we have had men of his sort over us. Have you no qualms about joining the rabble we have governing us now?"

Nathaniel flushed at the scathing tone. "Since the rabble is supported by Yankee troops, it seems to me to behoove us to use legal means of nullifying their power. By that I mean putting men into office who can be depended on to set things right."

"By right I assume you mean back the way they were?" Theo inquired.

"Well, no. That won't be possible." Nathaniel's eyes widened in amazement as he regarded Theo. "I'm afraid anyone who thinks it is, is either misguided or willfully blind. We are entering into a new era . . ."

"Yes, a new era of mediocrity," Theo interposed.

"An era wherein men will excel and become greater through personal effort instead of birth or the sweat of others."

"A fine thing, I'm sure."

"I think so, yes," Nathaniel said with simple candor.

"You are entitled to your own opinion," Theo said, "but I doubt there are many who will agree. Most favor the solution posed by the Knights of the White Gardenia."

"Your local nightriders?" Nathaniel smiled. "I hope they ride for many a night to come."

"You do?" Theo sat back with his wineglass in his hand, surprise making his face blank.

"Indeed I do. The intention of this group is to spread fear, to make the elected officials think twice before they indulge in legal robbery and oppression of a helpless population. The trouble with that is, the men who start such activities can't control them. Anybody fortunate enough to still own a set of bed linens can use them to further their own ends. One group, in all self-righteousness, takes a carpetbagger out and gives him a coat of tar and feathers before sending him North on a rail, next time another group takes out a wifebeater and gives him a taste of the whip, and a week later we have a sheeted outlaw robbing an old couple of their life savings. People become afraid. Nobody knows who belongs to the nightriders, where they will strike next, or why. In desperation, people have to stop this kind of thing. The best way is to remove its reason for being, the basic injustice. And the way to do that is through the political system. So you see, the more the men in sheets ride, the faster I'll benefit."

"I'm surprised you don't put on a sheet and lend them a hand," Sophia said, smiling across the table at Nathaniel.

"No, no," he answered, taking the joke, if that was what it had been, at face value. "I'll just let them hang themselves."

It occurred to Amanda that Theo, with his hint of support for the nightriders, might be the man she had seen riding homeward in the dawn. After a moment, she dismissed the idea. If he was he would surely have the sense to remain quiet on the subject.

Involuntarily, she glanced at Jason. He sat playing with his wineglass, his narrowed eyes holding an expression bordering on contempt as he stared at Nathaniel. It was, she thought, the contempt of the man of action for the purveyor of slow, dry legalities. It might also be, a part of her mind whispered, the contempt of the man who, like her grandfather, unlike Nathaniel, refused to compromise his honor to profit by base deeds.

Abruptly Jason set the glass to one side. "You applaud individual effort, Sterling, and yet you are willing to use other people's money to put yourself in office?"

"Unfortunately, it is necessary," Nathaniel said, his voice grave. "The expense is more than one man can bear."

"Granted, the expense is great, that is exactly the point. Why should you expect someone else to bear the burden?"

"I don't believe I understand what you are getting at, sir," Nathaniel said stiffly.

"I'm questioning the wisdom of using Amanda's patrimony to finance your ambitions," Jason said, his tone quiet, even gentle.

"By what right?" Nathaniel demanded.

"I see you don't deny it. My right? Why, that of her nearest relative. The connection is by marriage only, but I feel a certain responsibility."

"Do you indeed? I find that odd, I must say, under the circumstances."

"Must you? But then, you do not know me well."

"As well as Amanda does."

"True," Jason conceded.

"In any case, Amanda is of age and scarcely in need of your concern or aid."

"There I cannot agree with you," Jason said, his gaze watchful.

"Be that as it may," Nathaniel said, his face growing alarmingly red, "I am her fiancé and perfectly able to advise her in the use of her inheritance."

"For her advantage or your own."

"As my wife she will, naturally, benefit if I am elected."

"And if you are not?"

"Then I will support her, as any husband would do! See here, I will not tolerate anymore of this impertinence. What I can't understand is how you came to know of Amanda's financial position."

This was said with an accusing look in Amanda's direction. When Jason made no answer, she said, "I told them, Nathaniel. It was hardly a secret since Amelia was involved in the disposition of my grandfather's estate."

"I still don't like it," he said petulantly.

"Like it or not, you will have me to contend with in this matter," Jason told him, his voice rising for the first time as Nathaniel continued to frown at Amanda.

Nathaniel sent him a glance totally lacking in his usual urbane calm. "I don't see what you have to gain from it."

"No," Jason agreed, "I was sure you wouldn't."

Amanda's fiancé went rigid. He looked uncertain whether to issue a challenge on the spot or get up and walk away.

"Nathaniel, please . . ." Amanda said.

He glanced at her impatiently, then recalling that he was at his host's table, he gave a laugh of false heartiness, saying to Jason, "I suppose I must be glad that you will not be one of my constituents. I can see I would not be able to count on your vote!"

The clink of silver against china seemed loud in the quiet interval. Amanda played with her fork. "Has anyone seen Carl this morning?" she asked finally.

A flush rose under the tan of Theo's face, but he went willingly into the conversational breach. "He was seen sneaking away toward the woods. With any luck he will be gone two or three days."

"He has formed quite an attachment for you, hasn't he, Amanda?" Nathaniel said with an attempt at lightness as he glanced at her across the table.

"It isn't for me at all. I told you, he seems to think that I'm Amelia."

"Ah, well," he answered comfortably, "it's harmless enough, I suppose. So long as he is the only one to make that mistake."

Amanda could feel the color mounting hot to her face. His remark might have been innocently made. Still, in view of what had just passed between Jason and himself, it had the sound of a warning. She was acutely conscious of the interested gaze of the others at the table as, staring at her plate, she replied in a tense voice. "There seems little likelihood."

Still, though she scarcely realized it, the emotion the incident had aroused in her affected her conversation with Nathaniel later. She had been embarrassed before everyone, and the smothered resentment over that fact made her less amenable to suggestion than she might have been otherwise. When they were alone in the sitting room across the hall from the parlor, she gave him her cheek when he bent to kiss her.

"My dear Amanda," he said, "you are rather pale. I think you should rest this afternoon."

"I'm not at all tired, Nathaniel."

"Quite frankly, you look it, my dear," he insisted brutally. "I think you are trying to rush things. There is really no need. You are comfortably settled here."

"I don't like to take advantage of Jason's hospitality any longer than necessary. I would like to leave here as soon as possible. The quicker I regain my strength, the sooner we can be gone."

"It would be unwise to leave too soon simply because you dislike the company."

She sent him a slanting glance. "I would have thought you would be anxious to depart as soon as possible."

"Not if it means injuring your health. I feel, in some sense, to blame for this, you know. If I had come with you when you asked, it might not have happened."

In her present mood she felt this was too true to be denied. "You . . . you needn't stay, Nathanial—not if you would rather go."

"I wouldn't think of leaving at this juncture, my dear. Besides, I have it from Theodore that Jason is finding our visit a welcome distraction. He told Sophia's brother that he thought it would be a shame if we didn't stay at least until after this candle thing at Hallowe'en—that we were more than welcome to stay longer if we wished."

"Oh, yes, but after all, what else can the man say? He can hardly throw us out on our ears."

"You think not? I wouldn't put it past him if he really wanted to be rid of us. There is something ruthless about Jason Monteigne, don't you think?"

"Ruthless? I haven't seen that much of him, but it's hardly the word I would have chosen."

He looked pensive. "Perhaps you're right, but there is something odd here. This house, that ferocious beast outside, his own brooding spells. It doesn't add up to a happy man."

"Oh, Nathaniel," she smiled. "It isn't like you to be melodramatic. You sound as if you think him another Byron, '. . . mad, bad, and dangerous to know'! It's scarcely polite. He is your host, and he has been very considerate under the circumstances."

"If I didn't know you, Amanda, I'd think you had a partiality for the man."

"Don't be ridiculous—just because I refuse to run a man down behind his back!"

A shocked look came over Nathaniel's face at the irritation in her voice. "Amanda! This only proves that you need to retire. You are not yourself at all."

"And I tell you I have no need to rest. I wish you would all stop hovering over me like mother hens!"

"Very well then, if that is your wish. Theo has invited me to join him in a hand of cards. If you need me you can send to his room upstairs."

"Nathaniel, this is so petty," she said, but he had already gone, his back ramrod stiff, from the room.

Their quarrel had brought a faint throbbing to her head, and she put a hand to her brow, frowning a little as she massaged it. She knew that Nathaniel was right. She should go up and lie down, but pride and a kind of irritable obstinacy that was foreign to her nature kept her from doing what was sensible.

Thinking that perhaps a breath of fresh air would rid her of her headache, she stood up. Moving with weary footsteps she went from the room and across the hall to the front door.

From the dining room there came the sounds of Proserpine removing the dishes from the table. But for the cook, the lower part of the house seemed deserted. Outside, the day had grown warmer with the ascent of the sun. The wind that blew across the gallery had a softness that reminded Amanda of spring even though it carried with it the drifting whirl of fallen leaves.

She looked around her nervously for the dog, Cerberus.

Not seeing him, she hurried down the steps and along the brick wall to the gate. She stopped to fumble a moment with the catch, then she spun through the opening and clanged it shut behind her.

At the sound the great gray-black dog came loping around the side of the house, the bristles on the back of his neck rising. As he saw her standing beyond the fence a growl began to rumble in his throat. He gave a short warning woof, then stood watching with malevolent eyes as she walked away.

The grass that brushed against her skirts and was trodden beneath her feet gave off a smell like new-mown hay. The ground underneath it was still somewhat damp, but the grass itself was dry. In some places near the house it had been flattened by trampling feet, but farther away it stood tall and thick, waving gently in the wind.

Walking aimlessly, Amanda skirted the house and set out across an open space that had the look of an overgrown field. Near the line of the trees she stopped. Looking back the way she had come, she could see the rear of Monteigne, one or two storage buildings, fig bushes and pear trees.

The house stood four-square with its white walls gleaming and its gray roof silvery in the sun. As Amanda stood there looking at it she began to feel that behind that blank, too stolid, exterior something was concealed, much as the impassive face of the gambler hides both triumph and defeat, trust . . . and trickery.

But was it really the house, or was it the things that had been hinted, the things that she had heard without being able to understand? There was Amelia's illness. Was it real or faked? There was her distaste for the possibility of children, her relationships with the people in the house—intense relationships filled with love or hate. And then there was her death. That Amelia should take her own life, whatever the reason, seemed so unlike her. But in the past few days she had begun to feel that she had never known Amelia at all.

She shivered suddenly and once again put her hand to her head. As she brought it away, she stared at it, surprised to see the trembling that shook her. The wind that had felt so good a few minutes before now had a chill edge. Her knees hardly seemed able to support her.

She should try to get back to the house. She was weaker than she had imagined. Even as the thought was formed she sank down upon the thick grass.

For a moment she rested, leaning on her arm, then it gave way and very slowly she lay back closing her eyes.

She could feel the sun, warm against her face and the roughness of the grass under her fingers. Here, close to the ground, the wind could no longer strike her and, half hidden among the tall sedge, she felt curiously safe. As the seconds passed she could hear the minute rustling and crackling of the grass around her and the faint buzzing of a yellowjacket.

Then, as it had happened once before, she felt herself receding, moving back farther and farther within herself. It was as though somehow she was being forced out of her rightful place. After that, a grayness, like a cloak settling over her, blotted out the bright glow of the day, leaving her in darkness.

She awoke slowly, stretching, laughing softly to herself, her eyes dancing with victory. She ran her gaze down the length of her body and frowned. Then she shrugged, a rueful smile curling her mouth.

She sat up and looked around her. There was no one in view, nothing to see but the house before her.

She felt a tightness about her neck. Raising one hand to her throat she felt the constriction of a high collar tightly closed. Smiling a little she began to unfasten the buttons down the front of the polonaise and then those of the blouse. She pulled the wide wings of both collars open to a deep vee that exposed the soft curves of her breasts.

Lifting her fingers she began to pull the pins from the coronet on top of her head. She ran her hands through the long, russet strands, letting it spread out like a cape upon her shoulders.

She raised her skirt and dropped the pins into the pocket of her top petticoat. Then, letting it fall, she got slowly to her feet.

As she stood looking about her, her gaze moving around the brilliant pale blue sky of autumn, she undid the buttons of her sleeves and folded them back to her shapely elbows. She shook her hair back loving the feel of the wind blowing through it. She was still, her face lifted, her eyes closed, then with a mischievous smile curving her mouth, she started toward the house.

She paused at the gate, watching the front door with eager anticipation. But then as the sun went behind a cloud a shadow of doubt flitted across her face.

At that moment the great black dog got up from where he had been lying in the shadowed end of the gallery. He shook himself, then stood, his ears pricked forward, watching her.

"Cerberus," she cried, swinging through the gate, slamming it behind her.

For a long moment the dog did not move. Then, he gave a short bark and began to pad toward her. His stride grew longer, his tail began to wag, and then he was leaping about her, uttering sharp ecstatic barks of welcome, his long pink tongue lolling out as he jumped up, trying to reach her face.

She caressed him, scratching his crown, pulling his ears, and swinging his massive head from side to side. She spoke to him softly in a voice he obviously recognized and loved.

The dark figure of a man moved from the open doorway of the house. He crossed the gallery and stood with one hand braced against a square, white column.

"I would never have believed it," he said, shaking his head.

She looked up and a smile came and went on her face. "Theo," she said, and pressed the dog down to stand beside her with her fingers just touching his head.

"That dog hasn't been that friendly in months. I would have wagered he would have taken more than one bite out of a stranger like you."

"It seems you would have been wrong." She moved her fingers through the dog's fur without looking up.

"You must have had quite a walk."

She was silent so long that he began to think she was not going to answer. Then she slanted a quick glance at him. "Yes."

"If you had told me you were going I would have walked along with you."

"It is kind of you to say so."

The wind, sweeping around the corner of the house flattened her skirts against her and blew a strand of hair across her eyes. Reaching up, she caught it back and then suddenly lifting her eyes to Theo she gave him a slow, enchanting smile.

Theo pushed away from the column and descended the steps toward her.

"For the first time I believe I see the resemblance between you and your cousin."

"Oh?"

"When Amelia first came here she, too, used to come back from her walks with a high bloom on her cheeks and as windblown as a gypsy."

"That is bad?"

"I didn't say that. I liked her wildness. It made her seem natural and unaffected, less the . . . the Lady of Shalott that Jason wanted."

She looked up sharply, her eyes narrowing. "What . . . oh, I see. Pale and wan, lying on a bier . . . I don't think I like that comparison."

Theo shrugged and refused to be drawn, staring beyond her toward the stable and barn. The slight movement of a facial muscle, the twitch of an eyelid, made her follow his gaze.

Turning her head, she saw Jason coming then, his hands swinging at his sides with his free and easy stride. A smile curved her lips. She made a move as if to go forward to meet him, then she checked herself, following him with her eyes, ignoring Theo's frown.

Opening the gate, Jason came toward them up the path. She could feel his eyes on the flush that deepened in her cheeks, on her disordered hair, and the deep opening of her bodice. She wanted to laugh in sheer pleasure, but she knew it would sound mad. Still, she could not resist dropping him a mocking curtsy.

Deliberately she turned away to smile at Theo. "Shall we go in?" she asked, her voice low and somewhat husky as she took his arm. There was time enough for that other matter, as important as it was. It was so good to be alive, to see, and be seen. There was no hurry, none at all.

It was then that the third man stepped out onto the porch. He was a stern-faced man, with little sensitivity.

"Amanda," he called, his voice tinged with impatience. "Where have you been? I've been searching for you this past quarter hour and more."

He lowered his head as he hastened down the steps, then, as he looked up again, he seemed to realize the disorder of her clothing and hair, for his eyes widened.

"Amanda!" he exclaimed accusingly, grasping her arm, looking as if he wanted to shake her.

"Nathaniel . . ." Theo cautioned, his eyes on her white face. No one paid him any heed.

She stared as if she had never seen the man before her. Her eyes closed. She raised one hand, gropingly, toward her head, pressing against her temple.

At her side the dog was growling deep in his throat. He dropped into a crouch, slowly backing away, his hackles rising.

Jason stepped forward between the girl and the dog, his voice carrying a warning as he spoke. "Down . . ."

"Jason," she said, her eyes mirroring a frightening distress as she turned naturally toward him.

Would she have fallen? She was not sure, still she sought like a child the safety and haven of Jason's arms.

"Well, I'll be . . ." Nathaniel exclaimed. "I said all along she should have been in bed. She is not at all herself yet, not at all!"

Chapter
Seven

AMANDA lay listening to the sound of the guitar. The music Jason played had a plaintive sound. A Spanish piece, it had a hint too of *la soledad,* a bitter poignancy that seemed to match her own mood.

She was lying on a settee, a lightweight patchwork quilt across her knees, her back resting against a pile of pillows. After what had happened this afternoon, they had not wanted her to come down. But she had been adamant against Nathaniel's irritable concern, Sophia's jibes, and Marta's nervous apprehension. So far as she knew, only Jason had put forward no objection to her coming down. She was obscurely grateful to him for it.

Still, even here in the parlor she could not escape Marta's determined surveillance. The nurse sat to her left, comfortably ensconced in a heavy chair. On Amanda's right was Sophia, and among the three of them, before the settee, they had set up a table. On its surface was scattered quantities of black jet and crystal beads, lengths of wire, and a large pair of shears. There was also a pile of colored paper that had been cut into the shape of flower petals.

Marta was engrossed in the task of forming the bead-strung wires into flowers and then shaping the single flowers into bouquets. When complete with a beaded ribbon, they would be taken to the cemetery on All Hallows' Eve. Sophia had the more delicate job of turning the paper petals into full blown roses that, later, would be dipped into hot wax to make them permanent.

Amanda, although she still felt weak, was unused to idleness and, as she lay back against the pillows, her fingers were busily sliding the jet and crystal beads onto a piece of wire.

It was not the most congenial company or, for that matter, the most congenial occupation, but Amanda was satisfied. She had tried to lie down alone in her room earlier, before supper, but she had not enjoyed being alone with her thoughts. They were much too disturbing.

She could remember nothing from the time she had sat down on the grass on the rise overlooking Monteigne. She could not remember letting down her hair or opening the neck of her dress. She could not remember playing with the dog. The very thought sent a chill of horror through her. She could recall none of the things she had said to Theo or Jason. Despite what Nathaniel had tried to tell her about her actions, her first cohesive memory was of him, nearly shouting her name at her, his fingers biting into her arm.

She could remember well enough what had happened after that—Jason carrying her, the terrible anger that had made his arms hard beneath her.

The emotion she had felt then was relief mixed with sadness, and she had fought back tears as Jason took her into the house. But there had been, too, a black fear. It was a fear that came, she knew, from the grayness that settled around her when the blankness entered her mind.

When she had tried to tell Marta how she felt and why she had been near tears, the woman had made soothing noises. "It's only the concussion," she had said. "It's nothing to be afraid of." Her normal, emotionless voice had banished Amanda's fright.

She had almost been able to convince herself that Marta had to be right. Almost. Then she had found her hairpins. They had been placed in the handkerchief pocket of her petticoat.

She had held the pins in her hand, thinking back over the years. She herself had never been in the habit of keeping anything in the pocket of her petticoat except her handkerchief or, occasionally, a coin or two. But there had been someone who had always done so; someone who had a habit of stripping the pins from her hair to let the wind blow through her tresses, bringing them home in her petticoat pocket. That someone was Amelia.

From where she lay, Amanda could see Jason leaning back in his chair, his eyes half closed as he stared at the flickering fire, plucking the strings of the guitar. On a table at his elbow stood a glass half filled with liquor, and between pieces of music he would stop to refresh himself from the glass.

Near him Nathaniel and Theo sat over a small gaming table covered with green baize. The slap of cards and the murmur of their voices was a steady undertone to the haunting notes of the instrument in Jason's hands.

Watching Jason from the corner of her eye, she

seemed to remember that the sound of his guitar was concerned somehow with that other time, the time when she had awakened dressed in a nightgown not her own. But no, what connection could there be? It was only coincidence.

The fire crackled, there was a small snap of exploding resin, and a coal shot out onto the hearth and skidded across the floor.

Sophia jumped up and kicked the burning spark back into the ashes with the toe of her shoe. Then she glanced at Jason. "Can't you play something a bit more lively?" she asked with a coaxing smile. "Something we can dance to?"

He looked up at her but it was as though he did not see her, as though he had to force his thoughts to return from far away. Sophia laid her fingers on his arm pressing slightly, and he smiled, a slow curving of the lips, and sat up straighter in his chair. Without speaking he reached out and downed another inch of the liquid in his glass. He settled his guitar more securely under his arm and began to play a measured, but still faintly melancholy, waltz.

"Oh, Jason!" Sophia exclaimed with a hint of reproach, but he only smiled again, a peculiar smile that served to irritate the woman beside him. She withdrew her fingers from his arm.

"Theo!" she called imperiously.

Her brother looked up. She made a beckoning gesture, her arms held out.

With a murmured apology to Nathaniel, Theo tossed down his cards and went toward her.

They moved away from the furniture grouped around the fireplace to the clearer end of the room, near the front windows. Theo took his sister into his arms, and they began to whirl gently around the floor.

But soon Sophia was not satisfied with only her brother for a partner. She coaxed Nathaniel with a brittle gaiety to the far end of the room.

The draft from Sophia's whirling skirts, as she neared the back of the settee, made the petals of the paper flowers flutter to the floor. Amanda made a move to rescue them, then stopped. If Sophia could not spare a thought for her handiwork, why should she? Besides, to be honest, there was something about the woman enjoying the infectious rhythm of the dance, while she herself could not, that grated on her sensibilities. It was as if Sophia were flaunting her vigorous health, and Amanda found herself wondering how often in the past this tableau had been staged . . . the strange dark man with his proficiency at the guitar, the vigorous young woman with her abundant energy, the invalid Amelia on the settee? Was she imagining things if she assumed, on the evidence of only her own feeling, that it had been often?

Sophia seemed to be flirting with Nathaniel. They held a low voiced, and apparently amusing, conversation as they revolved around the small space. Once Nathaniel threw back his head and laughed, a startling sound from that more than ordinarily serious man.

Amanda found herself watching them over the back of the settee. She was not aware of any overt feeling of jealousy to account for her misgivings, and yet she was disturbed, more so, since now and then Sophia sent her a look half triumph, half expectation, as if she wanted some kind of reaction from Amanda.

Sophia cast a glance over Nathaniel's shoulder, now and then, at Jason also. Absorbed in the music that flowed from his fingers, the owner of Monteigne seemed not to notice.

Moments later Amanda was forced to reconsider her opinion of the last, for stopping in the middle of a measure, Jason stood up. He moved to the sideboard where he added bourbon to his glass and then poured small sherries for Marta and Amanda. He set the glass for the nurse on the table, but Amanda's he put into her own fingers.

Sophia sent Amanda a hard glance. "Jason," she admonished. "We were not finished."

He did not answer. He returned to his chair before the fire with his guitar across his knees, then lifting his glass toward Amanda in a salute he inclined his head, a tantalizing quirk at the corner of his mouth. Lowering his glass, he began again the melancholy tune he had first been playing.

Sophia stared at him, her face hard as if she suspected a deliberate snub, then with a switch of her skirts she took Nathaniel's arm and returned with him to the card table. With a faintly reckless air she accepted a hand of cards as Theo and Nathaniel resumed their poker game.

It was not long afterward that the last note of the guitar died away into oblivion. An intense silence fell. There were small noises, the flip of the cards, the hiss of the fire, the tick of the clock in the hall, the rattle of the beads on the table as Marta and Amanda searched among them for a particular shape or size. These sounds seemed only to emphasize the quiet, to draw attention to the currents of tension that flowed through the room.

Amanda leaned forward to hand Marta a short wire strung with beads to be twisted into shape. Their eyes met. Marta's gaze slid to Sophia, and a queer, satisfied smile flickered across the nurse's plain face. As she settled back she reached out and taking up her glass of wine that she had neglected until now, downed it in a single gulp.

Amanda was just beginning to think of the possibilities of escaping the strange atmosphere by returning to her room, when there came a scraping sound near the door.

Carl stood there, his hat in his hand and his sandy hair like strings of dust in the lamplight. He bobbed his head all around by way of greeting, one corner of his mouth pulled up in the travesty of a grin. With his rolling shuffle, he edged into the room and around the back of the settee to reach the fire.

"Must be getting cold out," Marta remarked to no one in particular.

Glancing at her, Carl nodded, then squatted on the hearth, his cupped hands held out to the blaze. He brought with him the taint of woodsmoke from a hundred old campfires and a wild smell that came, possibly, from the cap of opossum fur in his hands.

Theo made a sound of disgust in his throat but Jason only glanced at Carl absently, unseeingly, and looked away again.

Amanda wondered, since Theo had been so violently against Carl when he tried to visit her in her room the night before, why he didn't protest further. Then she remembered that Carl had the run of the lower floor.

The addition to their company did nothing to end the strain. If anything it increased it.

"I heard you playing the guitar, Jason. It has been a long time."

With a start Amanda recognized the voice, that soft, near formless voice, as belonging to Carl.

"You play best," he went on, "when you are half disguised . . . like now . . . and like that night."

Amanda found herself staring at Jason. Was he disguised, half drunk? He certainly didn't appear to be, but it was hard to tell. She turned back to glance at Marta for corroboration. Then, as she heard the rustle of her own clothing, she realized that the others in the room were gripped by a frozen concentration, waiting to see what Jason would answer.

The words came at last. "That night?"

"The night my Madame went away." And then as if there was some connection in his mind he said: "I have been to the graveyard."

Jason glanced at him sharply. "Why?"

"To see."

"To see? To see what?"

"The place. The hole they dug for the box they put my Madame in. It is still there, the place, the pile of dirt they left, with the stone they put above her. But my Madame has come back. How can it be?"

"Jason!" Sophia exclaimed, "are you going to put up with this?"

"It's monstrous!" Theo added.

Nathaniel sent a look of distaste and of disbelief to Amanda before turning back to Carl.

Jason ignored them all. "Listen to me, Carl. This woman is not your Madame, my wife. She is Madame Amelia's cousin. Madame Amelia is dead."

Carl stared at Jason. "She . . . she takes the place of my Madame?"

"No, no," Jason was forced to answer. "Soon she will leave and go back to her home."

Carl began to shake his head slowly from side to side. "No," he said. "No."

"I have told you the truth."

"No."

"I have told you many times . . ."

"No."

Theo got to his feet, color high in his cheeks. "I've had enough of this! The man's an imbecile!"

Carl rose up, and turning toward Theo, he stepped forward. "Not . . . not an imbecile."

Sophia stood up and moved in front of her brother, sending Carl a brilliant and forgiving smile. "Come. Let's not quarrel. You know, Carl, that you and Theo were always the best of friends before the war. Of course, he doesn't think you an imbecile. Don't even think of such a thing. It was a bad joke. Forget it, please. I expect you are tired. We all are."

She turned to Marta, her hands clasped together in a gesture of housewifely competence. "Marta, if you will, see that Carl has everything he needs in the stranger's bedroom."

When Marta had put down her work and left the room to do her bidding, Sophia glided toward Carl and took his arm. "Come, admit you are tired?"

"Y . . . yes," he stammered, though he sent Theo a far from imbecilic look from under his thick, sandy brows.

"And hungry too, I would imagine. Did you stop in the kitchen?"

He nodded.

"But I'll wager Proserpine didn't leave you dessert. She made a fig preserve cake this afternoon. Come, I'll find some for you."

It was not like Sophia to be so solicitous, Amanda thought as she stared after them. She felt uneasily that the woman had a reason. The most obvious one was to keep her brother from doing anything that Jason might disapprove of and at the same time, reinstate herself in Jason's good graces by a show of compassion. Still, Amanda had a niggling feeling that there was more to it than that, though what it could be she could not say.

She busied her hands, her head bowed over her work as she allowed the minutes to tick by to cover the misunderstanding. Once she thought of what Carl had asked . . . was she going to take Amelia's place? . . . and a faint blush stained her cheeks. She felt a pang of disquiet, then firmly dismissed it. She was silly to be embarrassed, and certainly missish to be disturbed by the suppositions of a man like Carl. However, the words seemed to linger uncomfortably in her mind.

At last her color returned to normal and she looked across to Nathaniel.

Jason seemed to sense her movement and almost as if he wanted to forestall her, he levered himself to his feet. "Would you care for another sherry? Or Nathaniel, would you like another drink?"

Nathaniel accepted but Amanda shook her head without looking at him as she threw back the quilt. "I believe it's time I went upstairs."

"Perhaps I can be of service?" Jason suggested, his face smooth and his voice holding nothing but a grave courtesy. "The stairs are steep . . . and you are a light burden."

As she saw the trend of his words she was compelled to look up at him. "Oh, no . . . no."

Nathaniel stepped forward. "I believe that is my prerogative, old man," he said with a false heartiness, touching Jason's shoulder.

Immediately Jason stepped back with a slight bow of acquiescence. But by that time Amanda had regained her composure. "I can walk perfectly well, if you will give me your arm, Nathaniel."

As they mounted the stairs, Nathaniel said in a low voice. "Peculiar, most peculiar."

"What?"

"This household, of course, my dear, but especially letting that mentally deranged fellow have the run of the place. I wonder why he does it?"

"Pity, I suppose."

"It's possible, though there are few people, in my experience, who would risk the danger for the sake of nothing more than pity."

"Danger?"

"You heard him. The man, Carl—he has a positive mania about this cousin of yours. And he's quite belligerent when he is provoked. You notice those hands? Strong. And he must have the constitution of a Missouri mule to live out of doors most of the time as he does."

"Yet he seems a gentle creature. As for his devotion to Amelia, I find it touching."

"Do you indeed? I never knew you wished to be worshiped."

Amanda sighed, wishing Nathaniel did not have this habit of bringing everything directly back to the personal. "I don't wish to be worshiped. I don't wish for anything other than respect and friendship . . . and . . . and to be valued for myself."

He paused outside the door to her room and turned to face her, a serious look in his hazel eyes. He slid his hand from her elbow to her hand capturing it between both of his. "And is that all?" he asked.

She looked up at him, feeling the warm pressure of his fingers. She knew what he was asking, and yet she could not force the answer he expected past the tightness of her throat. "What . . . what else should there be?" She posed the question in the rather cowardly hope that he would help her, that he would make it unnecessary for her to have to say that terrible word herself. Love.

His face went still then he relaxed, giving her a smile with a hint of forgiveness in it. Leaning close, he brushed her lips with his, lingering for a moment at the corner of her mouth. When she made no move to prolong their embrace, he sighed, and pressing her hand slightly, walked back down the stairs.

She watched him for a few seconds as he disappeared from sight down the stairwell, then with a shake of her head, she turned the doorknob and went into her room.

A lamp burned on the washstand. Blackened logs smoldered sullenly on the firedogs in the fireplace. Seeing them, she moved to take up a poker and prod them into life.

When they caught, she turned her back to the blaze, and for the first time noticed that the daybed Marta had found for herself, and her own four-poster, had been turned down for the night. It was plain that Marta had come upstairs after seeing to Carl's comfort in the stranger's bedroom below, but where could the nurse be?

It was doubtful that she had returned to help Sophia with Carl in the kitchen. In the first place Marta was afraid of Carl, and in the second, Amanda was certain she had heard Sophia's light footsteps going up the stairs minutes before she had decided to call it a day. Once out of Jason's sight, it had not taken her long to finish with Carl.

There was no use worrying. Marta was a grown woman. She would come when she was ready. It was not as if she had any real right to Marta's services as a nurse or a lady's maid.

Moving toward the bed, Amanda lifted her hand to the top of her head, pressing the soft silkiness of her hair to find and remove the pins. As the coil began to loosen and slip onto her shoulders she rubbed at the soreness of her scalp where the pins had held her hair's weight so tightly. When, she wondered, was she going to be well? When would it all end? For the moment, her single joy was the disappearance of her headache. Perhaps she could sleep the entire night away without waking. That would be worth something.

A frown drew her brows together as she unbuttoned her gown. It had been a long day and a distressing one, beginning at dawn with the nightrider and ending with her change of attitude toward her fiancé. She was thinking of Nathaniel and their conversation outside her door. What was the matter with her? Why was she so stiff with him, so unable to respond naturally as she had before? Had she changed so much? Was it, as Sophia had suggested, that she had been trying to run away from him? Could whatever was behind her restraint have gone back that far? Or was it, perhaps, that her illness had changed her? That her surroundings and their strangeness had contributed to her lack of openness?

It was always possible that it was Nathaniel himself who had changed, yet, thinking back, she could see no reason to suppose that this was so.

When she had undressed, she slipped into her dressing

gown, and taking up the hairbrush, began to brush her hair prior to braiding it. But then when the shining mass was smooth and even upon her shoulders she decided against the braiding. Already her scalp was tender, and any tension upon her hair might make her headache return.

She sat beside the fire for a time, reading. At last, when the logs had burned down to nothing more than a bed of red, glowing coals, she was forced to consider the fact that Marta had no intention of returning.

And yet, there was her bed standing ready.

Amanda stared at it thoughtfully. Marta had planned to come back. What had made her change her mind? Was it something Sophia had said? One of her veiled insinuations? It was not a very charitable thing to consider, but it was hard to ignore. Then again, it might be Jason's order that held her back. He was not likely to approve a bodyguard for her in his home. The idea was, on sober reflection, preposterous.

What could she do, go to bed, ignore the absence of the nurse? No, if Marta was suffering under some prohibition, it would be best, both for Marta and for her own peace of mind, to go to her and try to straighten the matter out.

She laid her book aside and got to her feet. The swiftness with which she moved to the door seemed, even to herself, to give the lie to her careful rationalization. There was something more that tugged at her mind, a feeling of distinct unease, a feeling that made her listen carefully at the door before she turned the knob and pulled open the panel.

She glanced up and down the hall, noting that there was no longer a glow of light at the stairwell coming from the floor below. Everyone must have already come upstairs to bed. It was dark except for the light behind her from her own lamp and also from an open doorway on the right farther down the hall.

The other lighted room belonged to Sophia, she found as she passed the door. Though the woman was nowhere in sight, the dress she had worn that evening lay across the foot of her bed.

There were six bedrooms upstairs; four large bedrooms and two smaller back bedrooms lined three deep on each side of the wide, central hall. On the left, on the front of the house, was her own with Jason's behind it. Beyond Jason's room was the one Marta used. Across from Marta, the other back room had been allotted to Nathaniel. Sophia's room was next on that side, and then that of Theo, on the front.

She hesitated outside Marta's bedroom, gripped by the feeling that she was interfering in what did not concern her. Then as she heard the sound of heavy footsteps inside the room she raised her hand and knocked.

She thought for a moment Marta did not intend to answer. The footsteps ceased and there was a long silence. Then the knob turned slowly and the door eased open to a slit.

"*Ja?*" The single word was long, drawn out. Marta's pale blue eyes stared fixedly through the crack.

"It's just I . . . Amanda. Are you all right?"

Again that single word came. "*Ja.*"

Amanda's brows drew together in a slight frown. She could not push in where she was not wanted, and yet something urged her to do just that.

"May . . . may I come in?"

Marta hesitated, then she stepped back just enough to allow Amanda to enter.

Closing the door, Marta turned to her, her face blank. Amanda reached out and put a hand on her wrist. "Are you sure there is nothing wrong? You . . . didn't come tonight, and I was sure you were going to."

A glazed look passed over the face of the nurse, as if she was concentrating on something which had nothing to do with what Amanda was saying. "Ah, my duty. I had forgotten. *Fräulein,* forgive me." She leaned toward Amanda, swaying forward.

An overpowering smell of raw spirits assailed Amanda's senses. She turned her head slightly, taking a deep breath as comprehension came. The woman was drunk.

"Marta!" The word slipped from her lips, filled with reproach, before she could catch it back.

Marta's shoulders slumped, and she raised one hand in a feeble gesture of helplessness.

Glancing around the room, Amanda saw a bottle, more than half empty, sitting on a bedside table.

"The drink . . . it was here when I came into the room. I . . . I could not help myself, fräulein. Truly, I could not. I have had this weakness for some years . . . four, five . . . since that time . . . " she trailed off, looking away.

"How did it get here? Where did it come from?"

"I don't know. I did not think. I was angry, a little, at that woman for ordering me about like a parlor maid. It was weak of me, I know. But I could not help myself. I will do away with it, I won't drink any more. I promise you this, *fräulein.*"

Her words were slurred, almost unintelligible. She tried

to take a step, as if to reach the bottle, then she swayed, her feet planted, as she nearly lost her balance.

Immediately Amanda grasped her arm. Leaning upon her, Marta was able to shuffle as far as the bed. She sat down heavily, then reeled back against the pillows, her eyes closing. Amanda lifted her feet and then stood beside her, undecided what to do next, afraid the woman was unconscious.

"Ah, *fräulein*," Marta said, opening her eyes, moving her head from side to side. "It is a sad thing to be old and alone, without family, without friends. Life, *fräulein*, is not worth the pain. All those I have loved are dead, those I have cared for have died . . . and I am to blame . . . I am to blame."

She rocked her head back and forth, tears rising to her eyes, tears that were partly of self-pity, caused by the drink, but tears that were also formed by a true sadness, or so it seemed to Amanda.

"Secrets I know, *fräulein*, terrible secrets I dare not breathe for my safety. I keep them all, my own and those the others lay upon me, knowing I cannot tell because I fear to go to the authorities." The watery blue eyes fastened on Amanda and for an instant the nurse seemed to recognize her presence for she reached out to grasp her arm in sudden fright. "You will not tell that I spoke of the secrets. Promise me you will not!"

"No, of course I promise," Amanda said soothingly. She could not understand above half of what the nurse mumbled.

"If they knew I had told, something horrible would happen. The horsemen would come for me. I would be blamed for all, everything. I am always blamed, always." The nurse moaned, her voice fading, before a species of drunken anger caught her. "No! No, I don't care what they say! The old lady . . . it was not my fault. And my poor, beautiful *liebchen,* if I had not had this weakness she . . . and the babe . . . But no, I must not think of that. I cannot think of that or I will go mad, as mad as that creature, that scarecrow with his candles."

Marta's fingers slid limply from Amanda's arm, still Amanda did not move. "The babe?" she queried softly.

"My *liebchen,* Amelia's baby."

"You mean . . . she was going to have a child?"

"*Ja. Ja,* no one knew of it, only Madame Amelia and myself. Ah, poor *liebchen,* she was so afraid. She was so afraid that night and in such pain with her head. It was past bearing, and she was not brave, not strong. She begged me for help with tears in her eyes. And I . . . I could not help her, for all my skill. I could bear her tears and her entreaties for merciful death no longer. I came away here, to my room. That night, like this, there was a bottle waiting. I drank. My weakness overcame me. I thought once I heard her call to me, and I tried to go to her, but I could not, and in the morning she was dead."

The horror of the pitiful tale held Amanda silent. Marta stared up at her set face and her eyes grew wide.

"You . . . you won't tell what I have said? You must not. *Herr* Jason would be enraged if he knew. I would be forced to leave. No one must know. Promise me. Promise me!"

"Yes, yes, I promise," Amanda said to still the rising hysteria.

Marta sank back. "Sometimes . . . sometimes she comes to me, wringing her hands. Behind her is the other, the old one. They come in the dark of night and I must do something to . . . to . . ."

Her voice sank to a drunken mumble, and though she rambled on and on, Amanda could not understand the words.

She would have liked to offer sympathy or some kind of reassurance, but there seemed nothing she could say that the woman could understand in her condition.

There was no fireplace in the back bedroom. Amanda covered Marta with a quilt folded at the foot of the bed. There was nothing more that she could do, and so she left, closing the door quietly behind her.

She started down the hall, the heaviness of depression tugging at her mind. The things that she had learned made little difference. What did it matter that Amelia was with child when she took her own life, or that the nurse who was supposed to be attending her lay in her own room in a drunken stupor?

Wait. Was that true?

A woman with child usually had a heightened awareness of the value of living. Her most vital impulse was to protect her own life for the sake of the child, not to take it. The bottles had not appeared in Marta's room by themselves. It looked suspicious indeed that Marta had been unable to attend her patient on the night she died.

Her mind was so filled with the things she had discovered that she started violently as a white form appeared in the darkened hall ahead of her. She stopped, one hand going to her breast, before she recognized Sophia. Theo's sister wore her white dressing gown open over a thin nightgown. Her unbound hair, like spun cotton, was a fluffy cloud about her shoulders. She seemed unaware of Amanda as she flitted across the drafty hallway to pause outside the door to the bedchamber directly opposite her own. Smiling a little, she listened, then tapped softly on the panel before pushing it open. No light shone inside, an indication, surely, that the occupant had retired to his bed. This did not deter Sophia. Throwing back her hair, she stepped inside the dark room, closing the door softly behind her.

At the finality of that sound, Amanda drew in her breath. Averting her eyes, she moved quickly, silently, down the hall to her own room. She did not need to look to know which room Sophia had entered. It was the bedchamber of the ex-Confederate soldier, the widower of three months, the master of the house.

It was Jason's bedchamber.

Chapter
Eight

SHE did not sleep. It was not fatigue that kept her awake, staring up into the canopy above her where the glow of the slowly dying coals in the fireplace gleamed red-orange on the silver tissue cloth. It was a disturbed mind. The more she learned of Marta, the less she was inclined to trust the woman. For all the strength of her body, she was basically weak. She knuckled under to a stronger will, such as Sophia's. Her affections were easily engaged, which argued a shallow nature. She apparently had no self-control, or it would not have mattered that a bottle had been left in her room. Amanda thought of the doctor and his insistence that Marta's face was familiar and of Marta's references to the death of the old lady. Had the doctor some knowledge then of the death of the elderly patient, a knowledge that Sophia shared since she appeared to have a hold over the nurse?

Equally damning was the fact that she had betrayed a confidence, the knowledge of Amelia's pregnancy. Unless the woman had brought the bottle upstairs herself and concocted this whole implausible tale, she was consumed with guilt, remorse—and yes, fear over the death of Amelia.

Why? Was it because she knew that she had been derelict in her duties? Or was there some deeper reason?

Suppose that someone in this house, knowing of Marta's weakness, had placed the bottle in her room the night of Amelia's death? Suppose that someone had then gone to Amelia's room, poured out the fatal dose of laudanum, and given it to her cousin—a woman beset by pain who was used to accepting medicine without question? Had she realized in her last seconds of life that she had been given a poisonous overdose? Had she then called for her nurse in vain? But again, why? There had to be a reason.

Reasons were not hard to discover. She thought of what she had seen, of Sophia's entering Jason's room. How long had that affair been going on? Could it have begun before Amelia's death? Sophia admitted that she had loved Jason for years. It would be human nature, under the circumstances, for Sophia to covet Amelia's place. Or alternately, if Jason had preferred Sophia, it would have been plausible for him to speed his wife's death.

Still, why would it have been necessary? If Amelia was dying they had only to wait a few weeks or months. But in a few months Amelia would have had a child.

Did that fact, then, put a new face on the situation? Was it possible that her murderer had not wanted to risk the possibility of an heir?

Why should that have mattered? Amelia herself had nothing to inherit, nothing other than the collar of Harmonia. The child would have been Jason's heir, but since Jason was in perfectly good health, why would that have mattered? Unless, of course, Sophia had preferred her own child to inherit Monteigne.

What if Amelia's illness had been a sham? What if she had not been dying? It need not necessarily be a deliberate charade. In spite of Sophia's caustic comments, it might have been that the pain was real enough but without physical cause. That the fatal illness had been only in her mind.

Amanda shook her head. Amelia's pregnancy was a complication. It hardly seemed possible that Jason would kill his unborn child or engage in a plot to have someone else do so. There were two others who lived in the house, Theo and Carl. But try as she might she could find no reason for suspecting them. No, it came back, always, to Sophia.

She sat up in bed to fluff her pillows, then lay back down again, a frown between her eyes. It was odd, but she found that her most dominant feeling was anger. It was all so sordid. Such a thing should never have happened.

She fell asleep toward morning. She was struggling, being pulled farther and farther into the smothering depths of a nightmare when suddenly she was awakened. She lay rigid in her bed, listening, until at last she recognized the sound that penetrated her dreams. It was the mournful howling of a dog. It was Cerberus baying at the moon, the harvest moon that sailed, round and full, glowing beyond the curtains at her window.

In that dark hour when the mind flows freely, unhampered by the inhibitions of the day, Amanda thought of Medea, in mythology, the wife of Jason, the wayfarer. Medea, who, on discovering that her husband wanted another woman, had killed her own children to spite him.

It was later, toward dawn, when she woke again. The howling of the dog had stopped, everything was still with that silence which fills the soulless time between the last of the night and the first of the morning, the last of the hunting owl's time and the first of the crowing rooster's. What, in this time of quiet had awakened her then? She could not say, but as she lay there a sense of terrible urgency communicated itself to her. She had to get up, to leave the darkened room. She did not know why or where she was going, she only knew she must obey the impulse. She had an impression of wasted time that must be recovered at once, before it was too late.

She slipped her arms into the sleeves of her dressing gown, fumbling in the dark. She could not find the belt and so great had grown her distress that she left it, only holding her dressing gown closed across her chest.

There was no one in the hall when she opened the door. No sound betrayed any other wakeful presence in the night. But a draft swirling about her ankles drew her attention to the double doors that opened out onto the upper gallery. They stood ajar, one of the panels swaying gently in the soft breeze.

Without hesitation she walked toward them. For a moment she thought the long open space of the gallery was empty, then a shadow moved in the darkness to the left down where the chinaberry pushed its branches through the railing. She went toward that movement, guided by the sureness of a need.

She stopped a few feet away and spoke in a soft, inconsequential voice. "Good morning, Theo."

He leaned against the end column, his head turned to watch her approach. "You are up early," he replied.

"Something woke me." She managed to suffuse her voice with the disgruntled sound of someone drawn reluctantly from the covers.

"Go back to bed then. No one expects you to get up to greet the dawn."

She shook her head, staring beyond him into the gray blackness. "I can never go back to sleep once I'm awake, not at this time of morning."

"Sorry, if I'm the cause."

"I didn't have the best of nights so it doesn't matter. I really don't know what roused me." But even as she made the easy rejoinder she grew unsure. It seemed that Theo might be the cause. Something about his stance there in the dimness of the gallery, as well as her own actions, made her uneasy. It was not fear, a physical fear for herself. It was the strangeness of the impulse that gripped her combined with an apprehension for the man who was so studiously avoiding her eyes.

"Did you hear Cerberus then?" he asked.

"Yes, I did. It's an eerie sound, a dog howling in the night."

"Blood-chilling. You should have heard him after Amelia died. We thought he would grieve himself to death. Instead, he simply destroyed whatever heart he might have had, became mean. It's strange, isn't it, the instincts of animals?"

She agreed and he went on. "They aren't as infallible as we have been led to believe though. Look at Cerberus yesterday afternoon. He was fooled, wasn't he? He was so sure you were Amelia he was almost comical when he discovered his mistake."

"I . . . I'm sorry. I can't seem to remember what happened. Marta thinks it's because of the blow to my head. I can't understand it. I feel fine except for being a little weak."

"That's a shame. It was a revelation to me. I would never have dreamed it could happen."

Amanda could feel him staring at her, waiting for her to bring forth some explanation. She managed a laugh. "You make me sorry I missed it. But I don't know why people expect animals and children to be oracles of wisdom. They have less to go on than we do. Have you never seen a perfect crook, like a gypsy tinker, being fawned on by your favorite hound and followed by a parade of youngsters?"

He smiled in agreement. "And it's usually the most shiftless, do-nothing hand on the place who has the best watchdog."

"I wonder what set Cerberus off last night?" Amanda pursued the subject more to ward off silence than from curiosity.

"Who knows? The moon, your presence . . . if dogs have memories . . . or maybe just something in the atmosphere. There are times when I feel like throwing back my head and howling myself. Can you understand that?"

Did he expect an answer? She could not tell, but she pretended that he was making a wry jest by smiling at him with a touch of compassion.

"Pay no attention to me. It's just the time of night. Depressing. Marta tells me this is the time when most people die. Having made it through the dark watch of midnight they cannot quite find the strength to face the morning. I often think of Amelia at this hour."

Amanda looked up to meet his eyes, dark, unreadable hollows in the shadows with no trace of their normal light color. A constriction of pain and sadness rose in her throat. "Is this the hour she died?"

"I think it must have been," he replied quietly, and in the silence turned away to brace his hands on the railing and stare out toward the imperceptibly lightening horizon outlined by a serrated edge of trees.

As he leaned forward something heavy slipped from the pocket of his riding coat. It fell to the floor with a clatter that raised dull echoes around them. Theo stooped immediately to retrieve it, but not before Amanda recognized the shape of a pistol.

Her eyes widened as she saw the furtive gesture of concealment, broken off, that Theo made. Still her voice when she spoke held only self-reproach. "You were going hunting and I stopped you! You should have told me, not let me go prattling on, keeping you from the woods."

Slowly he returned the pistol to his pocket. "It doesn't matter," he said at last with an effort at his usual gallantry, "I was by no means sure that I really wanted to go. One of those good ideas that seemed not so good on closer inspection. I would much rather stay here and talk to a lovely lady."

"I'm afraid I will be dull company."

"Then you will exactly match my mood. Shall we compare our melancholia?"

Amanda searched his face. Was she going demented or had self-destruction been on Theo's mind? Could a man still leaning in that direction joke of his melancholia? Now the tension was gone, only the calmness of composure lit his blue eyes. If Theo had contemplated going hunting for death, he had abandoned the quest. A small soundless sigh of relief left her before she smiled. "I think I would rather hear about Monteigne before the war, and of you and Sophia and Jason, if you don't mind."

They talked for a time, slow, desultory conversation, memories mainly. Theo seemed to know a great deal about her childhood, gleaned from Amelia, she supposed. Somehow they returned again and again to the things she and her cousin had done together in the days before they had gone away to school, the days when they had been inseparable, dependent on each other for the companionship of childhood in that elderly household of their grandparents.

When one of the long periods of quiet descended, after enough time had passed that she would not seem to be anxious to leave his company, Amanda made her excuses. It had struck her that this tryst at daybreak might have an odd appearance, especially to Nathaniel, and she did not care to put herself in the postion of having to make explanations that could only sound like feeble excuses. She was that uncertain of her reasons for joining Theo.

But when she entered her room a few minutes later, she had the feeling that she and Theo were not the only ones abroad. The tatting Marta had left on the chair had been unraveled and strewn over the floor, the doors of the armoire stood open, and the clothes inside hung askew as though someone had been fingering them. Amanda's trunk, against one wall, was open, its lid thrown back, and the contents tumbled about, while curious fingers had surely tampered with her reticule lying on the removable top drawer.

Taking up her petit point bag she opened it, expecting

to find herself poorer, but no, she was enriched. Enriched by a half dozen polished stones and one bright brass button.

She held them in the palm of her hand for a time, then she returned them to the bag. A thoughtful frown on her face, she began to set the room to rights. She was becoming more involved with the people at Monteigne than she had expected. Involvement brought its rewards, but it also carried its penalties . . . and its debts.

The morning dawned finally, bright and clear with more than a hint of warmth in the swiftly rising sun. With the coming of day Amanda found that the events of the night had a quality of unreality. Her instinctive reasoning seemed improbable in the extreme, if not impossible.

She was a practical person and practical people are apt to look for normal, ordinary solutions to their problems, but despite her misgivings it seemed that the normal answer to the problem of Amelia's death no longer applied.

She was confused, and though she did not consciously admit to remembering the handkerchief left tied like a signal to her bedpost or the hairpins left in her petticoat pocket, they were there at the back of her mind. With them was the knowledge of the complicated emotional involvements between the people in the house and her dead cousin.

Suicide or murder? She did not know. She only knew there was a great deal about the matter that needed explaining and she would not be able to rest until she had uncovered the last detail. Practicality, and perhaps even decency, rejected the idea of delving into an affair that might cast an unpleasant light on her cousin's character and the character of the man she had married, but for the sake of the health of her own mind, a mind playing with the idea of possessing spirits and presentiments of death, she must look deeper into her cousin's death. She must step warily, allowing no one to influence her judgment for good or ill. And she must act quickly. She would be only a little longer at Monteigne, a short time in which to learn enough to still the frantic voice of doubt that clamored in her mind.

She came to this decision in the early morning. At the breakfast table she was given her first chance to put her decision into effect when Jason, with friendly hospitality, asked her what she would like to do for the day.

She looked up from her plate somewhat coldly as she said, "I would like to visit Amelia's grave."

The room seemed to grow abruptly still, but no one argued with her. It was not such an unusual request after all. Visiting the cemetery was a duty performed by all relatives, especially the females, and a drive to the cemetery and back was considered a nice outing for a fine Sunday afternoon. It was not Sunday, but since no one expected her to linger much longer at Monteigne, it did not seem too much to ask.

For all her determination, when the time came to set out on the excursion, Amanda was aware of a deep reluctance to leave the house. She refused to acknowledge it, however, even to herself. It was late afternoon. The sun still shone with a pale, lemon-colored light, and a fitful wind blew the clouds around the horizon.

"It feels as if it's blowing up a cloud," Nathaniel said, as he climbed up beside her and picked up the lines.

"Do you think so?" Amanda answered. "It feels like a drying wind to me." She took a deep breath. "Is that smoke?"

Nathaniel followed her example. "Could be. Long way off though. Somebody clearing probably. Hope they're watching close, a day like this."

Amanda nodded but did not speak, for Jason came trotting toward them on a black stallion from the direction of the stable, Theo and Sophia behind him on a pair of chestnut geldings.

Sophia, perched on her side saddle, cried, "Let's go!" and the riders streamed down the drive.

Nathaniel slapped the reins across the horse's back, clicked his tongue, and they began to move.

The hooves of the horses ahead of them stirred the white sand of the road into a powdery dust. It was not a problem for long, however, for they soon outdistanced the gig.

This cavalcade was not what Amanda wanted. She had thought perhaps she and Nathaniel could go alone. Once the plans were set in motion, however, she saw no diplomatic way to stop them. She thought, too, that she would see what there was to see and be back before the midday meal. She was foiled there also. First Sophia had not been able to come because of some vague household duty, then Theo and Jason had been called to the fields for an emergency so that now, when at last they were started, the sun was coasting down the sky. The dimness of the gathering evening lay thick under the trees overhanging the road, and there was a coolness in the air that made Amanda pull her shawl closer around her.

There was something wrong, like an intrusion, about visiting the cemetery when the shadows were lengthening over the tombstones; something disturbing, too, in arriving at the cemetery breathless from the swift passage, with dust clinging to their clothes. The time of day could not be helped, but Amanda was content with the sedate pace Nathaniel set that allowed them to fall behind.

If Amanda had considered, she would have realized it could not be far to the cemetery. A private cemetery near the house was the usual burial place to make upkeep easier and to protect it from marauders, both two-legged and four-legged. Failing that, the graveyard next to a near-by church was chosen. As a small white chapel surmounted by a simple cross appeared around a bend in the road, Amanda touched Nathaniel's arm to call his attention to the horses lining the hitching rack before the church doors.

He pulled the gig into the sandy drive, scattering sparrows that scratched, like small chickens, in the grain spilled from Sunday feedbags.

The cemetery was to the rear of the building. It was completely enclosed in an iron fence very like the one at Monteigne.

As Nathaniel pulled up, Jason walked to meet them, while Sophia and Theo stood talking near the fence, their heads close together.

Jason gave her his hand to descend from the gig as Nathaniel climbed out on the other side. There was something odd in his manner, and as she stepped down she glanced at his face to find it set in harsh, forbidding lines.

She was not left to wonder at the reason for long. Theo came striding toward them, his fists clenched at his sides.

"That damned Carl!" he exploded. "I could kill him with my bare hands."

"What seems to be the problem?" Nathaniel asked,

moving to loop the reins over the hitching rack before joining them.

"It's desecration! There's no other word for it," Theo declared.

"We have no proof." Sophia, strolling up, sent a sidelong glance to Jason.

"Who else would do such a thing? It's the work of a madman!"

"I don't understand," Amanda said, looking from one to the other.

"You will have to see it to believe it," Theo said, and turning on his heel, led the way back to the fence. Lifting the latch on the gate he stood aside to let them pass through. Reluctantly Amanda brushed past him with the others.

The cemetery was not large. Scarcely more than a dozen graves were scattered about in the long grass. There was no need to search for the desecration that had upset the others; it lay before her.

A great, gaping hole had been dug into the center of the caked, red mound of a fresh grave. The dirt lay scattered about as though the digger had been either deliberately malicious, or in a hurry. A large flower vase had been toppled to one side, spilling out its brackish, algae-filled water and the blackened stems and dead heads of the mass of roses it had held. At the head of the grave the white marble marker had been thrown from its pedestal to lie with a smear of mud obscuring the name. Still, there was no need to ask whose grave this was. Their consternation told her. It was Amelia's.

"In all the years since our fathers donated the land and built this church," Sophia said slowly, "there has been nothing like this. Why now? On top of everything else?"

The evening wind swept whining through the leaves of the trees that surrounded the isolated little chapel. No one bothered to reply to Sophia's question. There seemed to be no answer.

"Can't have been long ago," Nathaniel observed.

"Oh? Why not?" Sophia looked at him, wide-eyed.

"Well, see for yourself. The ground is still a bit damp where the water from the vase soaked into it. And the soil in the bottom of this hole still has a darker color, hasn't dried out quite as much as this on top."

"You mean . . ." Theo began, then raised his head. Suddenly his gaze fixed on a spot among the trees and undergrowth on the far side of the church.

"I think . . . look, there!" He pointed in the direction he was staring.

"Yes!" Sophia cried. "It's crazy Carl!"

"Come on!" her brother exclaimed, and pelted out of the cemetery, his face grim with determination.

Were the leaves rustling unnaturally there where Theo had pointed, or was it only the wind? Amanda could not tell.

Nathaniel had been holding Amanda's arm as if he expected her to need his support. Now he dropped it, starting forward.

Jason looked at him. "Get her back to the gig first," he said. "And Sophia . . ."

"I'm coming with you," Sophia interrupted him.

He did not stop to argue with her but turned toward the gate, a frown drawing his brows together.

As Nathaniel hurried her from the cemetery, Amanda

watched them over her shoulder. Theo, in the lead, was already disappearing in the deepening shadows of the trees. Jason followed, and then came Sophia behind him, the skirt of her riding habit draped over her arm, out of her way.

"Oh, Nathaniel, what will they do to him?" she cried, a terrible dread catching the words in her throat.

"You needn't trouble your head over him," he answered shortly as he held the gate for her to pass through.

"But he isn't responsible, he didn't know what he was doing."

"He knows more than we think, if you want my opinion."

"Nathaniel, you've got to go with them, now, before they find him. I'm all right, truly. Just go and do what you can to keep them from hurting him."

"If you are certain . . ."

"I'm certain," she said impatiently. "Just go!"

He swung away at once, hurrying after the others. She could hear the thrashing sounds of their progress through the woods, but though she strained her eyes into the dusk and moving shadows, she could catch no glimpse of them. Picking up her skirts, she turned in the direction of the gig.

As she neared the door of the small white chapel, a dark figure moved in the doorway. Amanda halted, her nerves jangling, before she recognized the cassock of a priest.

He turned from locking the double doors of the chapel, then gave a visible start at the sight of her. An instant later he moved toward her, a small, rotund man with graying hair and a sane and friendly smile.

"Good evening, my daughter," he said as he drew

near. "I thought once I heard voices without, but while at my prayers I am deaf to all else."

Amanda returned his greeting, a slight frown between her eyes as she wondered if the priest might not be of help should Carl be caught.

"May I be of aid?" he asked, glancing about him at the same time, noting the gig and the lack of any one else accompanying her.

"Yes, I think you might," Amanda answered, telling him who she was in a few short sentences, and what had taken place.

The priest gave a shake of his head when she had finished. "I regret you had to see the condition of the grave. I had meant to see to it this morning, but was prevented by a burial elsewhere today. This, you realize, is only one of several small churches in the parish for which I am responsible. To the best of my knowledge, the damage was not done today, but yesterday or perhaps even the day before . . . though the vase may have been blown over by the wind this afternoon. That poor creature, Carl, may have done it indeed, I could not say."

Of course he had. Why had she not remembered? He had told them plainly only the night before that the box they had put his Madame in was still there. How else could he have known if he had not dug into the grave?

"I expect you are right," she said after a moment.

"If you will accept my advice, you will not trouble your heart overmuch for Carl. He knows these woods, the trails, the hollows and ridges and swamp areas, as no other. He will be difficult to catch on what has become his home ground."

"Yes," Amanda said, a relieved smile slowly curving her lips. "I'm sure you are right."

"You . . . are very like the late Madame Monteigne," the priest said. "I spoke often with her before she died. She was a convert, you know."

"I had not realized." Amanda tried to visualize Amelia accepting the sober tenets of Catholicism and failed.

"She was afraid, poor child, as all of us are when we hear the wings of the death angel. She was always regular in her attendance at Mass, regardless of the hour celebrated, and it is often irregular, since I must go from church to church of a Sunday. Twice, no three times, she sent for me before the end. I am not certain I helped her, though I tried with all my being."

The sadness in the voice of the priest marked him as yet another who had been drawn to lovely Amelia.

"Did she . . . did she ever talk to you about the people at Monteigne—her husband, and the others?"

"Often."

"Tell me, did she mention . . ."

"Forgive me, child, but I cannot discuss it. So much of what she said is protected by the seal of the confessional. You understand? You need not be troubled in your mind about her. I was with her on the afternoon before her death. She sent for me, knowing the end was drawing near. She died with her soul at peace and her sins forgiven, which is all that God's children—the strong as well as the weak—can ask."

"Yes, of course." The reproof was gentle; still it could not be disregarded.

"I regret that I cannot stay longer with you, but my horse waits for me at the spring just yonder through the woods. I have been long already, making ready for the Mass of the Candles. If I am much longer, she may leave me here afoot while she seeks her stable in town."

174

Amanda accepted the excuse though she thought the priest was just as anxious to escape the possibility of further questions. They exchanged the usual pleasantries of farewell, Amanda explaining that she would not be in the vicinity on the Night of the Candles and therefore could not attend the Mass. And so they parted.

Her brow knit in thought, Amanda made her way to the gig and climbed into the seat. In the time since they had arrived, the sun had set, leaving a gray-blue twilight. The air was cooler, and the wind had dropped so the leaves hung motionless on the trees. When the sound of the priest's horse had died away, a dense silence descended.

Amanda glanced around her uneasily, drawing her shawl close about her shoulders. How much longer would the others chase after Carl, if it was Carl they were chasing and not some figment of Theo's overwrought imagination?

One of the saddle horses, impatient with standing, stomped a hoof and blew through his nostrils. Amanda frowned. She thought that in that second of noise she had heard something move in the underbrush near her. There was a flurry of wings, and a flight of crows, disturbed from their perch, rose with a raucous sound from the trees. Crows, the bird that outlives nine generations of men, or so the ancients thought. Amanda followed them with her eyes. At that moment something struck the side of the gig near her head.

It fell to the ground and she looked down to see a sweet gum ball in the dirt just rolling to a stop. There was nothing so peculiar in that; it was the time of year for the gum balls to fall. But then as she glanced above her she saw no sign of the shiny, maplelike leaves of a sweet gum tree. The balls were much too heavy to have been windblown . . .

Suddenly a fusillade of the spiked balls showered upon the buggy. They stung Amanda's face and arms and struck the sleek rump of the horse.

He reared violently in sudden fright at the attack, straining the length of the tied reins. The gig rocked back and forth as he plunged. Amanda clutched the brace and grabbed for the seat as another fusillade of balls were aimed straight at the horse. Once more he reared, neighing.

Abruptly the reins snapped in two. The maddened horse swerved, throwing the buggy against the hitching rail. For a moment the axle caught, then with a grinding noise they were free, and the horse was off, nostrils flaring, his eyes wide with terror.

The wind whipped her face, and her teeth clattered with the jolting, rattling ride. Her fingers ached with the tightness of her grip, and her knees, as she braced against the dashboard, felt as if they were on fire. The thought flashed through her mind that she should scream to bring help, but her throat was too constricted to force the sound from it.

Mercifully the horse broke into the open road. There was some possibility that he would run himself out, that the weight of the vehicle behind him would act as a brake as he grew tired, slowing him to a stop. She fastened her mind on the chance, knowing that with such a headstart, even if the others learned of her predicament, there was little other hope.

Then she saw flashing toward her a great, gnarled tree root snaking into the sand of the roadbed. She shut her eyes tightly.

The right wheels struck the thick root at full speed. The gig bounded up, hovered on two wheels, then went over with a crash.

There was a thundering noise in her ears, then pain exploded in a red-gold sunburst behind her eyes.

A shrill screaming of a horse in pain. The rise and fall of angry voices. A shot. The screaming stopped.

"Why did this have to happen? She was nearly well." Nathaniel. She recognized his voice.

There were firm, impersonal hands straightening her arms, her legs, searching for broken bones, for a heartbeat.

"I say . . ." Nathaniel protested.

Jason spoke above her. "Yes?"

"Nothing . . ." Nathaniel muttered.

"She seems to be all right, though I doubt this will do her concussion any good. Sophia's horse is carrying the least weight, Sterling. I expect you had better double with her."

"I prefer to walk."

"Suit yourself."

"Nonsense, give me your hand," Sophia said, her voice sounding faintly strident.

There was a creak of saddle leather then Jason spoke again. "If you will hand her up to me . . ."

She was lifted gingerly. "Careful!" a voice that sounded like Theo cautioned.

Strong arms caught her up. She felt the smoothness of the saddle beneath her and the cradling of warm, enclosing arms and a muscled chest.

She knew she should open her eyes, make some effort to help herself. But the movement of the black stallion as he started forward set ripples of pain in motion that, combined with a vague awareness of the invidiousness of her present position, held her mute and still.

"Marta! Marta!"

The moment they stopped the horses before the front gate Theo began to call, an impression of panic in his raised voice as though he doubted the ability of anyone there to deal with the situation.

Amanda stirred. During the ride back she had decided that except for having the breath knocked from her and the jarring shock of the fall, she was indeed all right. She must have been thrown clear and cushioned from further injury by the mat of leaves beneath the trees lining the side of the road. She seemed to feel crushed bits of trash in her hair. Now she made as if to sit up straight.

Jason dismounted in one smooth motion, holding with one hand to her arm, then he reached up for her. She stared down at him then with a resigned sigh she slid into his arms. He swung her up and strode along the walk, ignoring her automatic murmur of protest.

"Where can that woman be?" Theo fumed. "She's never around when she's needed. Marta!"

"For heaven's sake, Theo! Stop shouting," Sophia said irritably.

"How else is she to know we want her?"

"I will go."

"You do that," Theo said with a bellicose stare, stung, apparently, by his sister's disapproval. "I could stand a drink." He disappeared into the dining room as Jason began to mount the stairs, Sophia going before and Nathaniel trailing after them.

Jason placed her on her bed. He stood for a moment staring down at her, then he looked across the expanse of the covers to Nathaniel.

"I expect I had better see about removing the gig and the horse from the road," he said in an odd, indecisive voice.

"I will stay with Amanda," Nathaniel said quickly.

Jason nodded once. "You might see if you can find out what happened."

Nathaniel reached out and picked up Amanda's hand and covered her listless fingers with his own. "I will try."

Jason's eyes were bleak as he surveyed Nathaniel and his protective hovering, then a sardonic smile curved his mouth as he turned and left the room.

Nathaniel watched him go before he glanced down and found Amanda watching him. "How . . . how do you feel?"

"I'm not . . . sure. I feel peculiar but it doesn't hurt."

"I don't like your color. Much too pale. Some brandy, now . . ."

"No . . . no, I don't think so."

"Then . . . is there anything else I can do for you?"

It was comical. The mere asking of the question and the personal service that it implied, had made the color rise to Nathaniel's face. She shook her head.

"You are all right then, you're sure?"

This concern with her health was wearing. Once more she nodded an affirmative.

"Then tell me how it happened. I left you there beside the church, as safe as a babe in his crib!"

She frowned, trying to remember. "Sweet gum balls."

"What?"

"Sweet gum balls. They hit the horse. He shied, and the reins broke."

"Leather had dry-rotted, I suppose. Funny, you

wouldn't think a thing like that would be allowed at a place like this."

"No . . . but Nathaniel. There was no sweet gum tree."

"But you just said . . ."

"The balls were thrown!"

"Oh, now, Amanda!"

"They were. They had to have been. There were so many."

"Just as I suspected. You must have hit your head again. You don't know what you're saying. No one would do a thing like that."

"That's not all. I think . . . I think Amelia was killed."

"Killed . . . now Amanda, don't take on so."

"She was. Listen to me. The night Amelia died Marta was in her own room, inebriated. Someone had left a bottle. Amelia called out to her but . . ."

"Delirious, that's what you are."

"But it happened, Nathaniel. I know it did. Something inside me tells me I'm right, and Marta said . . ."

"Something tells you? You've made up a tale in your mind out of something that nurse said. I'd never have believed it of you, Amanda. You have always been so level-headed. Regrettable things of that nature may happen, but to other people, not to any of our connections. No, no. It must be delirium, plain and simple. Don't try to talk anymore. No telling what kind of damage . . . and no telling how much longer we will be stuck here while you are recuperating. What a thing to happen!"

Amanda opened her mouth to speak, but he raised a hand. "No, I won't hear anymore. You are only upsetting yourself to no purpose."

The door swung open before he finished, and Sophia swept into the room. Amanda closed her eyes.

"Is something wrong?" Sophia asked, her eyes on the stern lines of his face. "Besides the accident, I mean?"

"I couldn't say." Nathaniel put Amanda's hand down and stepped back. "Offhand I would think she was injured more severely than we thought. Her head, you know." His voice dropped to what he no doubt considered to be a whisper, and he moved a bit closer to the other girl. "She seems to think it was no accident but some sort of malicious design. Sweet gum balls! If that isn't raving delirium, I don't know what is. Did you find that woman Marta, or whatever her name is? If I were you I'd see about getting rid of her as soon as she is no longer needed. She has been feeding Amanda all kinds of nonsense, best I can make out. Something about Amelia being murdered . . . of course, that may be nothing more than moonshine, I don't know."

A sick feeling of helpless anger washed over Amanda as she heard Nathaniel's well-meant, but incredibly short-sighted comments.

"No, I haven't been able to find Marta," Sophia replied. "Cook said that she left the house some time ago with a basket over her arm." She made no reply to what Nathaniel had confided, and Amanda could not decide if it was discretion, thoughtfulness, or merely surprise that held her silent.

A basket over her arm. The image gradually filled Amanda's mind. It was not so far to the cemetery, through the woods. It was Carl, she thought, who had pointed that out. Suppose the nurse regretted confiding in her? A basket of sweet gum balls? A runaway that would never have been explained if she had died? It would have been easy. With two deaths on her conscience, what was one more? What would happen now she had failed? It would be easy enough for a nurse to complete the job she had started.

Where were her thoughts leading her? Poor, friendless Marta. It could be that Nathaniel was right. She was out of her mind. Proof, that was what she needed.

She opened her eyes. "Did you catch him?"

"What?" Nathaniel, staring at the bedpost with a look of concentration, seemed startled.

"Carl, or whoever did . . . did that to Amelia's grave?"

"Oh, no, he was too quick for us," Sophia said when Nathaniel did not answer. "And then we heard the commotion the horse was making and turned back."

"I wonder . . ." she began, then was interrupted as Marta bustled in at the open door, her gray hair windblown, with the rat of her own hair showing through her pompadour, and her cape twisted to the side.

"Fräulein!" she exclaimed setting the basket down and unbuttoning her cape. "That one in the kitchen, she says you have had an accident again. So unlucky."

"Where have you been?" Sophia asked in a cold voice.

"Why, I went for a walk. In the woods. It was a nice day . . . and I found some lovely Indian Pipes. You know them? I brought them back, roots and all. Can't you smell them, there in my basket? Such a delicate scent. They will last for quite a time on my windowsill."

"And where else did you go?"

"Nowhere. I swear."

"You were not near the church?"

"Not at all. I was never out of hearing distance of

the house." Marta's voice rose in vehemence as she saw the trend of Sophia's questions.

"I think you are lying, a habit with you. I have watched you and your ingratiating ways. I don't know what you expect to gain in the end, and I have no interest in knowing, but I think it would be best if you packed your boxes and left this house."

"No, *fräulein,* you cannot do that. There is a sick woman in the house. Who will care for *Fräulein* Amanda? Who will see after her and protect her?"

"Protect her? I don't know what you mean, but it need not worry you."

"It does worry me. She is my patient. I am responsible."

"This argument is pointless. I refuse to pursue it. You will send for one of the hands to drive you into town."

"No." Marta's face had shed its placid, bovine look. It wore now a grim obstinacy coupled with assurance. She drew herself up. "You would like me to be gone before *Herr* Jason returns. I will not leave. You cannot make me. Only *Herr* Jason has the right to discharge me."

"That may be, but I believe you will leave. I believe Jason will uphold my decision, especially when I tell him a thing or two about you."

"And what of the things I can tell him about you and your brother in return?"

"There is nothing you can tell him he does not already know. We have no secrets from Jason, Theo and I."

"Nor do I, *fräulein.* I have told him everything. So. Go to him with your tales. You will see! I will not be leaving!"

Chapter
Nine

MARTA was right. When applied to, Jason appeared to feel that the whole affair was a woman's quarrel that had nothing to do with him. Though he could not, in all truth, be said to have sided with Marta, the nurse still went about with a smug smile on her face while Sophia retired to her room in a rage.

Though she found a bruised swelling on the side of her head beneath her hair, Amanda, still in a state of numb suspension, insisted on going downstairs. She walked a bit slower than usual and her hand on the railing of the stairs felt cold, but she smiled a gay greeting to Theo as he turned from the fire in the parlor at her entrance.

Amanda, as a concession to her bruised scalp, had foregone her tight, braided coronet and allowed Marta to pile her hair in loose curls on top of her head, drawing forward several softening wisps.

As Theo rose and led her to a chair, his eyes were on her hair.

"I must say, Amanda, you grow more like your cousin every day."

"It is only the hair style, I expect," she said. "Marta tells me it was one Amelia favored."

"It helps, of course, but the bone structure is there, the shading of the skin."

"An inheritance from our French grandmother, no doubt," she returned dismissingly, made uncomfortable by the conversation. Then she was surprised at herself. Her likeness to Amelia had never troubled her before.

"You must allow me to tell you how much I regret your accident this afternoon. I'm afraid you're going to leave with a bad impression of Monteigne, after the things that have happened to you here. I would not like that."

"Oh, no, I'm sure it could not be helped," she murmured conventionally.

"It seems," he went on in a reflective tone, "that your family has never found Monteigne a lucky place."

"It does look that way," she agreed.

"I would not like you to come to think it as unhappy a place as Amelia did."

Amanda was silent for a moment then she took a deep breath. "I don't mean to sound like a . . . a Paul Pry, but there is something about Amelia that troubles me. I can't be easy in my mind about her. Won't you help me?"

"Why . . . certainly, if I can."

"You say that she was unhappy. In what way?"

Theo leaned back on the settee and picked up a cushion that lay in the corner beside him. "Well," he said, his eyes on his fingers worrying the long, silk fringe of the cushion. "It's hard to put into words. At first she and Jason were very gay. They went here and there, to New Orleans, St. Louis, visiting friends and relatives. Then at last the honeymoon ended. They came home to Monteigne. Jason became involved again with his concerns that he had neglected during his courtship. Amelia was understanding . . . at first. She occupied herself in refurbishing her room as you see it, dressing up of an evening in new clothes she had bought in New Orleans, and entertaining us all at dinner. But gradually she grew . . . she became . . ."

"You are trying to say she became bored."

"I would rather say discontented. She had no real vocation as a housewife. Oh, she tried but . . ."

"Yes, I loved my cousin, but I knew her well. It was hit-and-miss, was it not?"

"Sometimes she would make a tremendous effort, and everything would be perfect, meals, flowers, the house, herself. Then for weeks afterward, chaos. She had no organization, no energy, but most of all, no interest. Understandably, Jason became impatient."

"Yes, I see."

"Well, so did we all . . . and yet . . ."

"You forgave her."

"Amelia's gaiety, her frivolous nature, the contrast between her's and Jason's own rather somber personality, were the very things that attracted Jason to Amelia in the first place. Yet, immediately after they arrived at Monteigne, he expected her to change to suit his way of life. She could not do it. They could neither one change what they were anymore than this useless little bit of a cushion can become a large comfortable pillow!"

"And so, disillusionment?"

"Yes, and unhappiness, shouting, and tears." A piece of fringe from the pillow came away in his hands, and he, seeing the damage he had done, tossed the pillow from him. "The same old story."

"So you think they were not suited?"

"There can be no doubt. What Jason needed was a helpmeet. What he got was a doll, an exquisite, impractical, and oh, so fragile doll."

Fragile. Yes, Amelia had always given that impression, but she had never been weak, except, perhaps, in body.

"They quarreled?"

"Tempestuously," he answered with a wry smile, "but then made up in the same way, at least at first, until Jason grew tired of scenes. Then he went his way, and she more or less went hers. Until she became ill. But then, let me tell you, no man could have been more attentive than Jason."

"Would you say then that they were still . . . in love?" Why had she asked that question, she wondered as the warmth of embarrassment seeped into her cheeks. What possible difference could it make? And yet, it seemed important that she hear the answer.

"With Amelia it was hard to say. Jason, her dark prince, had rescued her like a maiden from a tower. She never spoke of it, though we talked often, especially in those last days. She died in the middle of the summer, the busiest time of the year on a plantation. She said something once about Jason, however. Something that stuck with me because . . . I suppose because the meaning seemed especially clear to me at that moment. She said that what Jason showed toward her was the other side of the coin of love. It was compassion and the guilt that stems from the fact that it is a lesser emotion."

She glanced at Theo from beneath her lashes, seeing his strong farmer's hands and his broad, pugnacious face beneath the shock of blond hair. She had never expected him to be so eloquent. Was it possible then that it was a subject that touched him deeply?

"You . . . seem to have been fond of Amelia," she said tentatively.

He looked up. "Is that so odd? Jason was out about the fields. He is not a man who can delegate authority easily, and I hadn't much to do other than running errands to town. We were thrown together, and Amelia was . . . lovable."

Amanda looked at him measuringly with little taste for the implication of his confession. A man in love with another's wife? The man's sister in love with the husband. There was reason for murder in that three times over.

"I'm not sure I understand," she told him. "Marta seemed to think they were so very happy."

"Oh, Marta."

"Meaning?"

"Well, you know, an unattractive, middle-aged spinster living a rather dull life at the beck and call of others. She is apt to romanticize her patients. You have to allow for that with Marta, take what she says with a grain of salt."

"Are you saying that Marta is a liar?"

"Oh, no. I wouldn't be so blunt as that. But we all have a tendency to make ourselves more interesting or knowledgeable in other people's eyes."

She smiled and conceded, "You have a point." But the implication of falsehood lingered.

At the dinner table Amanda was quiet, staring at the

centerpiece, a cornucopia of porcelain from which spilled autumn nuts and fruits, pecans, and chinquapins, pears, pomegranates, and persimmons. Cornucopia, in legend the horn of river god, Achelous, torn from his head by Hercules, a mighty feat. But was it any mightier than the one she had set herself, that of discovering the truth about the death of Amelia?

She thought of what Theo had said, of the unreliability of Marta. Well, surely that was no surprise? She knew of her weakness for drink, a thing that made her every action suspect.

Playing with her food and her wineglass, she considered what Marta had told her of the bottles that had appeared in her room. Was that strictly the truth? Might it not have been an excuse hastily concocted when Amanda had seen the half-empty bottle sitting on her washstand, made plausible because she insisted that it had happened before? Even so, it did not prove that everything Marta had said was a lie. If she had discovered Marta's weakness, who else might not have done so?

No, what Theo had said changed nothing.

She returned to her room after supper escorted with all tender solicitousness by Nathaniel. When she had shut the door upon him, she walked to the window and stood staring out into the darkness.

After a time there came from below the faint sound of Jason's guitar. There was a haunting regret in the sound that brought her near to tears as she leaned her head again against the window frame.

As on the night before, Marta did not attend her. She had been downstairs for supper. Perhaps, emboldened by her victory over Sophia, she had decided to stay a while longer in the smoke-laden atmosphere of the parlor, where she was the only woman. Or it was possible that something or someone else had prevented her from coming, as last night? There was no real need for her, of course. Before coming to Monteigne Amanda had never had a personal attendant. But as she climbed into bed she felt deserted somehow, as if an important source of strength and support had been withdrawn.

She fell asleep suddenly, heavily, with a feeling almost like distress in her mind.

She opened her eyes with a smile of triumph. It was becoming harder each time, almost as though "she" had a suspicion of what was taking place and was fighting her. It could not be helped. Pray that her weakness lasted a little longer.

Darkness. Night. That was why it was easier. The body has less resistance during the dark hours, during sleep or the shock of injury. Convenient.

She stood up. She wanted to move swiftly but she was wary, now, of imposing her own sense of well-being on this body so recklessly. It was hard to resist. An urgency gripped her. She must succeed this time.

Still, she could not change her character, she found, as she surveyed her attire with a grimace. Vanity, she supposed, but she could not masquerade in such a dowdy costume.

A change was quickly made; the cream gown with green ribbons was near to hand with her own dressing gown of cream lace. The hair, for once, was passable.

She found herself moving on tiptoe as she neared Jason's door, and she caught back a tiny laugh of amusement mingled with joy. She sobered, taking a deep breath, and touched the handle. It was locked. She twisted the knob back and forth unavailingly. Locked, on Jason's side, and there was no key here in Amanda's side of the door. Strange. She glanced toward the empty bed with its covers thrown back, her eyes narrowing. Strange, but it did not deter her.

With a sure stride that sent the dressing gown billowing about her feet, she crossed to the other door, pulled it open and stepped outside, closing it carefully behind her. She looked up and down the open space, but it was empty, echoing with darkness and silence.

She moved a few short paces to the left, to Jason's outside door, lifted her hand, and knocked.

The door opened at once. Fully dressed as if he had never gone to bed, Jason stood framed in the light from a lamp burning behind him, staring at her. His hair was tousled, his eyes red-rimmed, and a grim smile curved his mouth.

"*Facies non omnibus una, Nec diversa tamen, qualem decet esse sororum.*"

"If that is Latin, Jason, you know . . ."

"Don't you recognize it? I was sure you would . . . *Their faces were not all alike, nor yet unlike, but such as those of sisters ought to be.* Ovid was speaking of sea nymphs with green hair but for me the allusion has a different ring."

"To sirens, I suppose. If I were Amanda . . ."

"Yes?"

"Nothing. Nothing, Jason. Don't be like this. There is something I must tell you."

"Haven't you done enough?" he asked with a bitter weariness.

"Jason!" Her voice was stern with the importance of her mission. "Jason? Do you know me?"

"Tomorrow . . . in the light of day . . . I will deny

the idea, but now with the fumes of the liquor I have drunk dancing behind my eyes, I cannot see the gray of yours . . . Amanda."

"I am Amelia."

His eyes widened a fraction, but he did not answer.

"I am Amelia," she insisted. And then when he still did not speak, she moved closer. Slipping her arms around his neck, raising her lips to his, she whispered, "I am Amelia, your wife."

Her lips beneath his were warm with the memory of shared passion. But his were cold, unmoved and unmoving. He reached up to catch her wrists and drag them down.

"Stop this! Now."

She drew back, stunned by the revulsion in his voice. "I only wanted . . ."

"It doesn't matter. Go back to your room and bed. No matter who you say you are, there is nothing you could say that can change what has been or what will be."

"But I must tell you. It's about that night . . . the night . . ."

"You needn't pain yourself with the words. I know what happened that night."

"You . . . you know?"

His grip tightened on her arms that he held against his chest. "Yes, I know. If you will remember, I was there." His eyes grew dark. "I poured out the medicine and put it in your hand."

"Jason . . ." The word was a whisper. "Not you . . ."

"I and none other."

A look of horror flickered across her face. "You are wrong," she cried, reaching out to catch his arms, giving him a shake in her distress. "There has been a terrible mistake, more terrible than I dreamed. I have come to explain because I cannot bear to see anyone innocent of real harm imprisoned, perhaps hanged, for my sake. I came to you, Jason, because only you can make the authorities listen to reason. You must help me do this or I cannot rest. Promise me you will . . ."

"What is this?" Sophia demanded.

So intent were they upon themselves they failed to hear her approach. They swung to face her while Jason's arm encircled the woman beside him in a protective gesture. Sophia strode within a few feet of them, her eyes going suspiciously from one to the other.

"Well?" she exclaimed impatiently.

"Amanda wished to speak to me," Jason told her evenly.

"Oh, yes," Sophia sneered. "I saw that at once. If that is your idea of a quiet conversation . . ."

"I would like to know," the girl at his side said in a faintly haughty tone, "what gives you the right to ask?"

"What gives me . . . ? Why, you fraud! Pretending to be so ill. As if you didn't know!"

"I haven't the least idea what you mean." Her manner was distant, aloof.

"Now that I can't believe. I made sure you saw how things stood between Jason and me."

"You . . . made sure?" She looked at Jason, as if for help.

"You made sure?" he repeated in a hard voice, his eyes narrowing dangerously.

"Well, she saw, that is . . . she was in the hall when I . . . Oh, Jason! She had to know how things were meant to be between us!"

The girl smiled gently. "It's always a mistake to involve a man in your plotting. They hate it, you know."

Rage at her own mistake and jealous resentment surged to Sophia's brain. As quick as a striking snake, she reached out and slapped that smiling white face.

With a gasp of shock Amanda raised her hand to her burning face. She stared with wide incredulous eyes at Sophia, then she looked up at the man who stood with his arm about her in a protective embrace. A throbbing pain began to grow within her head, bringing tears to her eyes.

No one spoke. Jason stared at her, a frown drawing his brows together.

Sophia stood, appalled at what she had done.

Suddenly the strangeness of the scene and the blankness of her mind swept in upon Amanda. A cry of fright catching in her throat, she twisted out of Jason's grasp and ran, straight back to the haven of her room.

The night was not done. Perhaps an endless hour of time had ticked past when the crisp night stillness was disturbed by the distant thunder of hoofbeats. Horses, hard-ridden, at least a dozen or more, Amanda thought. The sound drew nearer, growing in volume and with a sense of hard purpose.

Below in the fence-enclosed yard, Cerberus began to give voice. The rumbling roar of hooves braked, slowing to a clatter.

Amanda levered herself into a sitting position, listening to the milling clops of horses' hooves, recognizing with a thrill of dread the moment when the sound ended before the front gate of Monteigne. An instant later, a shot exploded, whining away in the cold, frosty air.

Cerberus went mad, his barking and growling taking on eager viciousness. Somewhere a woman screamed. Running footsteps were heard out in the hallway.

Amanda waited no longer. She slid from the bed with one arm already in the dressing gown lying across the foot—Amelia's dressing gown. The thought made her pause, then she gave an angry shrug. If she made herself free with it while she was sleepwalking, why not while awake?

The double doors out onto the upper gallery stood open to the moonlight night. Framed in their opening was Nathaniel. He wore an ankle-length dressing gown of turkey red satin with black velvet lapels over his nightshirt. His feet were bare beneath the hem, and his hair was covered by a nightcap dangling a red silk tassel.

Amanda stared at the man she was going to marry in a kind of suspended fascination, aware of an almost uncontrollable desire to laugh. Only the sound of a second rifle shot brought her to her senses. It was followed by a shouted challenge, a harsh demand for the owner of Monteigne.

At the other end of the hall, Sophia stood in the door of her bedchamber talking in a low voice to Theo. From her room Marta could be heard panting and moaning. After a moment she appeared in the hallway with a dress dragged on, unbuttoned, over her gown.

Only Jason was not present. Hard on the discovery, he appeared, mounting the stairs from below with quick, light steps, a rifle balanced in his hand. His hair was tousled from sleep, and he had pulled on his trousers, leaving his shoulders and chest bare.

A reassuring smile curved his lips as he caught sight of

195

Amanda. "Stay back out of sight," he cautioned and then moved past her to step boldly out onto the gallery.

Shouts rising to a full-throated roar greeted his appearance. As if drawn by invisible bonds, Amanda crept closer to the open door, close enough to see and to hear.

She had known what to expect, and yet she was unprepared for the terrible, anonymous menace of the sheeted, hooded figures on horseback. They milled below the gallery, the blank faces with holes for eyes turned up toward the man who confronted them. The moonlight gave an unearthly glow to their white covering and silvered the sweating shoulders and flanks of their horses.

Nightriders!

What could they want here at Monteigne? What business could they have with one who sprang from the same ancient, privileged class they sought to protect?

Hard on these questions came a realization she had been too stunned to allow into her consciousness. If Jason Monteigne was here, within the house, while the nightriders milled on his front doorstep, he could not be one of them. By the same token, Theo with his nightshirt tucked into his trousers, must also be held exempt. Nathaniel had not truly been suspect, of course.

Her relief was so great she found herself smiling, and sobered instantly as Nathaniel turned to give her a puzzled stare. Only the sound of Jason speaking outside prevented him from making some comment she was certain she would not have liked.

"What may I do for you, gentlemen?"

The leader of the nightriders rode closer, staring up at Jason who stood with his hands braced on the gallery railing. "We hear you're harboring a scalawag lawyer name of Sterling. We'd like to have a little . . . er . . .

talk with the gentleman about his politics with a view to changing his mind."

"Come tomorrow in broad daylight, share a meal, and a drink with us like gentlemen, and you may talk with Mr. Sterling about anything you like."

"I'm afraid that will not be convenient," the other man said. "We prefer to have our discussion now."

A murmur ran through the other horsemen, punctuated by a coarse call or two.

"It would scarcely be polite to wake a guest for anything less than a matter of great urgency."

Rising in his stirrups, the other man uttered a curse. "You are stalling, Monteigne, and you damned well know it. Are you going to give us Sterling or not?"

"Even if I wanted to do so, I would not . . . as a matter of principle."

"To hell with your principles!"

"Along with yours?" Jason asked, his quiet voice easily overriding the other's strident tones.

Now a second hooded rider joined the first. "We have nothing against you, Monteigne, but you don't know what you're up against. We mean to point out the error of his ways to this two-bit lawyer, and we won't be stopped by anyone. If you're not with us, then you're against us, and will have to look to yourself if you get in our way."

This speaker had the sound of being older than the first. His words came slower, but carried more weight.

Near Amanda, Nathaniel stirred uneasily. Afraid he was about to step out and offer himself up as a sacrifice, she put out her hand, laying it on his arm. Jason, she knew, would not allow Nathaniel to become a martyr to save himself from a clash, and the sight of Nathaniel might bring out the violence that Jason had managed to control until now. The glance Nathaniel sent her held no small degree of gratification, but she hardly noticed.

Jason had leaned his rifle against the railing. Now with movements slow and deliberate he picked it up, allowing the butt to rest on the balustrade with his fingers inside the trigger guard. "This," he said slowly, "is a Springfield repeating rifle, a gift from my late wife while we were traveling in the northeast. As much as I would hate to see it turned on my own kind, I will use it if you leave me no choice."

The uneasiness that ran over the group was readily apparent. There were rifles among them, their stocks protruding from saddle boots here and there. There were none to equal the repeating Springfield, the gun that had helped to turn the tide against the South in the recent conflict.

The saddle of the first rider creaked as he swayed sideways to speak to the older man. The latter nodded, and the first rider turned to signal to the others. The horsemen began to spread out. For an instant Amanda thought they were retreating, then she saw that their movement would make them harder to pick off.

Regardless of the quality of his weapon, Jason was one man facing overwhelming odds. As he stood at the railing with the moonlight pouring down upon him, grimly watching the deployment of the nightriders, Amanda knew a painful constriction in the region of her heart. Without conscious thought she removed her hand from Nathaniel's arm, releasing him to go to Jason's aid.

He did not move. His face pale and eyes wide, he stared out at the nightriders.

From whispers behind her, Amanda thought Sophia

was remonstrating with Theo, whether to keep him from going or urge him on, she could not tell. Something had to be done quickly—at once—or it would be too late.

"This is your last chance, Monteigne," the older man was saying. "We can settle this easy, or we can do it the hard way."

The timbre of the voice was calm, unhurried. It came to Amanda that its owner was positive that when it came to shooting Jason would not turn his gun on them. She, watching his grip tighten on the Springfield, was just as certain he would.

Without conscious thought she lifted her chin and stepped out onto the gallery. She moved unhesitatingly to Jason's left. The moonlight threw her shadow behind her, and yet it seemed to be noiselessly flitting at her side.

"Good evening, gentlemen."

Her voice was low and musical, awakening curious, murmuring echoes in the sudden stillness. Jason made an abortive movement, as though he would shield her, then relaxed.

"A bit late for a ride, wouldn't you say?" she went on. "Still, the autumn moon makes one restless." Wry amusement curved her mouth. There was a singing strangeness in her veins as she stared down at the riders on horseback, one after the other, and saw them look away. She felt a power beyond the physical within herself. Though she swayed a little where she stood, she had the feeling that if necessary she could leap the railing and land on the ground below with all the gentle grace of a falling leaf.

"Jesus!" a rider muttered. "I thought she was dead."

"She is," another said. "I know she is. I saw her buried."

She bit her lips. She caught her breath and held one

fist to her midsection. It did not help. The soft trill of her laughter rose, joyous, infectious, so that Jason turned to stare and could not forebear smiling.

Before the sound had died away Theo joined them, and then Sophia. The blonde man hoisted one leg up to sit on the railing. Eyes narrowed, he surveyed the men below before giving a nod or two, almost as though he recognized and greeted the men under the hoods.

Finally, when it seemed nothing could release them from the odd spell which gripped them, Theo spoke: "Permit me, Amanda, to present to you the Knights of the White Gardenia. Gentlemen, this lady is Madame Monteigne's cousin, Miss Amanda Trent, the fiancée of the man you are seeking. This lady, with Mr. Sterling, will soon be leaving us. Her beauty, and the folly of man she is to marry, will no longer trouble us. That being the case, don't you think your efforts tonight to encourage her fiancé to re-evaluate his thinking, will be enough?"

The two men who had constituted themselves the leaders of the group looked at each other. The elder made a chopping gesture and gathered up his reins. For one long moment more he stared from Jason to Amanda, then he wheeled his horse and galloped away. The others followed after, streaming down the drive to the road. Seconds later, all that was left was the distant rumble of hooves and a cloud of silvery dust boiling in the light of the moon.

Amanda shivered, closing her eyes, and wrapping her arms about her rib cage. Firm hands turned her back toward the hallway, and she was aware of the warm support of an arm about her shoulders. Jason, she thought, and did not question the certainty of her knowledge.

Nathaniel, fully dressed, was just emerging from his

room. "I refuse to let them take me in my robe," he said, settling the watch chain across the front of his waistcoat.

"They have gone," Jason told him.

"Gone?" Nathaniel sounded vaguely cheated, as if he felt he had gone to the trouble of dressing for nothing.

"Gone," Jason repeated, and moved past him with Amanda in the circle of his arm and Sophia trailing grimly behind.

"But how? Why?"

Theo clapped him on the back. "Let me find you a drink, old man, and I'll tell you."

Back in her bedchamber, Amanda climbed the steps up to the high mattress of the tester bed and turning, sat down. Despite the fact that Jason had seen her in nothing more than her nightgown before, she had no intention of divesting herself of her dressing gown in his presence.

"Are you all right?" he said, eyes narrowed as he peered into her face, trying to see her expression in the light of the candle Sophia had lit.

Sophia tossed the spent sulphur match into the fireplace, then turned. "Why shouldn't she be all right? She has just played the heroine. Did it never occur to you, dear Amanda, that you might make things worse instead of better by appearing on the gallery in your nightclothes?"

It was a minute before Amanda took her meaning. "No," she answered simply.

"It should have. A fine thing it would have been if Jason had been forced to protect you as well as himself. Anyone but a ninny could have seen that at once. It was my first thought."

"If a man must fight," Amanda said, choosing her

words with slow care, "I hardly see what it matters how many he is called upon to save by the battle."

"Your presence was a distraction. He could not have concentrated on returning their fire because of his fear for your safety."

A wry smile touched Amanda's mouth. "I am afraid such logic was beyond me at that moment. The idea, in so much as there was one, was to distract the others."

Jason made an abrupt movement as Sophia opened her mouth once more. "You succeeded, for which I am grateful. We will let it go at that for the moment, I think. You are not in pain?"

Amanda shook her head. Surprisingly, she was not, though she was aware of a strong need to lie down before weakness overcame her.

"Good. Sophia, don't you think you should see to Marta? She was beside herself with terror."

"Marta? Anybody who makes their room and board seeing to other people ought to be able to take care of themselves."

"Nonetheless, I think you should look in on her."

Sophia stared at him, suspicion in her light brown eyes. He returned her gaze with silent, unrelenting strength of will. After a brief struggle, she moved her shoulders in a petulant shrug, then sauntered from the room.

Jason waited until her footsteps had faded. He stepped nearer, bracing one hand on the post at the foot of the bed. "It will be a long time before I forget this night," he said, his eyes dark as they rested on her upturned face.

The breath caught in her throat. She tried to smile, but the effort went sadly awry. "It was nothing," she whispered. "I only did what I had to do."

"I wonder." Reaching out, he touched the frill that

edged the yoke of the dressing gown she wore—Amelia's dressing gown.

When he did not go on, she said, "Yes?"

His eyes held hers for a seemingly endless time before they moved to study the expanse of her forehead, the straight line of her nose, and the tender curve of her mouth. "Amelia might have joined me on the porch; she might have laughed, but she would have expected praise, gratitude, some appropriate acknowledgment of her effort."

"Would she?" Amanda whispered, her voice no more than a thread of sound.

"She would. And now, at this moment, she would be teasing, trying to force me to admit my debt, demanding payment."

Amanda's eyelids flicked down, and she turned her head away. "That doesn't sound very . . . nice."

"Amelia was not always nice. She tried to be, but often the feat was beyond her."

The face of the priest, and his hint of sealed confessions passed through her mind. The idea distressed her, and she gave her head a shake, as though she would dislodge it.

"You disagree? Even though it has been at least three years since you last saw her? A great deal can change in that length of time."

"I . . . I did not disagree," Amanda said, putting one hand to her head. Confusion crept like a cloud into her eyes, and she swayed a little as she sat.

Suddenly Jason pushed away from the bed. "Lie down," he said. "Forget what I said, forget everything. Perhaps tomorrow will be different. It doesn't hurt to think so."

The pained cynicism of his tone only added to her distress.

Her fingers trembled as she tugged at the knot in the sash. Tears, weak, useless tears hovered behind her eyes, threatening to blind her.

For long moments he watched her unavailing struggles before he stepped forward. His capable fingers released her with ease. Face impassive, he stripped the sleeves of the dressing gown off her arms. When she lay down, he reached for the covers where she had thrown them back earlier and drew them up to her chin.

"Good-night," he said, his voice abrupt, almost harsh. Turning, he went quickly from the room.

He had left the candle burning. Amanda lay for a time watching the living flame dance upon its wick, mesmerized by the warm yellow glow. Even when her eyelids fell, she seemed to see the flickering point of fire.

Candle flames. Carl. On the edge of sleep she remembered the capering figure beneath her window only a few nights before. Tonight he had not been in evidence. That did not mean he was the nightrider from Monteigne, for on that memorable night when he had held his vigil she had seen both him and the sheeted rider from her window. Who, then, used the barns at Monteigne to hide his nocturnal rambling, if all the men were accounted for?

Morning came at last. Despite, or perhaps because of, the overwhelming events of the night, she had slept. She did not feel particularly rested, or able to deal with what was happening at Monteigne, still she felt stronger than she had the evening before.

In the light of morning the runaway gig, the sleepwalking incident, the visit of the nightriders, had a feeling of unreality. That they had actually occurred seemed beyond explaining. That there was no apparent reason for them made them even more frightening, though Amanda would have been hard pressed to decide which incident distressed her more. Marta was not in evidence. With fingers that trembled, Amanda put away Amelia's clothing and took out a day gown of blue cambric piped in gray. The costume did nothing to add color to her face but, since it was doubtful anything less than a rouge pot would help in that area, she did not allow it to trouble her.

She descended the stairs with a slow but firm step. The smell of frying bacon hung in the air, and the doors closing off the ends of the central hallway had been thrown open. Still she could find no one about, though she peeped into the dining room, the sitting room, and the parlor.

The brilliant gleam of sunlight drew her out onto the gallery. The air was cool, making her draw her shawl closer about her shoulders, but a softness in the atmosphere hinted at a warm midday as the sun climbed higher. She moved across the gallery to the steps, keeping a wary eye out for the huge watchdog who sometimes made his bed on the sun-warmed floor at this time of day. The brick walk with the gate at the end beckoned. A walk in the fresh air seemed a good idea. It might clear away the last vestiges of her headache while giving her, at the same time, an opportunity to be alone to think. The dog was not in sight. She would chance it.

At the end of the walk, with one hand on the gate, she went still. The sound of a low growl raised the fine hairs on her arms and drew her gaze irresistibly to the corner of the house.

Cerberus, his curious marbled eyes fastened on her face and the fur ruff around his massive neck raised, stalked into view. The muscles beneath his dull gray coat rippled, tightening for a lunge before he was checked by the weight of a hand. Crazy Carl, walking beside him, did no more than place long gnarled fingers on his neck, but it was enough.

Amanda took a deep, trembling breath, her lips moving in a feeble attempt at a smile. She cleared her throat.

"Good-morning."

Carl stared at her in what appeared to be total surprise.

"Morning," he muttered, dropping his head, kicking at the ground with the toe of his shoe. Abruptly he looked up again. "All right?"

"Yes, I'm very well."

"I saw you yesterday."

"You saw me?"

"At the church."

"Then you were there."

He nodded, a smile slowly moving over his face. "They all ran into the woods, even Jason."

"Yes."

"They didn't see me."

"Not . . . not at all?"

Shaking his head, he smiled again, then with a quick, childish swing of emotion he frowned. "I saw the wagon turn over."

Wagon? He must mean the gig, Amanda thought. "Did you see . . . whoever it was that threw the sweet gum balls at the horse?"

He stared at her without blinking. "Other side."

"The other side?" she asked patiently.

"Other side of the churchyard. Them."

206

"Oh, I see. You were in the woods on the other side of the churchyard from me?"

He gave a quick nod. When she did not immediately begin to speak again, he looked about him and then, with a word to the dog, went to sit on the steps with Cerberus at his knee.

Slowly, thoughtfully, Amanda retraced her footsteps. After a moment's hesitation she sat down on the far end of the step.

Carl had pulled his begrimed cloth bag into his lap as he sat, and now his long fingers, with their nails thick and yellow as cow's horn, played with the flap. With her eyes on his fingers, Amanda said slowly.

"Who would want to hurt me?"

"Miss Sophia," he answered promptly, "maybe Theo, maybe that other man."

Surprise at the list held her quiet. Then she asked, "Why?"

"Miss Sophia because you're pretty and young and Jason watches you. Theo for his sister. The other man . . ."

"Nathaniel?" Her voice held disbelief. "But he has no reason."

"I don't know."

"You must have some idea. You can't accuse someone for no reason."

"He is afraid. He has something to lose."

"Oh, but . . ." she began, then stopped. He could lose her . . . and her money. Was Sophia right then? Was she too stupid to see that Nathaniel cared more for material things than he did her? Was that why he had come after her so quickly? No, she could not condemn him wholly on the supposition of a wild man. She was letting her fears run away with her.

"Marta is afraid," he conceded as he leaned to scratch behind the ears of the dog.

It was ridiculous. She was listening to this man and weighing what he said as if his strangeness gave him the wisdom of an oracle. But though she chided herself silently, she did not leave him.

"Carl," she said thoughtfully, "where did you sleep last night?"

He slanted her a secretive glance. "You always ask me that."

"And . . . do you ever tell me?" she asked carefully.

He grinned quickly and turned back to the dog.

"You couldn't have been in the house."

"No?"

"It would have been unwise. They were angry about the grave."

A cloud seemed to cross his face. He went still, then sat up straight, putting his hands on his cloth bag.

"Did you sleep in the woods?" she persisted. "Did you hear the men who rode up to Monteigne in the middle of the night?"

"Men in sheets. Silly."

"No doubt, but also dangerous."

"They never see me," he told her, a smile she could only describe as superior flitting across his thin face.

"But you see them?"

He nodded. "I see them."

"Do you know who they are?" She could not resist the question.

"Some." He shifted, darting her another quick glance.

"Do you know the one who rides at night covered by a

sheet and comes home to Monteigne to stable his horse?"

"I see him, he don't see me. When he comes, I go into the woods. Safe there."

That was not the answer she sought. "Was he with the riders who came last night?"

Carl's brow wrinkled as he thought. His lips moved as if in silent speech, and he tugged at his gray-streaked beard. It was long minutes before he brought an answer forth. "Saw him, after you, all the others, asleep. Watched him walk down the road a way, not long, not short. Talked with the men in sheets. Laughed. Walked back."

A feeling of revulsion ran through her. "Are you saying this man met his friends away from Monteigne, arranged for them to come, and then walked back to the house so . . . so he could be there, on hand, when the visit of the nightriders was made? That's terrible! Who was it? Which man met the riders in sheets?"

He did not answer. He stared out over the fence toward the drive, his eyes narrowed. He looked from side to side, then he scrabbled in his bag and brought out something wrapped in a greasy rag which he offered to her.

"What is it?" she asked, accepting it reluctantly.

He made a motion with his hand, and, remembering the polished stones and the brass button she had found in her room before, she began to unwrap the odd gift.

As the rag fell back she drew in her breath. "Why, it's the collar of Harmonia! Where did you get this? What are you doing with it?"

She turned on him, unconsciously accusing, her voice sharp.

He jumped up and, grabbing the necklace, stuffed it into his bag again.

"Here, wait! That's my necklace, mine, do you hear

me? Give it back!" She got to her feet, her voice rising as he danced out of her reach.

She took a step forward, and he retreated, but then he stopped, gazing at her with wide eyes. "You . . . you're not my Madame Amelia. The box was there . . . under the dirt. You're not my Madame. Where is she? Where . . . is . . . she?"

He was screaming now, capering as he had that night below her window, in a maniacal rage. The dog stood still, but a low growl began in its throat as it sensed the direction of Carl's fury.

Then she was aware of men running, of shouting. Carl turned his head and saw Theo and Nathaniel pelting toward him from the direction of the barn. A grim amusement seemed to touch him, then with easy strength he ran to the iron fence, placed a hand between the spikes of its top and vaulted over it. Long before they had reached Amanda's side, he had merged with the shadows of the woods.

Once again she was in the position of having to explain what had taken place. She was obliged to answer a number of exasperated, and exasperating, questions and to endure Sophia's expression that said as plainly as if she had spoken that she thought Amanda was asking for attention. It might have been an act of cowardice to leave them for the quiet and safety of her room; it had instead the feeling of self-preservation.

"You have a visitor."

Sophia, stepping into Amanda's bedchamber to make the announcement, seemed unusually subdued.

Amanda closed her book and set it aside. "Who is it?"

"Father Metoyer."

"Oh?" Automatically Amanda smoothed her hair as she slipped out the door past the other woman.

"He is the priest for the church we visited yesterday," Sophia supplied, turning toward the stairs. "He says he spoke to you as you were leaving."

"Yes, of course."

"It is kind of him to call, but then he was often here for Amelia, and I expect you remind him of her. She had a great interest in theological matters just before she died, you know. Not unusual, under the circumstances. Death-bed repentance is so affecting, isn't it?"

There was no time to answer that cynical jibe, for they were at the parlor door. Murmuring something about refreshment, Sophia moved away down the hall, leaving Amanda to greet the priest alone.

Father Metoyer come forward at her entrance to clasp her hand. "I am so happy to see you looking well, my child. I heard of your accident and was horrified that it should have happened so soon after I left you."

"Thank you. It was good of you to come. Won't you sit down?"

Amanda indicated the settee while she took one of the Federal armchairs. When they were seated Father Metoyer shook his head. "I cannot get over how much you look like your cousin. I find it uncanny, almost as if she had returned." At the look which moved over her face, he hurried on: "Pay no heed to me. I have a habit from many years of riding from place to place with only my horse to talk to of thinking out loud. I meant no harm, I assure you."

"No, I'm sure you didn't," she said, forcing herself to smile.

He tilted his head slightly to one side. "Other than

surface similarity, I don't believe you are like Madame Monteigne. Hers was not a gentle personality, nor a restful one."

"Not gentle?"

"No. I say that because she fought so hardily against her illness. She wanted badly to triumph over it."

"Then you do think that she was truly ill?" Amanda asked, her every muscle tense as she waited for his answer.

"Certainly," the priest answered, his eyes puzzled.

"You do not think there is any possibility that her illness was feigned, or even imaginary?"

"In my vocation we deal with human nature. I would say that your cousin would not have had the patience to feign such a lengthy illness. She enjoyed being active too much to submit willingly to the restriction of an invalid's bed. As for imagining it, no. I have seen much pain, and hers was real, though she tried for as long as possible to smile and make little of it."

Amanda chose her next words with care. "Has it ever occurred to you that my cousin may have found her pain too much to bear, that she put a stop to it in the only way she could?"

"Suicide? If I had thought so, my child, Madame Monteigne would not be buried in hallowed ground. Come, what is this? Why do you torture yourself with such questions? Your cousin was the victim of a malignant growth in her head. This we must accept."

"Must we? Since I came to Monteigne I have heard so many different tales of how and why she died that I can accept nothing. I have given you some of them in the hope that you would be able to help me decide what is, and is not, possible. There is still one other I have not mentioned."

"And that is?" His face was blank, his eyes wary.

"That she was killed, murdered by degrees with some form of poison or addictive medicine, and then given a final overdose."

Long seconds ticked past before he answered. "I understand that you have been injured twice since coming to Monteigne," he said.

"That is true," she answered, her voice stiff as she thought she saw the trend of his question.

"Is it possible you have let these accidents influence your thinking? I ask this for I cannot believe you would stay here if you believed in your heart that your cousin was murdered. Because if she were, it is all too likely that your own accidents were not so . . . accidental."

"The thought had occurred to me."

"And yet, you are still here, you have not called in the sheriff. Therefore, you do not really believe what you are saying can be true."

Was he right, or was it just that she did not want to believe it? "Perhaps not," she said.

"In any case, your cousin felt death was coming near, a phenomenon one associates with natural causes, not with murder. She repented of the great wrong she had committed and received absolution. Though I knew, or at least suspected, that she embraced the Catholic religion solely for the sake of her husband on the eve of their marriage, and though I realized that her character was not unflawed, I venture to believe that she found peace in God as the end drew near."

It was apparent that the priest did not wish to entertain

the idea that he might have failed a member of his flock in so desperate a situation. "Great wrong?" she inquired.

"Forgive me, I should not have used that phrase, would not if I had taken proper thought."

"Yes," Amanda murmured, "the seal of the confessional."

"Yes."

The priest did not stay long after that, pausing only for the time it took to drink a cup of black coffee and eat one of the pastries Proserpine provided. Amanda watched him go with a tight feeling in her chest. Had Amelia found his kindly, practical presence a comfort? It was possible, if she had never begun to suspect that someone intended to ease her way to death. But if she had, she must have looked in vain for aid from a man so good in soul that he refused to consider even the possibility of evil.

What was this great sin Amelia was supposed to have confessed? Did it, perhaps, have a bearing on the manner of her death? It was useless to ask herself such questions. There was little hope of gaining answers when they were withheld from her by a man's solemn vow and by death.

"What did he want?" Sophia asked. She did not trouble to hide either her curiosity or the fact that she had been hiding in the depths of the hallway, waiting for him to leave.

"Exactly what you thought, he heard of the accident and came to see how I fared."

"You were a long time talking."

"If you had joined us, you would know exactly what kept the conversation going," Amanda said with an edge in her voice.

"Amelia, I expect. Why not? She made such an affecting penitent."

Amanda's fingers curled into fists as she curbed her revulsion. "What did she have to repent?"

"Greed," Sophia answered and gave a sudden sharp laugh.

Above them the stairs creaked.

"If *Herr* Jason were in the house you would not say such things," Marta said, holding tightly to the rail as she descended. "It is you who are the greedy one, wanting for yourself all that my *liebchen* had."

"Drunken old fool!" Sophia said. "Why don't you go back to your bottle? You can hide in it from everything unpleasant, such as dying patients and nightriders. What did you think last night with your crying and screaming, that they had come to mete out the punishment you so richly deserve?"

"Don't say such things," Marta said, paling as she glanced around them.

"Why not, if they are true?"

"There are many truths which are better left unspoken. They cannot harm the dead but may hurt the living."

"Such as?" The sneer was plain in Sophia's tone.

"Such as the fact that *Herr* Jason feels nothing but pity for you. Madame Amelia knew this, that is why she was never jealous. She said you were alike, you and her, both loving a man who could give only pity in return. The woman he would love, she said, would have to be stronger and purer in heart than either of you."

"I don't believe it!" Sophia exclaimed.

"Because you are a fool wishing for something you will never have," the nurse replied, her pronouncements given more weight by the owllike solemnity of her manner. If she had been drinking, it was only enough to give her courage and a certain facility with words.

"Why, you maudlin cow. I'll see you whipped out of the state before I'll let you talk to me like that!" Sophia stamped her foot, beside herself with rage.

"That may be," the nurse said, nodding with a faraway look in her eyes. "But I would be careful. They might look for others to punish."

With immense dignity, Marta descended the remaining stairs and turned toward the hallway and the direction of the kitchen. Sophia stared after her, a brooding look on her face, a look tinged also by something like fear.

Jason returned to the house perhaps an hour before the noon meal. The dust of the fields clung to his clothes and powdered the brim of his hat. He was regaled by Theo with the story of Carl's near attack on Amanda while he was still sluicing his arms and face clean in the pan of water provided on the back gallery.

With the doors of the house thrown open, Amanda, who had descended to the parlor with her novel, could not help overhearing. She winced a little at the curt tone Jason used to cut across Theo's diatribe against Carl, and though she heard Jason mention her name, she stayed where she was. It was a quarter of an hour later when he sought her out. He had used the time to change and seemed to have repaired his temper along with his appearance.

"I understand you have had a busy morning," he said as he came toward her.

Amanda put her book aside. Though she did not mean to smile, she found her lips curving as he came toward her. "My own fault, I'm afraid," she said ruefully.

"I find that hard to believe."

"Nonetheless, it's true."

"Perhaps you will allow me to judge for myself," he

said, holding out his hand to help her to her feet. "Come into my study where we will not be disturbed, and you can tell me all about it."

Amanda had known this moment must come. To the others, when they asked why Carl had turned on her, she had said merely that he had shown her the necklace and became upset when she tried to take it from him. Such an explanation would not do for Jason. He must know the full reason for Carl's action, because if the evidence she gave suggested that he had attacked her without real provocation, then there was a stern streak in the owner of Monteigne which might cause him to cast off that poor derelict. She did not want that on her conscience.

On the other hand, she felt an overwhelming need to give Jason himself the benefit of the doubt. The night before, when Jason had faced the nightriders, she could have sworn the tension and danger in the air was real. How could that be if Jason had arranged the midnight visit? He was the obvious suspect, the landowner, former Confederate soldier, who was having to fight for his very existence against a hostile republican government. Still, wasn't that very vulnerability to suspicion reason enough for him to hold himself aloof from such clandestine activities?

There were two other men in the house. Two others with reason to encourage a visit from the nightriders. Theo, with his support of the group, was the perfect choice. He had been incensed with Nathaniel for his stand against them. What could be more in order than an attempt on his part to give Nathaniel a scare, at the same time encouraging him to think twice before taking an opposing political stand. The other possibility was Nathaniel himself. Considering his aspirations and his views on how they could be gained, martyrdom at the hands of the nightriders would be a convenient thing. If he could be made to appear a victim without any real danger or inconvenience to himself, then it could not but help his cause. The common people who were frightened by the excesses of the nightriders would look to him for leadership, while at the same time, to be their target could not hurt his cause with those currently in power in the carpetbagger government.

When the study door had closed behind them and she faced Jason across the oak table which served him as a desk, she found it harder than she had thought possible to make her explanations. The expression on his face was grim when she had finished.

"So," he said, leaning back in his chair. "Carl gave you no answer to your question?"

"No. I'm not sure whether he did not know who it was and was trying to placate me, or whether he did, but preferred not to say. He was obviously trying to distract my attention by giving me the necklace."

"I should have guessed Carl picked it up," Jason said. "He likes pretty, bright-colored things. He collects them like a magpie, and with little more understanding of their worth or the complications of ownership."

Amanda said, "When I saw the necklace I was so surprised I practically accused him of stealing it."

"And he became violent."

Amanda nodded. "He snatched it back and began to shout that I was not his Madame Amelia. He said something else, something about her grave, and the box that was still there. Father Metoyer seemed to think it was

Carl who disturbed Amelia's grave. I am almost certain he is right."

"I never doubted it," Jason said, "or the reason for it."

"And yet, you went after Carl with the others that day at the cemetery?"

"For his protection. Theo is not always accountable where Carl is concerned."

Amanda was forced to agree. "And after all the upset, I'm still no wiser as to who the nightrider may be."

If what she had told Jason increased his knowledge, if he guessed, or knew, who rode from Monteigne, he did not intend to tell her. "No," he said, his green gaze steady as he stared at her across the table. "And that being so, I am honored that you have confided in me."

Amanda looked away, staring at the Sheraton bookcase against one wall. It was filled with leather-bound volumes and yellowing farm periodicals. The glass doors which closed them in were smudged and powdered with dust. There was a brass Athenian owl on one of the shelves, and beneath it, a handwoven Indian basket of black and natural cane. She was aware of Jason's eyes on her averted face. The soft rustle as he took up a sheet of foolscap and tossed it down again was loud in the silence.

"Amanda . . ."

He said her name in the firm voice of one who has made a difficult decision, then he stopped.

"Yes?" she said after a moment.

He stood up and moved to lean against the desk, standing over her where she sat in the armchair.

"There is something you must know, but I find I don't know how to start, how to tell you." He made a small, helpless gesture.

"About Amelia?"

"Yes."

"You . . . you don't have to tell me," she forestalled him as he started again to speak. "Marta already has."

"Marta?"

"She told me that there was something peculiar about her death. Isn't that what you were going to say?"

"Something like that," he agreed, and yet Amanda had the impression that he was surprised.

More in response to the expression on his face than to any prompting, she quickly told him all that Marta had said to her in her drunken stupor.

While she spoke Jason kept his head down, and his arms crossed over his chest. There was a white line about his mouth when he looked up.

"Marta came to me a few days ago and told me about the old woman. She was a bedridden patient who had been ill for years. She lived alone, had no close relatives other than a nephew who, six months or so before her death, hired Marta to look after her. When the old woman died suddenly one day, Marta claimed the cause was heart failure. The nephew charged her with negligence. The doctor in the case upheld Marta's diagnosis, but he claimed that he found the old woman in such circumstances that he could not absolve Marta of the charge against her. Marta claimed that her patient had been in the midst of a deliberate portrayal of austerity designed to persuade her nephew to increase the amount of money he was paying to support her. The nephew could not admit this possibility without looking as if he was a skinflint, of course, and so he gave out hints that Marta had been stealing from her helpless patient. How Amelia heard the tale, I don't know. She just came bringing Marta home one day, another of her strays mistreated by the world. The tale Marta told me is substantially the same as the one Amelia gave out when she established the woman here."

"A terrible story. It is almost enough to explain why Marta drinks."

"Yes, if it's true, and I have no reason to doubt it. But I did not know of the drinking. Marta forgot to mention that in her confession. And I certainly never knew she was not with Amelia when she died. In fact, Marta went to great pains to make me believe she never left Amelia's side that whole night through. She swore, on that basis, that other than herself I was the last one to see Amelia alive."

Amanda frowned. "Marta could hardly be sure of that if she was lying in drunken sleep in her room. No doubt she said it to excuse herself, because she knew she had failed in her duty."

"That is possible," he answered, but there was a look of such fierce concentration on his face that Amanda had the impression his thoughts were concerned with something entirely different.

Jason had returned his gaze to his booted feet. Amanda, studying the damp waves of his hair, the sun-bronzed planes of his face, and the strength of his fingers as they gripped his arms, sensed the disturbance he felt. She wanted to help him but knew herself to be powerless. That feeling was not unknown to her. In some mysterious way, it was connected with what had occurred in the early hours of the night before; obscured by the dangers of the visit from the nightriders, it had been almost forgotten. Now it came back to her in fragments of memory that brought the quickening of excitement to her veins.

Amanda cleared her throat. "About last night . . . ."

"Yes"? He glanced up, the expression in his green eyes wary.

"Earlier last night, before the riders came, we were in the hall, you and Sophia, and I. Could you tell me what . . . what happened? I know that sounds odd, but I can't remember. I . . . I think I must have been sleepwalking!" She brought the last words out in a rush, and felt the relief that they were said wash over her.

"You are sure you can't remember?"

She shook her head. "It is a frightening thing. I know I have been walking and talking, but I can't remember where I've been or what I've said . . . and deep inside I have this feeling of . . . of guilt."

He gazed at her a few seconds, then said carefully, "Last night you came to my room."

"What?" She got to her feet slowly.

"You knocked on my door and said that you had something to tell me."

He paused expectantly, and she shook her head again. "I couldn't have."

"You insisted that you were Amelia, but you were shocked when I told you that I was responsible for your final, lethal measure of medicine."

Disbelief gripped her, making her mute. For a moment there seemed to be an echo in her head, as if she had heard that pronouncement before, then the feeling was gone, and she was left with a stricken look in her gray eyes.

It was a long time before she could speak, but he did not move or look away. "Are you trying to say you killed Amelia?"

"I have lived for three months with the knowledge that I must have."

"How? Tell me."

"It was a night like so many others. Amelia was feverishly gay, trying to hide her fear of death and the pain that lived inside her. She held court from her bed until she became overwrought, railing hysterically against fate, life, our marriage, me, everything. Marta calmed her down, finally, but we were all exhausted. Then in the middle of the night she began to cry, the most helpless, hopeless weeping I have ever heard. It haunts me still." He paused a brief moment, then went on. "I went to her. Her face was wet with tears and her hair in tangles from her twisting and turning. Her drowned violet eyes begged for relief. Marta . . . she was deathly tired, at her wit's end. She had given Amelia her laudanum only an hour and a half before and was afraid to give her more. We waited nearly another forty-five minutes, then I saw she could not endure the pain much longer without going mad. I took up the bottle, measured the dose, and watched her drink it down. She slept finally. In the morning she was dead."

"Was the dose more than . . . more than usual?"

"I didn't think so at the time, but it must have been. It was late, I was half out of my mind with the sound of her screams and moans, and I must admit, I had been drinking to deaden the knowledge that Amelia was dying and I could do nothing. Dozens of times before, when she would wake in the night screaming, I had felt the urge to help her toward a painless release. Where does the thought end and the deed begin?"

"Perhaps it was the effect of the second dose so soon after the first."

He shook his head. "I spoke to her doctor about that possibility. He said that a double dose given as it would have to have been, more than two hours apart, would have made her sleep for several hours, but it should not have killed her. No, I can't shift the blame. It is mine to live with, if I can."

He allowed a moment to pass before he went on. "But that isn't what I wanted to put to you. This may—no, it will—sound strange, even mad, but I can't help thinking . . . country people, most of our Negro workers, believe in possession, by devils—by the dead. The Catholic Church has a ceremony for casting out the one who has taken possession. No! Don't answer! Last night you looked, walked, talked and . . . reacted like Amelia. You were not yourself at all. You cannot remember what you said and did. You took things that were not yours, acted as I'm sure you would never dream of acting when you are yourself. Is there nothing to show that, when you are asleep, or weak from the effect of the injury you sustained, Amelia possesses herself of your body for some purpose of her own?"

It was unbelievable, so beyond thinking that her mind would not function. Her concern fastened on what he had said before. "How did I act? What can I have done to make you say such a thing?" she whispered.

Without haste he moved to take her into his arms. "Only this," he murmured gently as his lips touched hers.

Chapter
Ten

THE moment she fled the study she remembered that she had not mentioned to Jason the hairpins in her petticoat pocket or the handkerchief tied to her bed. But she could not go back, not after what had happened between them. The feel of his lips lingered on hers. Her heart still beat uncomfortably fast, the effect, she was sure, of the possibility he had disclosed to her. She frowned as she stood in the hall. Could it be that she had been in his arms before? That Amelia had used her body without her knowledge? It did not seem possible, but how else was she to explain her lack of memory of the events described. No. She could not go back after her precipitate flight from Jason and his incredible theory. She would have to wait. There might be an opportunity to tell him of this slight evidence supporting his theory at another time.

She moved up the stairs and along the hall to her room with her mind in confusion. She was just opening the door when Nathaniel came down the hall toward her.

"Wait, Amanda. I want to speak to you."

His voice was curt with a hint of command. His manner set her back up a little, but she turned courteously enough.

"Inside, please."

He pulled the door open and they passed through, then he closed it firmly behind him.

"Where have you been?"

A flush stained her cheeks, half from anger, half from the guilty knowledge that she had, in a manner of speaking, betrayed her fiancé, but she answered steadily, "With Jason."

"Oh?"

"He . . . he has some idea that . . . I don't know how to tell you without sounding . . . melodramatic . . . that Amelia . . ."

Nathaniel made a brushing gesture with one raised hand. "Never mind. What I want to know right now is, what were you two doing last night?"

"I . . . I don't know what you mean."

"Don't you? I find that hard to believe, but I will make myself clearer. Sophia tells me that she saw you and Jason . . . in a close embrace in the doorway of his room last night!"

"Oh." Sophia. She should have guessed that the venom of Sophia's anger would lead her to what she considered revenge. Abruptly she realized that was an odd way to put it. Wasn't it revenge that Nathaniel had called her to account for her actions?

"Is that all you have to say?"

226

"I'm afraid what she told you is true, but I can try to explain if you would care to hear it."

"I'm listening."

"I . . . I didn't know what I was doing. I thought later, when I learned of it, that I must have been sleepwalking . . . because of the drugs and my head. But Jason thinks because of the way I spoke and acted that . . . that it was Amelia."

"Amelia what?"

"Amelia . . . coming back, using me, my body . . ."

"Ridiculous!"

"But how else can you explain it, Nathaniel? It wasn't the first time I have awakened wearing her clothes, her perfume, wearing my hair as she did. I found the hairpins in my petticoat pocket, just as she used to carry them. And Nathaniel, you know me! I would never have dreamed of . . . of going into the arms of the husband of my dead cousin, not if I were well and myself!"

"Maybe . . ."

"Yes, go on." She gripped her hands tightly, afraid of what was coming even before he began to speak.

"Maybe you aren't well, aren't yourself, Amanda."

"What do you mean?"

"I mean . . . this head injury. Maybe you only fancy yourself as Amelia. I've said it before. There was envy between you . . ."

"No! Never to that extent, Nathaniel. You can't believe that!"

"No? Deny you envied Amelia the excitement of her runaway marriage while you stayed at home caring for those old people. Deny that your engagement to me seemed dull compared to the dashing stranger who had run away with Amelia. No. You can't deny it. I've seen it in your eyes whether you realize it or not. I'm not saying it's deliberate. I'm saying it could be all in your head, on account of the accident. You haven't seemed yourself to me, not since I came here."

"Nathaniel, I . . ."

"I don't mean to upset you, so there's no use staring at me with your eyes like plates. Nobody likes to hear the truth about themselves, but I can't allow you to listen to a lot of nonsense that can't do you any good. I tell you what I think. I think we should pack our bags and leave this place, just as quickly as we can."

"Leave?"

"Don't tell me the thought never crossed your mind?"

She ignored the edge of sarcasm. "I . . . I don't think I can."

"You seem well enough to me. We wouldn't hurry. We would stop often. Matter of fact, we might even get married along the way. You're of age. There's nothing to stop us."

"I'm sorry, Nathaniel, but I can't."

"Can't or won't?"

"A little of both," she answered, trying to be honest. "I have a feeling that I'm needed. I told you Amelia was killed . . ."

"Please. Don't start that again," he begged, his tone weary with tried patience.

"No, no, I won't, but I won't go with you either."

He stepped forward and took her hands. "Don't, Amanda. Don't say that. Believe me, it is concern for you that makes me seem . . . less than sympathetic. I can't stand to see you like this, to hear you say such wild, improbable things as though you really believe them.

Think about what I've said. Tomorrow is a new day, a new month, the first of November. It would be a nice day for a wedding. We could leave early, be married in town, and take our own time reaching home."

The first of November. She had not realized. Tonight was Hallowe'en, All Hallows' Eve, the Night of the Candles.

"Well, have you nothing to say?" Irritation laced Nathaniel's tone.

"I . . . couldn't. I don't have my wedding gown with me . . . Why, it's not even finished! And besides, you know I'm in mourning for Amelia."

"The gown doesn't matter," Nathaniel told her. "As for your mourning, I have every respect for the dead, but you must admit the relationship was not close either in degree or affection. It's been nearly three years since you saw your cousin last, three years! No one will blame you for putting your own happiness before the conventions in this case."

"No, I suppose not, if you look at it in that light."

Her expression was so much the opposite of the happiness he suggested, however, that he stiffened. "Of course, I may be assuming too much."

"Don't be angry, Nathaniel," she said with a small gesture of distress. "It's just that I'm so confused."

"Yes, I can see that," he said, softening at once. "But you will at least think about what I've said. Promise me that much."

She promised at last, to be rid of him, recognizing that a desire to see the back of her fiancé was hardly the proper frame of mind in which to consider his proposal.

She kept her promise. She thought of going away with Nathaniel in the morning, of marriage to him. There seemed no substance to her thoughts, nothing to grasp to help her make a decision. Absurdly, she kept picturing him in his long velvet dressing gown and tasseled nightcap. Even that vision could not keep her mind from wandering to other things.

She considered Marta—drunk, derelict in her duty as a nurse the night Amelia died—and what Jason had said. Marta had told Jason that he was the last person to see Amelia alive, but how could she know that? The answer was simply, she could not. She had told him what she had to, to protect herself, not knowing or caring that she condemned Jason to the belief that he was a murderer.

Perhaps he is. The whisper came from within. Perhaps Marta had spoken the truth. There was nothing to prove her wrong.

At least the reason why the nurse had stayed on at Monteigne was now apparent. Jason could not afford to let her go away so long as she clung to her version of the last night of Amelia's life.

She had moved to the window, staring out without seeing. Gradually she became aware of someone moving down below. It was Jason, walking toward the stables. Without conscious reasoning she moved from her room and, on impulse, skirted the stairwell and walked out onto the gallery that fronted the house.

It was dim and shadowy on the gallery, the effect of the overcast sky. A cool breeze swept across the high open space causing her to clasp her arms for warmth. A few dry leaves rustled as they were blown about over the floor and the sound of the wind in the branches of the trees seemed abnormally loud. She stood leaning against a column, staring at the stables, waiting, thinking idly of turning up the back of her skirt to use as a shawl against the coolness, letting a wry smile curve her mouth as she realized it would be a very Amelialike thing to do.

Then at last Jason led his horse from the stable, mounted, and rode toward the house.

As he neared, Amanda thought he looked up and caught sight of her. The fingers of his hand must have tightened for his horse sidestepped, then he turned down the drive and was gone without looking back.

Behaving like a schoolgirl, Amanda chided herself, breathing gently against the pain in her chest. What did you expect? A salute?

No, only a smile. Some acknowledgment of her presence. She was suddenly ashamed, and she had turned to go back into the house when she heard voices on the gallery below.

Nathaniel and Sophia, she thought an instant before they came into view, moving along the walk and out the gate. Their heads were close together, their voices low and intimate. Plotting. The word came unbidden though she could not hear what they were saying. She was surprised at herself. What could they possibly have to plot? The memory of the scene with her fiancé returned to her as she stood watching. Nathaniel had said that it was Sophia who had carried the tale of Amanda's indiscretion to him. She would, no doubt, want to know the results of her efforts.

A weight of dark depression moved in her mind. Stay or go? What was she going to do? One half of her felt as light as one of those dry leaves flying before the wind while the other felt as deeply rooted as the ancient oaks from which the leaves fell.

Go or stay? No one could help her. No amount of

plotting would influence her. The decision had to be made in the next hours.

Slowly she turned and went back into the house.

She found Marta in the parlor. Beads and wire lay scattered upon the table at her elbow, the last of the All Hallows' Eve flowers, but the nurse sat staring into the fire. It was so unusual to see her there in the dim room alone, in the middle of the morning, that Amanda stopped, then went forward purposefully.

"Marta, I want to talk to you."

The woman started. She turned to look at Amanda before forcing a smile to her mouth. "Of course, *fräulein.* Anything you say. But I think it might not be wise for you to come close. I feel sure I'm catching a cold in the chest."

"I'm sorry," Amanda acknowledged this excuse briefly. "I want to ask you about the night Amelia died. Tell me again, what was it you heard?"

"It was very little, *fräulein,* and not, perhaps, so unusual except that I found my poor *liebchen* dead next morning . . . 'twas only a scream."

"You were with her when her husband gave her the last laudanum drops?"

"*Ja,* standing right beside him."

"Amelia went to sleep then . . ."

"Why, yes, and *Herr* Jason returned to his room."

"And so you went to bed also?"

"It was to be for only a small nap. One must rest, and there had been so many nights without sleep except in snatches. I drank a part of the bottle I found, thinking it was meant for me, a kind of gift. I was asleep as soon as my head touched the pillow."

"You woke later when you heard Amelia cry out."

232

"Indeed. That was the way of it. But it sounded far off. I couldn't make myself move. I couldn't go to her. I tried. I did try."

"I'm sure. It was unfortunate. But tell me. What do you think happened then?"

"Why, I think she must have reached out herself for the medicine. Half out of her mind with pain, the sweet lady took too much. *Ach,* my poor dear. But 'twas best, 'twas best."

"But Marta, the other day . . ."

"*Ja, fräulein?*"

"You hinted there had been foul play."

"I? Oh, no, not I!"

"You did, you know you did, because of Amelia's condition."

"Condition?"

"The baby."

"The baby, *fräulein?*"

"You told me there was to be a child," Amanda said slowly, holding onto her temper with the greatest difficulty.

"I don't remember."

There was nothing slurred or in the least weak about her words. The woman was not drunk, but still her eyes slid back to the fire as she finished speaking.

"Marta, I . . ." she stopped, then taking a deep breath, went on more calmly. "I did not make up what I heard. I know what you told me. I don't know why you are denying it now, but I will get to the bottom of this if it takes me all the rest of the year!"

"Perhaps, *fräulein,* you imagined it?" she said, her tone flat, her face stolid.

The sound of someone clearing his throat came from

233

the door and, as she turned, Theo stepped into the room from the outside hall. There was a faintly apologetic look in his eyes and a pale cast to his normally florid skin.

"I couldn't help overhearing," he said when Amanda did not speak. "I don't know what Marta has or has not been telling you, but I don't think Amelia could have been with child. She was under a doctor's care, was visited by him often. Such a thing could hardly have been a secret."

"No? Not even if it was of short duration?"

"I find it hard to believe Amelia would have kept it from . . . us."

Amanda stared at him. She had the impression he had been about to say "from me"; why should he have been privy to Amelia's secrets?

"You see," Marta was saying. "Depend on it, there is some simple explanation. It was likely something I said in my terrible English gave you the impression."

Amanda knew it was not so, yet she could hardly argue further with Amelia's personal nurse, someone who had been in the house when she died.

"Tell me what the trouble is," Theo said. "What brought on this discussion?"

"It was . . . nothing." For a moment Amanda had been tempted to explain, to tell Theo of her suspicions, before some inner caution took over, silencing her.

"Nothing?" Theo asked with a quizzical look in his eyes. But before she could form an answer, Sophia brushed through the open door and into the room.

"There you are, Theo. I wanted you to help me with the wreaths, set them out on the front porch ready to load into the wagon."

"All right," he agreed but made no move to comply.

"Well, Amanda," Sophia said, turning to her with a bright smile. "So you will be with us for the ceremony tonight, after all. Who would have thought it on the night you arrived here? Certainly not I."

"Nor I," Amanda said.

"You will come with us to the cemetery? And you also, Marta? Father Metoyer has promised to say the Mass for the Hallowed Souls for us this year. It will be late since he has at least two other small country churches where he is expected, but we will not mind."

"I don't know . . ." Amanda began.

"Don't tell me you don't want to pay your respects to Amelia. It is expected, you know. It will look odd to the others if you are still here and fail to come."

"There will be others?"

"Oh, yes, a few, I'm sure. The Monteignes built the church, but it is for the community, after all, even if the congregation's somewhat sparse these days. There will be a dozen or more people plus all of us, that is, if you and your fiancé are coming?"

"Perhaps we will, just for the Mass."

"Not for the Lighting of the Candles? Now, to me that is the best moment of all. Deliciously frightening but with a pious overtone."

"Sophia . . ." Theo seemed to find something objectionable in his sister's voice, but she merely smiled at him.

"First, we will eat, then have Mass, after which we will march through the cemetery with our candles and place the burning tapers on the graves. Some will depart then, most, in fact. A few will stay longer, lighting other candles from the first when it burns down. I have never, in the past, ventured to stay so long myself, but I thought I might this year."

"It would seem to be quite an occasion," Amanda said dryly.

"Yes, indeed. Proserpine is planning quite a picnic basket for our delectation."

There was a strange glint in Sophia's eyes, a sound of cracking glass in her voice. Amanda said, "I hope you are not going to any trouble on my account."

"Oh, no. We do this every year."

"We?"

"Theo and I. It is a family tradition, inherited from our Creole mother. Jason's father, Monsieur Monteigne, used to come, sometimes. Jason is harder to persuade, but he has agreed to put in an appearance."

"I'm sure it will be very . . . interesting."

Sophia's lips moved in a smile. "I expect you are thinking it will be grotesque, and you're right, of course. But it also gives one a sense of kinship with those who have gone before. No one can tell you; it is something you must experience yourself. Now you will have to excuse me," she ended abruptly. "I have a great deal to do yet."

"If I could be of help . . ."

"No, no," Sophia refused Amanda's help before the words were out of her mouth. "There is no need."

"I would help you, Sophia," Marta said querulously, "but I'm not feeling at all the thing."

"Never mind! Coming, Theo?" Sophia said and, turning, swept from the room.

"In a . . . few minutes," he called after her, his eyes on Marta.

"*Ach*," the nurse grumbled, getting to her feet. "I sup-

236

pose I had best go and help her, or she will not be fit to live with."

Theo waited until Marta had moved slowly, to show her ill health, from the room.

"Nathaniel tells me you will be leaving in the morning."

"Does he?" she said, wondering where Nathaniel was if Sophia had come into the house so soon.

"Amanda?"

"Yes, Theo?" She brought her attention back to him.

"Are you certain this . . . this marriage . . . is what you want?"

Her eyes were clear as she surveyed him. "Why?"

"I wouldn't like for you to . . . to be unhappy. I've seen enough of that kind of marriage."

"That kind?"

"The kind where after the first excitement of the honeymoon is over, neither has anything to give the other."

"You are speaking of Amelia and Jason?"

"Yes," he answered simply, his eyes calm.

"Tell me, Theo, how do you know they were not happy?"

He was silent a long moment. When he spoke his face was hard with some strong feeling held in control. "I know because Amelia told me. The marriage was a mistake. We . . . I was in love with Amelia. Before the growth in her head was discovered, we were planning to go away together."

Adultery. This then was Amelia's great sin. Amanda could think of nothing to say. Vague questions and comments formed in her mind, but they were too personal to voice.

At last he went on. "You see, you are so like Amelia that I want you, at least, to be happy, to be sure the man you marry is the man who can make you happy. I don't believe that you and Nathaniel are well-matched. I may be wrong, but if there is any doubt, then be very careful. You might save yourself, your fiancé, and the man who might someday love you, a great deal of sorrow."

Though she heard him she could not attend. A question rose to her lips that she had to ask. "How could you? How could you do such a thing to Jason?"

He made a short humorless sound that was meant to pass for a laugh. "We are a pair, Sophia and I," he said, turning his face away. "Each fell in love with someone we could never have. I with Amelia, Sophia with Jason. It was quite a family here while Amelia lay slowly dying. So much festering hate and cold despair. Not the least of it was guilt. There was the look in Jason's eyes, he blaming himself. And my own sister, quietly hopeful, and Marta, officious, driving Amelia mad with her fussing and self-importance and air of fellow suffering!" He took a deep breath and let it out slowly. "Unbearable, truly, it was unbearable."

"Why do you stay, now she is gone?" What had prompted that, a desire to rub salt into the wound?

"I stay because . . . because it is only three months, and something of her lingers. She lived here. She sat in that chair, slept in the room upstairs . . . I can picture her standing there, like you, before the fire. Where else could I find as much?"

"You look Jason in the face each morning."

"He had her over two years!"

"Was the child yours?"

There. That was the burning issue, and it was better to

238

blurt it out than to wait for better words or a better moment, and lose the courage to ask.

"I told you. I know of no child."

"Nor do I!"

That harsh voice came from the doorway, and Amanda swung toward it, the color draining from her face. She caught her bottom lip before she said, "You weren't gone long."

Jason refused the ploy. He had no intention of covering the subject that lay between them with polite conversation. His face twisted with contempt. "Not long enough, it seems. If I had known you needed the information, I could have stopped to tell you how far I was riding and when I would return."

"I'm sorry. I . . ." But she was interrupted.

"Curiosity, wasn't it? You could not stand to let it lie. You had to stir it all up again."

"That's hardly fair! Amelia was my cousin. Would you deny me the truth about her death?"

"The truth? You have the truth," he grated, anger and a kind of desperate pain flaring in his eyes.

"Do I? I can't accept that. I won't accept that . . . unless you want to be a martyr, Jason?"

He stared at her, his green eyes like stone, and then he sighed, lifting one hand to run it over his hair to the back of his neck. "No," he said, his voice low, almost husky. "Forgive me, Amanda, for lashing out at you. It's not your fault."

She would not be disarmed by gentleness. "You are not the only person who might have killed my cousin. Any one of the people in this house might have done it."

"The fact remains . . ."

"Does it?" she said scornfully. "Are you willing to take

the word of a woman who would lie about a thing so important as an expected child against your own memory? If you will, then I have no choice but to suppose you *want* to be blamed for Amelia's death because you feel guilty!"

Theo turned on his heel and left the room. Amanda glanced at his stiff back. She supposed he was hurt that she could have included him in her sweeping denunciation, or perhaps he wished to avoid confronting Jason and hoped he had not heard enough of Amanda's and his conversation to demand his return.

"So," Jason said when the door had closed behind him. "You would save me from myself? Why, I wonder?"

So did she. Made wary by the quiet, gentle tone of his voice, she searched his face for some sign of his mood. The things she knew about him, his household, his relationship with her cousin, tumbled through her mind, and yet, unlike her talk with Theo, she could not bring out the truth unmindful of his pride.

A part of her distress and indecision must have shown in her eyes and in her hands clasped together at her waist for he gave a silent laugh. "Don't trouble yourself, Amanda. There is nothing you need tell me, nothing to hide from me. You see, I know."

"You . . . know?"

"About Amelia and her flirtation with Theo. Their elopement plans. She would never have gone. But she could no more help attaching him to her, encouraging him, than she could help . . . the violet color of her eyes. She was beautiful and bored, loving and . . . lovable. She intended no harm."

"No. But it came to her."

"It was coming, slowly, hurtfully . . ."

"That doesn't make it right!"

"Still, I'm grateful."

"Grateful? To a murderer? Grateful enough to let them get away with their crime? What if they decided death comes easy? What is to keep them from doing it again?"

"Don't work yourself into hysteria. You don't know Amelia was killed by choice. It could have been an accident. And if it comes to that, for all your conviction, you still haven't proved I didn't do it."

"Does it come to this, you would rather not know? Why? Because it might be someone you cannot bear to part with?"

"No . . ."

"No? Marta admits she doesn't know what took place. She never saw you. She saw nothing, she only heard a cry in the night. She cannot even swear it was Amelia!"

Slowly he moved toward her and lifting his hand, touched her cheek. "What is it you want? Revenge?"

She shook her head. "Only . . . only to know. I cannot bear to think . . ."

"Don't. Don't think. Let it go. Leave it alone before . . ."

But she would not let him finish. "You know, don't you?"

He dropped his hand and turned to walk away.

"Jason!"

When he looked back at the door she asked, "Justice? Doesn't *it* matter?"

"It's a cold thing," he answered, his hard gaze meeting her soft gray eyes squarely, "and lonely."

Why was Jason so reluctant to bring home this deed without a name? The question nagged at Amanda as she stood staring out the window of her bedchamber hours later. The wind had fallen since noontime. The sky had grown more leaden. If the weather turned cold and rainy, perhaps they would call off the trip to the cemetery this evening. She did not want to go. Under the circumstances the idea filled her with repugnance. To stand at Amelia's graveside with the person who had murdered her? No. She was not looking forward to the All Hallows' Eve visit or the celebration of the Night of the Candles.

Whom was Jason protecting? The most obvious answer was himself. By his own admission he had been aware of Amelia's affair with Theo. That he could speak of it so calmly now did not mean that he had never felt jealousy or hate because of the betrayal. She would have thought that his rage would have turned against Theo in a situation of that sort, but Jason was a strange, silent, self-contained man. It was not impossible that he might consider the abrupt death of Amelia as a more subtle and fitting revenge against the man who had dared to love her. Or it might have been even simpler than that. Amelia stood in the way of his possession of a second wife, a healthy and more voluptuous mistress for his home.

Then there was Sophia. She could have come in the night to offer Amelia the overdose with quiet words and a soothing hand on the sick woman's brow. Who had a better reason than she? She wanted Amelia's place, Amelia's husband.

But she had only to wait, and they would have been hers in the fullness of time. Yes, but suppose Sophia had believed the lie of Amelia's child. She might not have been able to bear the prospect of Amelia's lingering into the early spring and bringing forth an heir who would displace the children God might grant to her and Jason.

Property, the land, Monteigne, meant much to Sophia who had lost her own heritage.

There was Carl, poor, mad, loyal Carl. Suppose Amelia, waking, had found him in her room and cried out in pain. Could he have had the sense, the intelligence to pour out a draught of her medicine and press it into her trembling hand, a draught too much? He was far from being as stupid as he appeared, Amanda knew.

And Marta, clinging to her job and its security in the fear and shuddering of a frightened, drink-soaked, middle age, dogged by something in her past. How far would she go to protect her position and herself?

As long as she was listing, consider Theo. Did he, a man content to live at the expense of his friend in return for a minimum of effort, have no motive for the deed? What if he had cared less for Amelia than he pretended? What if his devotion, now so freely admitted, was a screen? He might have dallied with Amelia, might have been charmed by her manner and her beauty, but in the end opted for the security of being the brother of Jason's new wife. It would not be the first time brother and sister had connived for gain.

Then suppose there was one other name to be added, one other name to couple with suspicion and deceit. Amelia. Amelia waking to a dark and silent house uncaring of her suffering, with no answer for her call. She might have struggled from her bed and reached for . . . oblivion.

There they were. No one, with the exception of Nathaniel, who had not been here, could escape the taint of suspicion. And of them all, who would have a reason for wanting to frighten or harm her, Amanda? There must be a connection.

Gradually voices raised in argument impinged upon her consciousness. She sighed, closing her eyes. Was there nothing here at Monteigne but suspicion and harassed tempers and discontent? Had this ever been a happy place filled with sunshine, the sound of children and laughter?

Those voices—one sounded like Theo in a rage while the other was . . . a woman—Sophia, Marta? Marta, she thought after listening a moment. She imagined Theo was taking the woman to task for lying about Amelia's condition.

Marta, however, sounded quite vehement. Suppose she had told the truth? Suppose Amelia had been carrying a child, Theo's child, with no one the wiser except her nurse? Would it change anything, this secret? Nothing, other than to strengthen her reason for suicide. Unless . . .

Unless the secret had been found out. Unless Jason had found out.

The implications of that train of conjecture were so unwelcome that her mind shied away from it. She found herself straining her ears, questing in memory for another time, another quarrel. It had not been long ago. Yes, of course. Here in this house, the night she came. A quarrel between Theo and his sister, a quarrel ending in a blow. Who had struck whom? Then it had seemed obvious, but she was no longer certain.

Nothing so definite ended this contretemps. The voices faded allowing her to shrug off the interruption and return to her own problem.

Who had tried to harm her, and why? She must be methodical and objective; still it was an effort to consider Marta first. Did the woman realize that she had mentioned the death of the old woman in her drunken ravings? Did she hope that fear would drive Amanda away before she could put the bits and pieces of the puzzle together?

Or could it have been Sophia, for the same reason . . . plus another—fear of Jason's attraction for Amanda's type? Amelia had taken him from her grasp once, and she did not want to risk its happening again.

That was flattering herself, she thought wryly, but it could not hurt to explore every possibility.

Carl had liked her, until he had discovered she was not Amelia. Surely he was not cunning enough in his madness to dissemble to that event. And Theo? She shook her head. It was possible, of course, but she did not like to think of it. Which left only Jason.

Jason. Would he stoop so low? Was he capable of such petty skirmishing, when he could have thrown her out of his home bodily at any time and remained within his rights. There might have been some community comments, but that would not have weighed with him, would it? Jason. It was difficult to feature him pitching gum balls at a horse. It was not . . .

A faint sound, like the furtive creaking of a board gingerly stepped upon brought her thoughts to a halt. She half turned, listening. The sound did not come again, and yet the quiet seemed to hold a tense, unnatural, hush. The sound came from the hall, she thought. A chill ran over her and glancing down she saw her fingers clasped together so tightly that the knuckles were white. Forcing them apart, she stretched her fingers, letting them curl naturally at her sides, then moved to the door.

She touched the cold doorknob lightly, then her grip increased as she turned it and eased the door open to a slit.

Marta, her head closely covered by a scarf, a dolman

cape emphasizing her width, was just descending the stairs. She kept close to the wall of the staircase where the treads were firmest.

When she had dropped down out of sight, Amanda slipped into the hall, moving with swift steps to the stairwell. From there she watched as Marta paused, glancing left and right into the empty parlor and the sitting room. Seeing no one, the nurse hurried to the front door, swung through, and closed it noiselessly behind her.

With swift, running steps Amanda gained the upper gallery to keep the nurse under observation.

The woman moved out the front gate and along the drive until she was lost beyond the screen of the woods. She did not look back.

Chapter Eleven

"AMANDA: There you are," Sophia said, coming toward her as she re-entered the house. "I've been looking for you. Would you mind lending me a hand . . . literally?"

"Of course," Amanda said, closing the door to the gallery behind her.

"I'm just finishing tying the bows on the last of the fresh bouquets of chrysanthemums. A person needs three hands for that," Sophia said with a smile as they made their way down the stairs to the sitting room. "Marta was to help me with them, but she's gone off somewhere and everyone else has deserted us . . . though you can be sure Jason will be back late this afternoon with some cutting remarks if we aren't ready to go."

Sophia's cordiality might be due to a need for assistance, but somehow Amanda doubted it. She accompanied her warily.

"If you will just hold the bunches of ribbon I have formed into loops, I'll wrap this wire around them and twist it, so?"

"Yes, I see." Amanda picked up the mass of yellow ribbon. Several loops slipped out of place and she carefully secured them. They worked in silence while Amanda waited. There was nothing here that Sophia could not have handled alone if she had so wished.

As Sophia twisted the soft copper wire, she glanced at Amanda from the corner of her eyes. "I suppose you will be leaving soon?"

"I imagine," Amanda answered.

"In the morning, perhaps?"

Amanda flicked a look from her lashes. "I'm not sure. Why?"

"I . . . thought maybe a small celebration tonight would be in order. We always have a late dinner on All Hallows' Eve, and I thought a bottle of wine, to toast the happy couple, would be in order."

"Oh?"

"Forgive me for anticipating your news, my dear, but you know you can't keep a secret in this house."

"You will be . . . disappointed, then, to hear that I haven't given Nathaniel my answer." That should give Sophia pause.

"The answer is yes, of course? You couldn't let such a worthy man slip through your fingers."

Worthy. Yes, that described Nathaniel. "I rather thought you were convinced Nathaniel is after my money?"

"That was before I met the man," she objected with a

laugh that had a forced sound. She moved to several bouquets that lay scattered on papers over a table where she began to wire the ribbon about the bare stems. "You do intend to have him, don't you?"

"I'm not sure."

"You don't want to keep him dangling forever. He might decide he doesn't care for the match either."

"In that case we will both be better off, won't we, if we are so changeable?"

"Oh, it's easy to be flippant, but marriage is a serious matter."

"Marriage? Or just being married?"

"I . . . don't understand you."

"Marriage to a certain man or just . . . being married?"

"Are you suggesting that I . . ."

"That you have a somewhat different point of view."

"So would you, my girl, if you had no money, nothing. If you had seen your youth slipping away with all the presentable men gone to war, and, at last, found younger women carrying off the matrimonial prizes!"

"Sophia . . ."

"Oh, spare me your enthusiasm, or your platitudes!"

"I will not rush into marriage."

"Rush? You have been engaged to this man for months."

"So I have. That should tell me something, shouldn't it?"

"Oh, very well then," she said in a tight voice, "do as you please. But don't blame me if you live to regret it!"

"No, I won't," Amanda agreed as she closed the door quietly behind her.

Though she had kept her temper and said nothing she

regretted while she was with Sophia, now anger slowly grew within her. How could Nathaniel have discussed his proposal . . . and his sureness of her answer! . . . with that woman? She was bitterly disappointed in him. It was a betrayal of their relationship, of their plans, and of the sane and sensible future they had laid out together.

Then why, a quiet voice within asked, was she angry? Why wasn't she hurt and disillusioned? Why did she have this urge to fly into a rage and create a final scene rather than to assuage her pain in his arms?

Her face thoughtful, she mounted the stairs to her room.

At last the time to leave for the cemetery drew near. A carriage and Nathaniel's gig stood before the gate. Hampers of food and drink; chicken, ham, baked potatoes, pie and cake, tea, chilled wine, and hot coffee, had been piled into the carriage along with all the beaded, paper, and natural offerings of flowers. There had been a kind of hectic gaiety about Sophia, like an excited hostess at a party, as she saw to the placement of everything carried out by Theo and Jason. She had dressed with extravagance also, at least to Amanda's eyes, in a many-flounced gown of dark blue taffeta trimmed with black braid and a black silk hat with white and blue plumes curling about the brim. Amanda, in her dress and matching cloak with a simple gray weave felt austere in comparison, nearly as plain as the men in their dark suits with black armbands.

"Are we ready?" Sophia asked then answered herself. "No. Where is Marta? Perhaps someone should go up . . . no, here she is. All right then . . ."

Marta had returned as stealthily as she had gone. Now, her face carrying a flush of high color and her eyes looking peculiarly determined, she sailed out of the door. Gathering voluminous skirts of an ugly brown about her, she followed Sophia's gesture and climbed into the carriage.

"Theo has said he will drive this vehicle. I will ride with Marta to look after my creations. Amanda, I'm sure you prefer to drive with Nathaniel in the gig. Jason . . ."

"My horse is saddled and waiting."

"Oh? I rather hoped you would come into the carriage with us. It looks so much like rain we may all be glad of a roof and doors around us before the evening is over."

Jason cast a glance around the pewter sky but he made no comment, and after a moment's hesitation Sophia climbed into the carriage and shut the door behind her with an irritated slam.

Then in a flurry Theo scrambled to the carriage box, Jason mounted, and Nathaniel handed Amanda into the gig and climbed up beside her. He slapped the reins against the horse's rump and with a jerk, the procession started.

For a little way Jason rode even with the gig talking in desultory fashion to Nathaniel, but finally he dropped back, and Amanda could hear his voice raised slightly as he spoke to the others above the noise of the carriage following.

The damp wind of their movements blew against her face, and she pulled her cloak more closely around her to shut out the penetrating chill. Like Sophia, she could feel the prospect of rain in the air, a cold rain presaging winter. The autumn was almost gone. The leaves had left nothing but the brown tatters of their spring costumes hanging on the trees. The weeds that lined the roads were dry and sere. Still, it was early for winter. Fall—the rich, pleasant Indian Summer that passed for fall of the year in the South—usually lingered until after Thanksgiving.

"Comfortable?" Nathaniel broke into her reverie.

"Yes," she answered shortly, remembering her anger with him.

She noticed the glance he slanted at her, but she averted her face.

"Amanda? Is . . . something wrong?"

"What could be wrong?" she asked perversely.

They drove on for a few moments in silence. "You are not yourself," he said decisively.

"I thought you were of the opinion that I have not been myself for some time?"

"Very true."

"I could almost say the same of you."

He considered that in silence. "Has something happened that I don't know of?"

Amanda allowed herself to remember the evening before when for a few short moments Jason had held her in his arms. A delicate color burned on her cheeks.

"I asked you a question, Amanda," he insisted, and because the pompous assurance of his tone annoyed her, she lashed out at him.

"I'm not sure you have the right to know anything of my affairs, Nathaniel."

"What does that mean?" he asked, frowning as he divided his attention between her face and his driving.

"It means I'm no longer certain anything that occurs or is spoken of between us will remain private."

"If I had some idea of what you are getting at . . ."

"I'm referring to the fact that you discussed your proposal to me with Sophia—I can only assume, before you spoke to me."

"Now, Amanda, it wasn't that way at all. We were talking and the subject came up and she mentioned what a good opportunity it would be . . . "

"So the whole thing was her idea!"

"I didn't say that!"

"Don't you see what she was doing? She was trying to maneuver us into marriage to suit her convenience."

"I don't see that at all. Why should she care whether we marry now or later?"

She should have foreseen that question. Now she did not know how to answer. "She is jealous and . . . and terribly possessive of Jason. She lost him once to a . . . a younger woman and would like to make certain it doesn't happen again."

She thought that for a moment he looked a trifle conscious of the force of her argument, then his face closed in and he began to defend his position.

"Utter nonsense. How can you think such a thing with Amelia barely in her grave?"

"It's true. Sophia as much as said so."

"Really, Amanda. You talk as if she had something to fear from you."

"No, but it may be that she *thinks* she does, which amounts to the same thing."

He shook his head emphatically. "I can't believe it."

He was so obtuse, so phlegmatic, he had to see something for himself before it became real for him. "Are you doubting my work, Nathaniel?"

"Not your word, but perhaps your understanding," he stated firmly.

"Nathaniel! You . . ."

"Please, let's not quarrel, Amanda. You aren't yourself . . ."

"Really!"

"You haven't recovered from your accident, and if the truth was known, I think you were more affected by Amelia's unfortunate death than you realize. Your nerves are strained."

"I am, in fact, a total incompetent! Given to daydreams and nightmares and with only a tolerable understanding of what goes on about me! Next you'll be saying I'm no better than poor Carl!"

"You're exaggerating . . ."

"I thought you, at least, could be depended upon to support and help me, Nathaniel. But you, you have to see the dragon first, don't you? You can't take my word that he is there."

"Are you going to harp back to that possession nonsense? If so, then yes, you're right. I will have to see it first!"

"I would like to accommodate you, but unfortunately I have no control over it."

"Then there's nothing more to be said, is there?"

"No," she agreed, her voice suddenly tired. "I don't suppose there is."

There were quite a number of buggies and wagons around the church; the horses held their heads down, their tails patiently switching at flies as if they had been there for some time. Women dressed in their best tie-back dresses, looped and braided, and wearing bonnets of questionable becomingness, stood talking in groups while a conclave of stern, bewhiskered men was being held near the hitching rack. Children ran here and there with a spotted mongrel or two chasing breathlessly at their heels. Hoes and rakes leaned against the fence, while within the railings industrious . . . or playful . . . young boys still plied whitewash on tombstones made of transported iron rock or raked the leaves that had been blown in drifts against the fence. Even from where she sat Amanda could see the bouquets of beautiful flowers that lay on the freshly scraped graves. New flowers, new earth exposed with every blade of grass removed. Was that supposed to be a reminder of the rawness of the loss of loved ones?

She almost opened her mouth to comment to Nathaniel, then she closed it. She doubted Nathaniel would agree, and she felt no real necessity to share her thoughts with him.

As they pulled up she jumped down unaided. Some of these people must have been here all day, she thought, as she noticed covered dishes and baskets reposing in the back of several wagons. A few people seemed to be taking their leave even now as the gray day imperceptibly darkened into evening.

As the carriage, with Jason beside it, drew up behind them, greetings were called. A few men came toward Jason with their hands outstretched, but Amanda was quick to notice that no such gesture was made toward Sophia though there was a tentative smile or two of recognition.

As Nathaniel was introduced into that masculine circle, she acknowledged her own presentation with a stiff nod. Nathaniel might smile and shake their hands, but she could not help wondering how many of these upstanding gentlemen had been clothed in a sheet in the front yard of Monteigne a short time ago. As soon as she could, she left them, drifting toward the feminine circle. Marta, like a large, silent shadow, moved beside her. The ground was uneven, and the nurse stumbled, recovered, then stumbled again. A foolish smile passed over her face, and her blue eyes focused somewhere beyond the graveyard. She swayed. "Let me . . ." she muttered, reaching out one large hand.

The sudden dead weight on her arm made Amanda sag. "Are you all right?"

"Yes, let me . . . just catch my . . . breath."

"Did you get down from the carriage too fast?" Amanda began sympathetically, and then she caught the smell of brandy fumes.

Drunk, her mind registered, but she stood still with Marta's fingers clinging to her arm as to a lifeline.

"P'raps if I could sit down," Marta suggested in a thick whisper.

"There is a bench over against the fence."

"Would you be so kind, *fräulein*?" she said, tugging on Amanda's arm.

Stifling a feeling of repugnance, Amanda led her to the bench. An elderly lady in rusty black was seated at one end, but it did not seem to matter to Marta.

"Must speak to you," she said, "of great . . . great import . . ." And she hiccuped gently.

"Yes, what is it?" Amanda spoke in a neutral tone but her attention was caught. Was the woman as drunk as she wanted to appear?

"I go. I have been told to go, and I dare not refuse, on pain of death."

"Go? Where?"

"I will not say. I have hired a man. He will come to-night, and I will run far, far away from this place of sad memories, this place of sad regret. I will go far and never return, perhaps to the homeland I will go. I have never seen it. My mother . . ."

"Marta," she interrupted this maundering recital. "Who told you to go? Who has threatened you?"

"The one I fear, have always feared. Madame Amelia never feared, no, never. It was . . . it was . . . a . . . pity." With shaking hands she reached for the net bag, an oversized reticule, that hung from one beefy wrist. Drawing the strings open with difficulty she plunged in a hand and took out a tonic bottle. Pulling the stopper she drank, shudderingly.

"What is that?" Amanda asked, watching her carefully.

She laughed with a husky, wheezing sound. "You know," she said with a bleary playfulness, lifting a limp finger. "You know, you know."

"If you keep this up you won't be able to . . . to leave tonight!"

"Don't worry. I'll do it. I paid my money. The man with the cart will come. I know. I know, I know." She laughed at her feeble joke.

"You haven't told me who ordered you away."

"No, not what I wanted. Wanted to tell you . . . I like you . . . A . . . Amanda. Wanted to tell you . . . what? Something. Have I forgotten? No. No, it was come. Come, too. Quick, quick. Before it's too late. You're not Amelia, not safe."

Safe? Amelia? But there was no time. "Marta, tell me something. Did you . . . was it a . . . something you made up . . . about Amelia and the baby? Was it?"

"Why? Why should it matter now? When we're leaving."

"Then it was a lie."

"No! Never said that. Never did. Never will."

"Jason denied it. And Theo."

Marta smiled, the heavy skin of her face creasing. "Men!" she said and suddenly burst out laughing.

"Shh. Be quiet," Amanda said and immediately the nurse sobered, but there was such a strange gleam in her eye that Amanda was half afraid to question her further, afraid that raucous, mocking noise would echo again across the silent mounded ground behind them.

Amanda sat beside Marta trying to think. But it was impossible in that gathering. She felt exposed, as if she was being eyed in curiosity. One or two women came up to her with their condolences as the news circulated who she was. They had known Amelia slightly, having seen her in town or at church. None were real friends, however, and when they learned that Amanda would not be staying in their community they moved away, satisfied that they had performed their social duty.

The Monteigne family plot had been cleared and the tombs scrubbed in readiness. Amelia's grave was neatly mounded once more, the vase standing firm, ready. Who had done that? Jason and Theo? Or had Jason merely issued the necessary orders? Not that it mattered. Perhaps that was where he had gone . . . was it only this morning? It seemed a hundred years ago.

She offered to help Sophia place the wreaths and bouquets but was refused. Like a general placing troops to the best advantage she parceled out the creations she had made on the various graves of the Monteigne and Abercrombie family plots.

Evening drew on and they straggled back to the carriage to eat their cold supper before the last feeble light had left the sky. They were growing chilled with nothing to do but stand and talk in increasingly hushed voices and admire the floral handiwork of the women of the community. A couple of bottles of wine brought to wash down the chicken and ham and potatoes, and the pickles, the spiced peaches and cake also took away the incipient cemeterial ague.

The glow they caused did not last long, however, as the autumn darkness closed in.

When the last of the food had been put away, the girandoles inside the church were lighted, and the people outside trickled into the building.

Small and unpretentious on the outside, the interior of the church was beautiful. The ceiling was arched in sections like ribs with spiral posts for support. The floor was of polished wood; the pews were curved to support the back and neck of the occupant, and cushioned with ruby velvet. Behind the altar was a reredos of carved wood that had been gilded and painted. It represented the Madonna and Child in the center panel with the figures of saints on either side.

Sophia was involved in a long recital of the difficulties Jason's mother and father had faced in having the reredos shipped from France as Father Metoyer arrived.

The mass for the suffering souls in Purgatory—who had to expiate the sins they had committed on earth before they could enter Heaven—was a solemn emotional experience. For Amanda, it was in the nature of a memorial service for her cousin whose name was read along with those others who had died in the past twelve months. More moving still was the moment when the priest took a candle and lighted the taper of the person standing nearest to him, who in turn lighted that of the next, until everyone in the building held a flame, symbol of rebirth and everlasting life, in their hand.

That done, they filed from the church, protecting the flames with their cupped hands as they emerged into the windy darkness. They made their winding way into the cemetery behind Father Metoyer who carried a small font of holy water with which he sprinkled the graves. As each grave was blessed, those who were related to the deceased placed a burning candle before the headstone. A few guttered out in the whipping wind, but most were protected enough to continue burning.

It was not long before they stood in the midst of dozens of glimmering pinpoints of light. The black night, the wind, the encroaching forest that crowded up to the fence enclosing the graveyard, the myriad flickering, dancing lights, sent a shiver along Amanda's nerves.

A final prayer, and Father Metoyer mounted his horse and was gone. Somewhere another congregation waited to hear a Mass for their dead. One by one, other families followed the lead of the priest, kneeling to say a private prayer, then climbed stiffly into their wagons and buggies, gigs and carriages, and rattled away, leaving their candles to burn down alone.

"When will we go?" Marta asked under her breath, not waiting for an answer as she once again had recourse to the tonic bottle in her net bag.

Sophia took her up sharply. "We will go last, of course. The party from Monteigne is always last to leave. Someone has to stay until the candles melt away to prevent fire and protect the church. It is a holy vigil—one never shirked."

They were quiet then, standing, the three men bare-headed, before the grave of Amelia. No one spoke, no one mentioned prayer, and yet, it was a moment of reverence, a moment of remembered loss, a moment to consider that in not too many years they also would be old bones beneath the cool, sandy earth joining those who had gone before.

In that silent, windswept moment they heard the last of the wagons roll away out of the churchyard, and they were left alone.

Marta sighed heavily and shifted her feet, then caught at Amanda's arm. Amanda felt the tremor of distress that shook her.

"Look, there," she said pointing into the darkness beyond the glow of the candles.

As Amanda swung her gaze in the direction the nurse indicated, a sweeping gust of wind swirled about them, and some of the far candle flames near the wood danced, flattened, and died. But there was nothing else to be seen in the darkness.

"Where? I don't see a thing."

"It's . . . gone now. 'Twere a demon . . . or a grendel."

"A what?"

"A . . . what is the word? An . . . ugly beast!"

Sophia, becoming aware of their conversation broke in. "Impossible! You're seeing things, and I for one can't say I'm surprised."

"No bickering, please," Theo said in a quiet, strained voice.

"Bickering? Who's bickering? This fool said something

about an animal of some sort over there." She waved toward the woods.

"Not an animal. A grendel . . . a . . . dragon. Beowulf tore off his arm . . ."

"Please," Theo's voice had turned sharp. "Remember where you are."

"I remember," Marta said with an attempt at a firm nod. "I remember, but I would like to forget." Fumbling in her bag she drew forth her small bottle and took a deep pull. "I would like to forget," she repeated, then taking a deep breath she muttered, "I will . . ."

Suddenly her eyelids fluttered down. She sagged, then like an aerialist's balloon collapsing, fell to the ground.

On reflex Amanda caught at her but her strength was no match for the weight of the nurse. She was nearly dragged down too before she stumbled, regaining her balance.

"What the . . ." Theo exclaimed turning, but he was too late to help.

Jason reached her in time to keep her head from striking the ground while reaching out a quick hand to Amanda to steady her. Nathaniel, as though he resented Jason's touching her, reached out and caught Amanda's forearm, sending Jason a hard look.

"Well, for heaven's sake," Sophia exclaimed angrily.

"Unconscious," Jason said after a cursory examination.

"Passed out, you mean," Sophia said. "If this isn't the most disgusting thing!"

"I suspected her tonic had a strong smell," Theo agreed.

"We can't leave her here on the cold, damp ground . . ."

"She's a hefty weight," Nathaniel said. "We ought to

see if we can bring her around. Neither of you ladies would have smelling salts with you, I suppose?"

Amanda shook her head. Sophia said, "Not on an outing like this!"

"Water then . . ."

"I doubt it would do any good. From the looks of it I'd say Marta has been at the bottle most of the day. She probably won't come to for half the night! Theo, Nathaniel, I have her shoulders. If you will just . . . that's right. Careful."

It was an awkward burden, that completely relaxed, large woman. Jason looked back. "Sophia, from the sound of her breathing I'd say she needs a little more air. Could you . . ."

"Probably laced within an inch of her life . . . for what good it does. Yes, I'm coming. I'm coming."

She would follow them in a moment, Amanda thought. Sophia might need help, and they would possibly go home earlier than they had intended, though not before extinguishing the candles surely.

But now she was glad to have this moment alone, a moment to try to sense the presence of the spirit of her cousin, not her ghost. . . she was not so superstitious, despite her growing belief in Jason's theory . . . but only the essence of her personality, remembered charm, and vitality. She would like to conjure up the vision of the girl she had been, not the woman she had become. She would like to think of the girl lying there not as Jason's wife but as her cousin, think of her . . . and bid her a last good-bye, among the flickering candle flames.

And so when the others were out of sight beyond the church she swung back, staring at the headstone of the grave before her.

AMELIA CONSTANCE TRENT MONTEIGNE
born March 14, 1852
died July 21, 1871
Beloved, death is a gentle keeper.

Perhaps it was true, what was written there, perhaps death was more gentle for Amelia than life.

She thought of her cousin, so gay and happy, and of Jason and their elopement. It was odd how seldom things turn out exactly as planned. "Happily ever after" was more than a matter of intent. It was work and tolerance and shared joy. It was love but not necessarily romance. When had the happily-ever-after turned into a faded dream? When had it become a nightmare?

Did it matter? It was over. Death had taken the fear as well as the happiness. Death. The gentle keeper.

With a sigh that caught in her throat Amanda bowed her head. Opening her eyes after a moment, she turned away, catching at her skirt to keep it from the dew-wet sand. The wind whipped among the trees with a mournful sound and came rushing toward her making her glance fearfully up at the dark sky.

When she looked back a figure stood before her, a figure whose rags flapped about him like a scarecrow, whose pale face shimmered in the fitful light of the sputtering candles, who had beside him, like some ancient guardian beast, the dog Cerberus. Marta's grendel.

Carl.

Chapter
Twelve

"CARL," she whispered. Then added more loudly, "You startled me."

The dog growled, and Carl put a staying hand on his head.

"What is it?"

Still he did not answer. He was real enough, she thought nervously, for she could see the glitter of his eyes.

"Did . . . did you want something? Jason? Or Theo?" Was that high-pitched voice hers? She must control that. It could not be good for him to suspect that she was frightened of him. Then she jumped as he spoke.

"Where is my Madame?"

"Why . . . Jason told you. She is dead."

"No. They put her in a box and shut the lid and carried her away. The box is there, under the dirt, but not my Madame, never my Madame Amelia. I won't believe it!

You took her place! But you are not my Madame! Where is she?"

"Please, Carl, you must believe me. She died."

"You. You sent her away from me. You came with the other man. You came to take the place of my Madame. You have her hair, her face. Sometimes I look and I see my Madame staring from your eyes. Where is she? What have you done to her?"

Fear mixed with revulsion crept over Amanda. "You don't know what you're saying," she whispered, her hands clenched so tightly that her nails were cutting into her palms.

"I know!" he cried. "I know!"

"No! I've told you but you won't listen. You don't want to know. Amelia is dead. She's dead, I tell you!"

Now Carl's face was contorted with an infantile rage. She could see his lips moving. She could see men, running, from the corner of her eye. She could see the bared teeth of the dog Cerberus, his raised bristles, and straining muscles. Did Carl give a signal, an infinitesimal movement of his hand? Or was it only the rage in his voice that unleashed the dog to the attack?

"If she is dead . . . then . . . you killed her!" Carl screamed and, obedient to the wish if not the command, Cerberus gathered himself and sprang!

Blood and bone, fur and fangs she saw him launch himself, saw his yellow eyes gleam red, burning into hers.

A shout, a strangeness in her mind, a blank, featureless moment when out of the past interdependence she cried, "Amelia!"

And the dog at the last moment turned his head. His body struck her, and they fell to the ground. They lay stunned a breathless instant. Then she sensed the movement as Cerberus rolled over on his belly and crawled toward her. In a moment she felt a warm roughness on her fingers as the dog licked her hand in repentance. She raised herself to touch his head in benediction, in forgiveness.

"Goddamned crazy idiot! What do you mean? I thought you had killed her!" Theo yelled as he came to a breathless halt, dropping to one knee beside Amanda.

"She killed my Madame. She killed my Madame! She killed . . ."

"Shut up that screeching! Amanda didn't kill Amelia! You did!"

The silence felt like a blow on the ears. Candles dimmed as the wind, gathering force, picked up sandy dirt and flung it, stinging, against them. Jason stepped forward to put his hand on the dog's collar, his eyes scanning quickly over Amanda as she lay braced on one arm. Sophia raised one hand to her eyes against the wind. They did not speak and, with her heart thudding sickeningly against her chest, neither did Amanda. She could not.

"No," Carl said shaking his head. "No."

Theo leaned toward him his lips drawn back, so intent on the thrust he was about to make and his pleasure in it that he was unaware or uncaring, that he had an audience.

"Oh, yes. Yes! You gave her medicine. You remember, medicine in a green bottle with a black stopper. I poured it out for you and you carried it to her room. You watched while she drank."

It was a long moment before Carl spoke, then his voice carried that chilling note of sanity he could sometimes evoke. "You . . . you let me kill her."

The aching horror in Carl's voice seemed to touch Theo with remorse. He put out his hand. "She needed to die.

267

She wanted to die, Carl. And I could not do it. I could not. You helped her, Carl, you helped her!"

But Carl backed away. "No, no."

Theo stood, took a hasty step toward him, but Carl stooped and swept up the lighted candle from Amelia's grave then two others in quick succession. Brandishing them at Theo in half defense, half aggression he shouted a wordless, animal sound of bitter, unbearable loss. The candle flames flared and dimmed but burned on.

"Carl!" Theo said, an arm before his face, anger overcoming his remorse. "Put those down!"

But Carl thrust the candles at him once more and then, as Theo fell back, he whirled and ran toward the woods, his terrible, crazed laughter sweeping back to them on the wind.

They watched him leaping, loping, rags fluttering in the weird light, saw him merge with the black shadows of the woods.

"Oh, Theo, Theo." It was Amanda's voice, chiding, pleading, commanding. But she had not meant to speak.

Theo turned to stare at her, his brown eyes wide and liquid. Then he straightened his shoulders with a deep breath and turned his face back toward the woods. He looked back one final time at Amanda, then he ran after Carl.

Beside her the dog gathered himself, his ears pricked forward as if to heed a silent command. Amanda, abruptly aware of the stiffness of his fur beneath her fingers, lifted her hand from his neck. Released from the last restraint he bounded to his feet and raced after the two men.

"Stay with the women," Jason told Nathaniel before he followed at a run.

The sound of their hurried progress through the underbrush came to those who waited for a few minutes, then all was quiet.

Nathaniel helped Amanda to her feet, and she stood, her fingers biting into his arm, listening.

It was Sophia who first smelled the smoke. It came on the wind, a faint acrid intimation of the holocaust to come.

The darkness hid the first gray plumes of smoke from them but soon they could see the sparks, like darting orange fireflies, rising above the black spikes of the tree tops. Then beneath the smoke soared the first shooting yellow arrows of flames, and with them came the ominous crackling of burning brush and dried foliage.

"That idiot has set the woods on fire," Nathaniel said unnecessarily. "This wind is fanning it right toward us. If we stay here we may get caught in its path."

"They'll all be killed," Sophia cried, her hand to her mouth. "Why don't they come out?"

"Jason." Amanda said the name softly, her thoughts crystallizing around that one word. With the smell of smoke in her nostrils she felt herself, her every sense alive to fear and a bitter, unbelievable, but undeniable truth. She had come, somehow, to care more for this man, her dead cousin's husband, in a few short days, than she did for the man whose arm she clung to so desperately.

Now the wind tore at their hair and clothes, carrying in its ferocity the heat of the fire, laden with black cinders and sand. Smoke swirled around them making their eyes stream.

"Come on!" Nathaniel shouted to make himself heard. "I've got to get you three women out of this!"

He dragged at Amanda. Sophia started back toward

the carriages, to the horses, who were plunging and neighing with a rising terror.

Amanda could not bear to leave. "The candles, we must put them out," she said, grasping at anything to delay. But then looking about her she saw that the wind had done that chore. The graves lay dark, huddled to the ground. The glow of light about them was from the fire!

But no, there was one candle left, a single candle shielded from the wind by a headstone and a large vase. Twisting away from Nathaniel, Amanda ran toward it, plucked it from its holder and upended it, ready to snuff it out in the soft earth. A gust of smoke caught her and she began to cough, turning away from the woods. Then as she looked through tear-filled eyes she saw a man stagger into the open.

"Jason!" she cried, seeing his burden only as she began to run.

His clothes smoldered, his hair and brows were singed, and the tracks of the tears of smoke irritation made white streaks in the grime on his face. The body in his arms appeared lifeless, the head thrown back and the arms and legs dangling helplessly.

"It's Theo," he said as she neared him, but she had to read his lips for his words were drowned in the thunder that rumbled overhead.

Lightning forked from the black sky as if trying to meet the leaping flames. Darkness closed in around them. There was no need for words of warning or hurry. Their danger was all too clear.

They ran, stumbling among the graves in the dimness, through the gate and past the church, orange-hued in the gloom as its whiteness reflected the fire, to the carriage.

Theo was lifted inside as great fat drops of rain began to fall. Thunder combined with a hissing sound of wet heat around them, and then they were moving at a runaway pace set by the terrified horses. Behind them clouds of steaming black smoke billowed like mountains into the sky. Behind them lay the fire. And somewhere in its seething, blinding mass, hiding and hidden, lay Carl.

They found Carl when the coals had died at last in the hearts of the trees and the smoke had blown away with the wind. His body was charred almost beyond recognition but he had died, so they said, of smoke inhalation. Was that meant to be a solace? It did not help nearly so much as the finding of the body of Cerberus at his side.

The funeral was held in the little church built by the Monteignes. Its back wall was somewhat smoked and the grass around it had crisped into sooty curls, but the rain, coming like a smothering wet blanket, had saved the building. Still the fresh white headstone they placed in the cemetery, near Amelia's grave, looked strange, out of place, among the other gray markers. In years to come when memories grew short, they would always be able to determine the date of the fire that nearly destroyed their church by the difference in the color of the headstones.

Despite a valiant effort and the suppurating wounds of his terrible burns, Theo did not die. He lived to lie on his bed and beg ceaselessly for death. Once, in his pain and despair and self-blame, he snatched the bottle of laudanum from Amanda's hand.

She struck it from his mouth before he could drink.

"Why?" he asked as he fell back gray-faced on his pillow, watching the dark medicine bubbling out onto the floor. "Why won't you let me die?"

"I can't. I can't do it. I can't make that kind of decision."

"I can," he said, his eyes hard.

She stared at him, remembering, accusing, wanting him to remember that he had made that decision once for Amelia and once for himself, but neither time had he been able to carry it out.

At last he turned away, his eyes closed, the lines of anguish deep about his mouth.

"You win," he said, but he added, "for today. Only for today."

"Theo . . ." she said in a soft helplessness. She could not hate this man for what he had done, she found. She could only pity him.

He turned to look at her, his eyes searching her face. He seemed to hold his breath. Then he let it out with the whisper of a laugh, set his teeth, and turned to the wall.

Nathaniel accosted her as she came slowly from the sickroom.

"How much longer are you going to stay here?" he asked without preamble. "I've got to be getting back to my office. Been gone too long already."

She looked down at the tray in her hands. "I don't know, Nathaniel. Someone must stay with Theo night and day to keep him from . . . doing anything foolish."

"The man deserves to die."

"I think, sometimes, that forcing him to live is the worst thing we could do to him," she said, making as if to pass him.

He put out his hand and caught her arm. "Why are you staying, Amanda? This man," he tilted his head toward Theo's door, "means nothing to you."

"I've told you. Someone has to stay with him."

"Then let his sister do it. Let Jason hire some help, another nurse, like that Marta who ran off."

"I couldn't. What would they think if I left while I was still needed?"

"That's just it. They don't need you. Listen to me, Amanda. I'm tired of being kept on a leading rein. I'm leaving in the morning. I want you to come with me. If not . . ." He took a deep breath, "if not, I'll go alone."

"Oh, Nathaniel, I wish you would try to understand . . ."

"I . . . think I do, Amanda. I wonder if you do?" His eyes were serious, but not patient. "I will be leaving at first daylight, in case you change your mind."

"I don't know what you mean," she said, but he was already walking away down the hall.

Before Nathaniel left, the emotion . . . whether pride, indignation, or merely exasperation . . . that had caused him to issue his ultimatum made him also bring the thoughts hovering in all their minds out into the open.

At the supper table that night he waited until dessert had been placed before them, then he leaned back in his chair. His voice, when he spoke, was quiet but firm. "I will be leaving in the morning, but before I go there are a few things I would like cleared up. For instance, this accident of Amanda's the first day. What really took place there? I understand this Carl was present. Was he responsible?"

Sophia toyed with her fork. Jason stared at Nathaniel, a thoughtful look in his dark eyes.

"Please, Nathaniel," Amanda said.

"No, I want to know. What's the use of keeping quiet?

I'm a little tired of these unexplained events and secret passions."

"Some things can't be explained."

"Hogwash!"

Jason spoke at last. "What do you think happened?"

"From what Amanda says, I would say she was given a little push!"

Silence.

"Why?" Jason's voice held nothing but curiosity, still there was a flatness in his tone that spoke of controlled anger.

"For the necklace, that's why."

"Oh, Nathaniel, there is no need for this. I told you Jason refused the necklace."

"All right, all right! I suppose it's possible it was an accident, but I beg leave to doubt it. There have been too many accidents and peculiar happenings around here, and I intend to get to the bottom of it."

Amanda's face was flushed with embarrassment. She looked at the wall behind his head, wishing there was some way she could make him stop.

"Well," he demanded of her, "can you deny it?"

"Perhaps . . . perhaps I only imagined much of it. It could have been all in my head, like the other times, the times I can't remember when I walked and talked and acted unlike myself . . ."

For a moment he appeared nonplussed, then he blinked and a look of rejection made his face blank. It was as if he refused to think of the possibilities her words conjured up, as if his refusal could deny the existence of such a possibility.

"Are you trying to say you imagined the runaway?

What about the gum balls . . . or whatever it was that frightened the horse? They were real enough."

"Nathaniel, I wish you wouldn't," she whispered miserably. She didn't know why talking about these things disturbed her so, but it did.

Nathaniel ignored her, leaning back in his chair.

"Nobody wants to talk? Well, I'll tell you then. That day of the runaway when you were all so set on chasing Carl? Well, I had nothing against the man. I sort of lagged behind after a minute or two. I saw who dropped back and crept around picking up sweet gum balls. Being a curious fellow, I decided to see what was taking place. By the time I could see what was going on the horses were off, and it was too late to prevent it. Luckily no great harm was done. I thought that I would be taking Amanda away soon. I figured no real harm was meant by a jealous attack like that. I'm not so sure now. At any rate I held my tongue but kept watch. I went out of my way to make a confidant of this person. And sure enough, I was enlisted in a plot to get rid of Amanda . . . in any way I could or would."

He stopped for a moment, his eyes on the table. Then, quite deliberately, he looked at Sophia. "I think . . . though I have no proof, mind, that this person gave Amanda just a little push that first night with the intention of keeping her around long enough to get hold of the necklace. It must have been a shock when it disappeared. But came the discovery of what proved the worst mistake. Amanda was not a milk-and-water miss like Amelia. She was dangerously strong in the kind of grace and character that appeals to a man. Hence, the decision to scare her away, an injured woman. It made little difference how

. . . or whether the experience proved fatal. If one thing did not get rid of her, try another. Work on her fiancé. Frighten him and maybe he would take Amanda away with him. Arrange a visit from the nightriders, not a difficult thing to do when a close relative, who rode with them as a solace to his grief and guilt, was cooperative."

"You don't mean . . . ?" Amanda could not finish the question. Theo. Nathaniel was trying to say without a blatant accusation that it had been Theo who rode with the Knights of the White Gardenia.

"Exactly," Nathaniel said, seeing her gray eyes fixed in horror on Sophia. "Fear didn't move the fiancé, then perhaps jealousy would be the lever? That one came close to working. Now, I could put a name to this troublemaker but after my subterfuge it hardly seems the gentlemanly thing to do. However, I will bend my principles a little if it becomes necessary for Amanda's happiness."

Abruptly Sophia's nerve broke. She slammed her chair back and jumped to her feet. "It's not true! Lies, nothing but lies! You made it all up out of whole cloth! Lies! Lies!"

"Now why would I do that?" Nathaniel said gently. "I have nothing to gain, nothing at all."

"You're a stupid fool, that's what you are, full of the notions of what is becoming in a gentleman!" Sophia attacked him bitterly. "You could have won if you had only had a little resolution."

"You can't force happiness, Sophia," Nathaniel said with a seriousness that made him more attractive than he had been at any time since his arrival. "Scheming and conniving, setting traps—only scare it away. I'm sorry for the hand I took in your plans but I changed nothing, Sophia.

Your chance for happiness was already gone. You saw to that without my help."

Nathaniel left as planned. Amanda walked out to the gate to wait for him. When he pulled the buggy up beside her, she gave him her hand. "I wanted to thank you, Nathaniel," she said, smiling.

"There is no need," he replied, retaining her fingers in his grip. "I owed you something for my blindness."

"I don't understand."

"Over the . . . the spirit of your cousin, or whatever you chose to call her effect on you. I shall never forget the moment when that huge dog leaped for your throat. I expected to see you torn apart, horribly mangled, before my eyes. Then you called your cousin's name, and that beast turned aside in midair. For a few brief seconds, I actually saw a change come over you, a change I cannot explain by logical means. Your face altered in small ways, as did your gestures, and there was a radiance about you. More than that, the dog recognized you, licked your hand, obeyed your unspoken command." He pressed her hand and released it. "If only I had listened to you. The only thing I can do now is ask for your forgiveness and take it as a lesson not to be so pigheaded in the future."

"You are too hard on yourself. I doubt seriously that I would have believed it myself if such a tale had been told to me in the bright light of day. Let us not speak of it anymore. Instead, let me apologize. I am sorry for everything, Nathaniel."

"So am I," he said, answering only the last. "I hope you will always be happy."

Now that she was free, Amanda found herself returning

his smile and his liking with genuine regard. "Thank you. I will wish you the same."

The last were banal words, but what else was there to be said? She stepped back as the buggy began to move. When it was out of sight, she went in to breakfast with Jason.

It was a strained meal with only the two of them. Sophia was gone; she had packed bag, parcels, and trunks, then fled in the night like Marta, except that she had demanded frigidly that Jason drive her and her brother into town.

"What of Theo? What will you do?" Jason had asked, but Sophia had hardly looked at him. "We have taken care of each other for some time. Why should now be any different . . . or of any interest to you?"

But for all her sarcasm, Amanda heard Sophia promise finally to allow Jason the pleasure of seeing that Theo was established with their doctor in his clinic, with nurses to guard him, while she herself was going to a hotel.

"You are very quiet this morning," Jason said.

Amanda looked up nervously. "Yes . . . I suspect it's the . . . letdown."

"You must be tired after all your interrupted nights lately."

She nodded. "Still, it's not just that. Everyone has gone. Everything has changed."

"Yes. You are ready?"

"Yes." She was packed, she wore her traveling dress, and her bonnet hung near to hand on the halltree near the door. She was ready.

"I would like for you to stay, if the situation were different."

She smiled her understanding. Yes, propriety. He had

returned from taking Sophia into town around three in the morning, but he had not slept under his own roof. The conventions. She was unmarried, unchaperoned. Nor had she slept.

"Are you sure you are well enough for this trip?"

Glancing up at him through her lashes, she was gratified to discover true concern in his face.

"Do I look so like a hag then?" she asked with a try at sprightliness.

"You look . . . lovely," he said, which might have been encouraging if he had been looking at her rather than his coffee cup.

She took a bite of biscuit, but felt as if it would choke her.

"So, you are not going to marry your Nathaniel?"

She swallowed with difficulty. "No, I . . . we are not suited."

"It was lucky you discovered it before it was too late."

"Yes . . . wasn't it?" she said only managing to prevent a quaver from invading her voice.

"Marriage is serious. It lasts . . . a lifetime, and it's very easy to be mistaken about the people you think you love."

"I . . . can see how it might be."

"For God's sake, Amanda," he burst out suddenly. "Help me. Don't sit there agreeing with me and saying 'yes, it is' and 'no, it isn't.' Say something."

She looked up, meeting his eyes squarely. "All right, I will say something. I will ask you, did your child die with Amelia?"

"No."

"You seem very sure."

"Why shouldn't I be? She had been . . . ill for some

279

time. I thought I married a woman and got instead a child . . . no, a doll, demanding unquestioning loyalty and worship, not just love. I was supposed to place her and her demands above all else, even our welfare, our security. I must bow to her will . . . or else. There is no tyrant like a beautiful, spoiled young woman. When I refused to bow, she looked elsewhere for subjects. I was too involved with my work, I will admit. I suppose it could even be true that she was neglected. But I will never believe there was a child—mine, or Theo's. I doubt, despite the prattlings of that pathetic old woman who called herself a nurse, that even Amelia believed in enslavement to that extent."

Amanda was not so certain, but she did not argue with him. What did it matter now? "I'm sorry. I shouldn't have brought it up."

Jason sighed, running his fingers through his hair; then he closed his eyes, turning his head to shut out the sight of her face. "No, perhaps not," he agreed.

Amanda pushed back her chair and stood up. "I guess we had better go," she said huskily, turning toward the door.

"Wait, I have something I wanted to give you."

She stopped in the hall, looking back. "Oh?"

He took something from his pocket as he moved toward her. It was wrapped in a silk handkerchief, and he unrolled it into his hand before he handed it to her.

"The collar of Harmonia . . ." she breathed. "Where did it come from?"

"While we were searching for Carl, I came upon his treasure bag. He must have lost it, or hidden it, there where he left the woods. The bag itself was . . . scorched, but the necklace is unhurt."

"I would have hated to never know what had become of it. Thank you, Jason. But are you sure?"

"You're not trying to offer that thing to me again, are you?"

"N . . . no," she said with a shaky laugh.

"Then we had better go."

She nodded but her gaze was still on the necklace. Poor demented Carl. She hoped it had brought him some pleasure. Little else had. To die in an agony of mind and soul and body . . . Carl, with the dog Cerberus. Theo had cast him in the role of Charon, the keeper of the ferry of death. A man with such a job would have needed to be a little mad.

"Don't think of it," Jason said softly.

She looked up to see him standing at the open door, her bag in one hand and an unfamiliar leather case in the other.

"There must be some mistake," she said, coming to his side. "That isn't my bag."

"No, it's mine."

"Oh . . . are you staying in town then?" In town, near Theo . . . and Sophia?

"No, I'm carrying you home, remember?"

"But . . . I thought you were going to take me into town to catch the stage."

"No."

"I . . . if I had known you were going to so much trouble, I could have gone with Nathaniel."

He smiled as he looked into her worried and slightly bewildered face. "Then what would I have done for company?"

"You . . . you were going anyway?"

He set the bags down and gently caught her arms. "Do

you think it will look odd if I stay a few days . . . if there is a room vacant in the hotel . . . visiting my late wife's only relative?"

"Not odd, I suppose."

"Suggestive?" he guessed with resignation.

"Of what?"

"Of a man in torment," he said drawing her to him with a sigh and laying his cheek against her hair. "Dearest Amanda, would you consider me unfeeling . . . if I told you I was thinking of marrying again?"

"Marrying?"

"You, if you will have me after we have known each other longer, and in more settled surroundings. After time has let the memory of these past days fade."

"Jason?" She lifted her head.

"Yes?"

"Are you sure? Are you sure what you feel isn't guilt and some kind of . . . continuation of your love for Amelia? Are you quite certain that, because of the strange things that happened, the times when Amelia seemed to . . . to make herself felt, you are not seeing her in me?"

"Amelia," he said, instead of answering. "Why do you think she came? Remorse perhaps, the desire to right the tragic wrong that had been done, or was it mere revenge?"

"I would prefer to think the first," she whispered.

"So would I. Tell me this too, then. Is she gone? Is this Amanda or Amelia I hold in my arms?"

She drew back, her eyes grave. "I am Amanda."

"And there is no trace of Amelia, no trace of what she might have felt for me?"

"No, Jason. I promise you."

"Then listen to me while I promise you that what I feel

is for you alone. For you, Amanda. I love you for your beauty, but also for your integrity; for the sweetness of your smile, but also for the honesty that shines in your eyes. You are a woman, not a child; someone to love and to cherish, not to worship blindly. You are everything I wanted in a wife when I married Amelia. You have the character that complements the beauty of your face. Oh yes, Amanda," he said, "I'm sure. You have my word. But because I want you to be as certain as I am I will wait a year . . ."

He smiled slowly, gathering her close against him, tipping her chin, his eyes on her smooth warm lips waiting for his kiss. "A year to come to know each other, a year to forget, to talk and to laugh and to draw close. Perhaps in that time we can discover some way to prove what we feel."

"Perhaps," she said, her lashes veiling her eyes before she looked up fearlessly, "perhaps we could begin . . . now."

And so they were married a year and two months later, at Christmas, 1872. Their wedding was small, held in the little chapel that had been built by the Monteignes so long ago.

Amanda wore white satin with pink rosettes draping the fabric, Jason wore gray with a pink rose in his buttonhole. Attending the wedding was Nathaniel with his wife of six months clinging to his arm, a young thing with fine, fluffy, blond hair. Sophia was there also, her head high and a bright smile on her face. She was accompanied by a florid gentleman with salt and pepper mustachios, and the expansive chest and humor of a successful town merchant. The ceremony was simple and very quiet, so quiet that as the vows were exchanged the sound of a seam ripping in a glove was audible in the back of the church. Sophia carried one glove of white kid in her hand as she left.

Theo was not among the guests. His burns had healed but his depression had deepened, strengthening his determination to end his life. During that past summer he had nearly succeeded in cutting his throat with his own straight-edge razor. The doctors, wise at last, diagnosed his condition as extreme melancholia, and Sophia was forced to commit him to the insane ward of the charity hospital in New Orleans. There he seemed to improve for a time, until he received a visit from a large Germanic woman in a nurse's apron, as she was described later, who came upon him sitting by himself in the common room. She appeared more than a little tipsy, they said, weaving back and forth, blubbering into her hands like a penitent might in the confessional.

When she was gone Theo sat still for a long time, then suddenly erupted, raving that he had killed them both, the woman he loved, and his own unborn child. In the strength of beserk grief he managed to break away from the attendants and ran out into the maze of busy streets. He was found next morning, floating in the river.

A wedding trip was undertaken, a fairly long one to the fashionable resort of Saratoga Springs in the East. But Jason and Amanda did not linger long. Monteigne was waiting.

Amanda spent her first year of married life redecorating the house. Theo's old room on the front was redone as a master bedroom of muted colors of brown and old rose, a popular scheme just then. It did not matter that the room was not one of a suite. She and Jason never slept apart in all the years of their married life.

Amelia's old room, stripped bare of her things . . . Jason did not say what he had done with them and Amanda did not ask . . . was done last. In shades of yellow with white, it made a sunny room, perfect for a nursery, though to Amanda a trace of violet perfume always seemed to linger in the vast armoire.

Amanda was never troubled again by the strange metamorphosis that had caused her to act and speak like her cousin. She and Jason did not mention it. Least said, soonest mended—Amanda always reminded herself of the wisdom of the old saying when the thought of doing so occurred. Perhaps Jason did the same.

Their lives moved on, passing by with steady measured ticking of the clock in the entrance hall. Their children arrived, the plantation flourished under Jason's management and the advent of better times.

When they had been married five years, Jason commissioned a family portrait during one of their visits to New Orleans. For the sitting Amanda wore gold satin, the new pompadour hairstyle, and of course, the collar of Harmonia. Jason stood behind her, distinguished, with just a touch of gray at the temples, an easy, relaxed manner about him. Their son, Aaron, beside him, looked such a copy of his father that Amanda always had to smile. The baby in her arms had been extremely good, his eyes solemn with the importance of the occasion, his long gown streaming down across her skirts to the floor.

But a troubled expression often came into her eyes when she gazed at the child who leaned against her knee. It was a little girl, a tiny princess with long auburn curls and purple pansy eyes. Such knowing eyes the artist had painted for her daughter, Amelina, though she was a gay and laughing child, a truly lovable little girl. Still, she could be stubborn. For this portrait she had insisted on wearing her favorite dress, a white dimity strewn with violets.

ABOUT THE AUTHORS

MARY BALOGH, who won the *Romantic Times* Award for Best New Regency Writer in 1985, has become one of the genre's most popular and bestselling authors. She has since won four Waldenbook Awards and a B. Dalton Award for bestselling Regencies, and a *Romantic Times* Lifetime Achievement Award in 1989. Her latest Signet Regency romance is *The Notorious Rake*.

MARJORIE FARRELL was born in New York City and currently resides in Massachusetts, where she is an assistant professor teaching psychology, writing, and literature. Her latest Signet Regency romance is *Lady Arden's Redemption*.

SANDRA HEATH, the daughter of an officer in the Royal Air Force, spent most of her life traveling to various European posts. She now resides in Gloucester, England, with her husband and daughter. Her latest Signet Regency romance is *A Country Cotillion*.

EMMA LANGE, whose latest signet Regency romance is *The Unmanageable Miss Marlowe,* is a graduate of the University of California at Berkeley, where she studied European history. She and her husband live in the Midwest and pursue interests in traveling and sailing.

MARY JO PUTNEY is a graduate of Syracuse University with degrees in eighteenth-century literature and industrial design. In 1988, she received the *RWA* Golden Leaf Award for Best Historical Novel, and the *Romantic Times* Award for Best Regency Author. In 1989, Ms. Putney won three awards for her Regency, *The Rake and the Reformer.* Her novel *Dearly Beloved* received the *RWA* Golden Leaf Award for Best Historical Novel in 1990. Her latest Onyx historical romance is *Silk and Secrets*.

SIGNET REGENCY ROMANCE
COMING IN DECEMBER 1992

Margaret Evans Porter
Road To Ruin

Melinda McRae
The Highland Lord

Mary Balogh
A Christmas Promise
